PRAISE FOR KIRSTIN CHEN

"*Bury What We Cannot Take* explores what it takes to survive in a world gone mad—and what is lost when we do. Kirstin Chen has written both an engrossing historical drama and a nuanced exploration of how far the bonds of familial love can stretch."
—Celeste Ng, *New York Times* bestselling author of *Everything I Never Told You* and *Little Fires Everywhere*

"In Maoist China, the family at the center of this propulsive, haunting story is fractured by the dazzlingly complex fallout of a single irrevocable act. This beautifully plotted, suspenseful, and deeply compassionate novel shows Kirstin Chen, whose work I've long admired, at her absolute finest. *Bury What We Cannot Take* is a vital book."
—Laura van den Berg, author of *Find Me*

"*Bury What We Cannot Take* fulfills the promise of Kirstin Chen's debut. San San's family flee Drum Wave Islet, leaving her behind. An epic story follows that explores gender roles, oppressive ideologies, sacrifice, and what it means to be free. All through the microcosm of one family. This is a book set in the past, on the other side of the world, that is more than relevant in today's America. Chen delivers a page-turner that holds a historical mirror up to our fuzzy, complicit world."
—Matthew Salesses, author of *The Hundred-Year Flood*

"This story will sweep you away. An utterly beautiful, entirely engrossing family saga. Chen writes betrayal and love with wisdom and nuance, attuned always to the complexities—personal, historical, cultural—of the human heart. *Bury What We Cannot Take* is an instant classic."
—Claire Vaye Watkins, author of *Gold Fame Citrus* and *Battleborn*

"The perfect blend of family drama, complicated romance, and behind-the-scenes artisanal brewing of the world's most unsung condiment."
—*Glamour*

"Chen's flavorful prose will have you thinking about the often dismissed condiment in a whole new way."
—*Metro*

"Chen keeps the action at a steady pace with well-placed dialogue and setting, making it hard to put down, even for sleep."
—*Webster-Kirkwood Times*

"Gretchen's journey of self-discovery forms the backbone of this story about family, tradition, and honor. Foodies will appreciate the behind-the-scenes look at the world of artisanal soy sauce, while others will enjoy Chen's tribute to her native Singapore."
—*Booklist*

"*Soy Sauce for Beginners* is Kirstin Chen's first novel, and it works like a good recipe, with smooth language and an easily digestible plot . . . a dialogue based page turner . . . Readers craving an engaging and readable foodie tale will declare themselves satisfied."
—*Washington Independent Review of Books*

"*Soy Sauce for Beginners* is an assured debut novel as light and flavorful as the condiment spicing its pages."
—*The Straits Times*

"A funny and heartfelt novel exploring the intersections of food, family, and culture."
—*Hartford Guardian*

"Chen navigates the culture with the insight of an insider."
—*San Jose Mercury News*

"Kirstin Chen's debut is a delicious page-turning treat. Chen captures the zeitgeist of Singapore's new generation in an engrossing, intimately layered tale of love, family, and the discovery of one's true calling. It will also turn every reader into an artisanal soy sauce aficionado willing to settle for nothing but the best."
—Kevin Kwan, author of *Crazy Rich Asians*

"*Soy Sauce for Beginners* is an engaging story about a young woman's journey through love and friendship, business and family as she seeks her own place in the world. A satisfying and insightful novel."
—Jill McCorkle, author of *Life After Life*

"At the center of this novel is a struggling family business, but its bright heart is the difficult business of family. Written with warmth, umami and humor, *Soy Sauce for Beginners* considers the intricacies of inheritance and the challenges of safeguarding tradition. Kirstin Chen has written a spirited novel of self-discovery."
—Amber Dermont, author of *The Starboard Sea*

"Kirstin Chen evokes with wonderful brio the conflicts of a family business, and of a family. Reading these vivid pages made me want to catch the next plane to Singapore. Or failing that read another absorbing chapter. A sparkling debut."
—Margot Livesey, author of *The Flight of Gemma Hardy*

BURY WHAT WE CANNOT TAKE

ALSO BY KIRSTIN CHEN

Soy Sauce for Beginners

BURY WHAT WE CANNOT TAKE

a novel

KIRSTIN CHEN

Text copyright © 2018 by Kirstin Chen
All rights reserved.

Published by Little A, New York

www.apub.com

Amazon, the Amazon logo, and Little A are trademarks of Amazon.com, Inc., or its affiliates.

ISBN-13: 9781542049702 (hardcover)
ISBN-10: 1542049709 (hardcover)
ISBN-13: 9781542049719 (paperback)
ISBN-10: 1542049717 (paperback)

Cover illustration by Olivia Bodor

Cover design by Faceout Studio

Interior map by Mapping Specialists, Ltd

Printed in the United States of America

First edition

For Asmin, my Paris

SUMMER 1957

1

When San San followed her brother inside, she knew something was wrong. The flat was too quiet. Mui Ah, who always met them at the door to take their satchels, was nowhere to be found. Her brother shrugged and dropped his satchel on the floor on his way to the dining room, and San San did the same.

Usually their grandmother would already be seated in the chair closest to the kitchen door, but this afternoon, though the pink pastry box sat on the revolving stand in the center of the table, Grandma's chair was empty.

Mui Ah emerged from the kitchen with the tea tray. Her eyes were bloodshot, as though she'd rubbed them with her fists.

"Where's my grandma?" San San asked.

Mui Ah busied herself with the teapot and cups. "In her room, I think."

San San's brother asked, "Is she ill?"

San San asked, "What's wrong with your eyes?"

Mui Ah waggled her head, halfway between a nod and a shake, and retreated to the kitchen. San San's brother lifted the lid of the pastry box, and together they peered in, as though its contents would provide clues. There were the same petits fours that Grandma had Mui Ah purchase daily from the baker who'd apprenticed with a real Frenchman, before all the foreigners had left Drum Wave Islet.

Her brother was pinching out the chocolate éclair when they heard the crash of shattering glass. San San's hands clapped over her ears, as though compelled by some outside force. The éclair landed on the table with a soft splat. Mui Ah appeared in the kitchen doorway with Cook close behind her.

"I'll go check," her brother said, pushing back his chair. "You stay here."

San San pushed back her chair, too. Twelve years old to her nine, her brother was constantly forbidding her from going places with him and his friends. Sometimes when he was particularly grumpy, he made her follow several paces behind when they walked home from school. This time, however, she wouldn't let him bully her. She stood and squared her shoulders, and he scowled but said no more.

They tiptoed out of the dining room, through the empty drawing room, and stopped before the study. The sliding door had been pulled almost shut, though not all the way. Inside the room, something thudded to the floor.

Her brother held his finger over his lips, and San San pulled a face. What did he expect her to do? Burst into song? He planted himself before the sliver of space between door and wall, blocking her view. Her nose was running—her grandmother scolded her for always catching cold, as if it were something she could control—and she wiped her nostrils on her sleeve so she wouldn't have to sniffle. She tugged on the back pocket of her brother's uniform trousers, and at last he stepped aside.

San San held back a gasp. On the opposite end of the room, Grandma knelt before the framed photograph of Grandpa on the family altar, her face buried in her hands to muffle her sobs. And then San San noticed the shards of glass strewn about the dark walnut floor, the claw and long wooden handle of the hammer partially hidden by Grandma's skirt. Above Grandpa's portrait, in the very center of the wall, the Chairman's gleaming face continued to preside over the room, smiling benevolently at all who gazed upon him, oblivious to the spiderweb of cracks that scarred him.

San San's fingers brushed the door handle, and then she pulled back her hand. She turned to her brother, but his face was pale, his eyes clouded with worry. He dragged her back to the dining room.

"You're hurting me," she said.

When he let go, she saw that his fingertips had left red spots on her skin. She winced dramatically and massaged her forearm.

"Sorry," he said quietly, even though he no longer had to whisper. He leaned in close. "I need you, please, for once, to listen to me."

San San stopped rubbing her arm.

"You didn't see anything. Neither of us did. Is that clear?"

San San nodded.

"Nothing at all."

She nodded again.

"We came home from school, and they told us Grandma was resting in her room, and we had our afternoon tea as usual."

"All right," San San said, annoyed.

Mui Ah came out with a broom and dustpan. "Does Grandma need help?"

In unison, San San and her brother shouted, "No."

Mui Ah narrowed her eyes.

"Leave her alone," her brother said. "She'll call if she needs help."

Mui Ah backed slowly into the kitchen.

Her brother took his seat at the table, and San San did, too, even though she was no longer hungry. He reached for the slightly squashed chocolate éclair, which Mui Ah must have returned to the pastry box, and held it out to San San. "You can have this if you want."

He'd never once offered up his éclair, and, regardless of her lack of appetite, San San wasn't about to turn him down. Before he could change his mind, she bit into the crisp chocolate-glazed shell.

"Good?" he asked.

She nodded and took another bite. "Thanks, Ah Liam," she said with her mouth full. As a small child, she hadn't understood why she was supposed to call him "Gor"—elder brother—when everyone else in the family used his nickname, and, after a while, the grown-ups gave up and stopped correcting her.

Ah Liam lifted out the pear tart that was their least favorite, which they usually left for their mother to eat when she returned from her residents association meetings. He nibbled at the crust.

As much as San San relished her éclair's spongy, slightly savory pâte à choux and creamy custard, her thoughts remained in the study with Grandma. Could the whole thing have been an accident? Could her grandmother have been aiming for something else? No, the damage San San had seen was purposeful, precise. Grandma must have tottered on her tiny bound feet beneath the weight of the hammer, drawn back her arm until her shoulder strained in its socket, and gathered every ounce of her meager strength to smash the Chairman's sacred face.

San San pushed the last nub of pastry into her mouth and chewed. "Do you think—" she began.

"How should I know?" her brother cut her off. He dropped the mostly uneaten pear tart on his plate and charged to his room.

San San took a sip of tea. She was surprised by his vehemence, but not by his words. All her life, her family had skirted her questions, turning away or simply telling her to be quiet. Once, she had asked Grandma why her father couldn't find a job closer to the islet, like the fathers of her friends. Even before the borders had closed back when she was three, her father had returned from Hong Kong only a few times a year. Grandma had clicked her tongue against her teeth and said, "No man will marry such a nosy girl," which, as far as San San could tell, was beside the point.

Another time, after San San's teacher explained that the Chairman had liberated Chinese women by banning the oppressive practice of taking multiple wives, she asked her mother whether concubines were still allowed in Hong Kong. Ma choked on a mouthful of tea and fled to the kitchen, coughing. Someone changed the subject. San San never got her answer.

She couldn't conceive of anything that could so anger her wise, unflappable grandmother. Then again, her family came from a long line of landowners and industrialists and capitalists. As she'd learned at school, bourgeois thought processes and behaviors had been bred into her kind through the generations. Could this tainted blood of theirs have somehow muddled Grandma's brain? Were all of them at risk?

When San San had trouble falling asleep, her grandmother sometimes sat by her bedside, recounting stories of the olden days. Once, Grandma mentioned an exorcism she'd witnessed in the adjacent courtyard. San San's eyes sprang open, causing Grandma to say, "That's a story for another time."

But San San begged and begged until she relented.

"The girl screamed so loud that all us neighbors came to our windows. She thrashed her arms and bared her teeth at the priest like a bloodthirsty wolf. Three grown men had to hold this slip of a thing down."

"Why?" San San asked, tightening her grip on her grandmother's arm.

"It wasn't her fault," said Grandma. "The demon inhabited her body and controlled her completely."

San San set down her teacup and hurried to her brother's room.

2

At school the following day, Comrade Ang wrote the political discussion topic on the blackboard with a stub of chalk: *Western goods are not superior to Chinese goods.* Ah Liam searched for an appropriate example from his own life. As one of two class monitors, he was expected to be a model for his classmates. And the sooner he spoke up, the sooner he could relax.

As usual, Ping Ping, the other monitor and the class's sole Youth League member, was the first to raise her hand. "None of us needs to be reminded that the bandit Chiang Kai-shek brainwashed the masses into worshipping all things foreign," she said, looking around the classroom and smiling.

Ah Liam hoped she would single him out, but the instant their eyes met, he looked away.

Ping Ping continued. "Because of our shameful history, we must be vigilant against our baser instincts."

Ah Liam studied her profile. How confidently she uttered those smooth, glossy phrases. How grown-up she looked with that elegant gold pin, emblazoned with new China's crimson flag, on the upper corner of her blouse—unlike the rest of them, with their childish Young Pioneer scarves knotted at their throats.

"Just the other day," Ping Ping said, "my father ordered our whole family to throw out our Western-made shoes." She stuck her foot in the air to show off a dainty canvas slipper. "Red Stars are the best shoes in the world. They're light and washable. What more could you ask for?"

Comrade Ang nodded firmly, the most he ever did to show his approval. The political discussion leader was slender and of average height, with flat, unremarkable features—the kind of person whom Ah Liam would have struggled to describe to his friends. But despite Comrade Ang's placid demeanor, everyone knew he tracked participation and scrutinized every word.

Ah Liam wiggled his toes in his own Red Stars and raised his hand. "Comrade Ping Ping is right about the need for us to question our behaviors. For example, my grandma would have continued her old habit of buying French pastries for tea, if I hadn't urged her to break free from the bondages of her background and her upbringing."

Ah Liam's seatmate, whom everyone called Pimple Face, grunted his assent. Across the room, Ping Ping gave Ah Liam a smile that hid her teeth.

He kept talking. "Besides, our local sweets, like *moa ji* and mooncakes, are equally, if not more, delicious. As the Chairman states, 'Whoever sides with the revolutionary people in word is only a revolutionary in speech. Whoever sides with the revolutionary people in deed as well as in word is a revolutionary in the full sense.'" Then and there, he resolved to talk to his grandmother as soon as he found the chance—and to never touch another French pastry.

When the session was over, Ah Liam headed for the door with his classmates, but Comrade Ang called his name. Ah Liam took a tentative step toward the discussion leader, who rested his palms on his wooden desk and looked intently at him. There was no way Comrade Ang could know that Ah Liam had made up his entire example, unless he'd spotted Mui Ah hurrying to the baker's and somehow known she was the Ongs' house girl. Had something in his words rung false? Why had he gone on and on like that? Why did he have to show off by quoting the Chairman?

Comrade Ang beckoned him close. "I've been watching you these past weeks."

Ah Liam swallowed hard.

"You consistently make thoughtful and interesting points that demonstrate your commitment to the Party."

Ah Liam relaxed. "Thank you, Comrade, for your encouragement."

"Now," Comrade Ang said, "your family background is problematic, to say the least, but it's clear you're able to think for yourself."

Ah Liam felt his cheeks color. His classmates were from well-off families, but only he had a father who was an Overseas Chinese in Hong Kong; only he lived in Diamond Villa at the very top of Tranquil Seas Road, although the bottom two stories had been requisitioned by the Party and leased to tenants, the servants' quarters converted into the People's Maternity Clinic.

Ah Liam wasn't sure if he should thank the discussion leader for the backhanded compliment, or apologize for his family. Before he could decide which, Comrade Ang reached into a desk drawer and withdrew a sheet of paper, pale yellow and tissue thin.

Ah Liam's breath caught in his throat. It was an application for the Youth League.

"I don't hand this out lightly," Comrade Ang said. "You know as well as I that joining the Youth League is the first step toward full Party membership."

Ah Liam nodded, unable to speak. He'd coveted that gold pin ever since he'd seen a team of tall, strapping boys from the senior middle school sweeping the streets by the marketplace while they sang "Red May" in robust baritones. Standing before the boys, Ah Liam had taken in the appreciative, admiring faces of the passing townsfolk—all except for his mother, who, in her typically bourgeois way, yanked his arm, saying, "What a waste of time. Don't they have sweepers for that?"

Comrade Ang handed over the sheet of paper. "Turn this in as soon as you can."

Ah Liam took the long route home, grateful that, for once, San San wasn't tagging along. With the whole family crammed into the top floor of the villa, along with the servants, he never had a moment to himself. But he knew it was wrong to complain, even if only in his head, when everything his family had amassed had been at the expense of the proletariat. Now that his uncles and aunts and cousins had left for Taiwan and the Philippines, it was only fair that all those spare rooms be returned to the people.

At the intersection, instead of turning homeward, he continued onto Eternal Peace Road, which led to the edge of Drum Wave Islet, away from the din of town. Years earlier, on his very first day of school, Ah Liam had learned that in ancient times, large hollow rocks had lined the stretch of craggy coastline down below. When high tides pounded the rocks, ghostly drumbeats soared through the air, frightening the early settlers who would give the tiny two-square-kilometer islet its name. Of course, the reef had long since disintegrated, which encapsulated all Ah Liam hated about being a child. Everything magical and exciting seemed to have happened in the past, before he was born, or would happen in the future, after he was an adult. Nothing ever seemed to happen now. Leaning over as far as he could without losing his balance, he watched the waves lap at the shore like the tongues of kittens. Playful, harmless, meek.

A few hundred meters away, across the channel, the dense, towering buildings of the city of Xiamen glittered beneath the late-afternoon sun. At that very moment, he imagined brand-new, multilevel dormitories rising into the sky, railroads unfolding across the land, swarms of people in buses and on bicycles hurrying to wherever they needed to go to play their roles in the construction of new China. Motor vehicles weren't even permitted on sleepy Drum Wave Islet. Teams of laborers lugged wooden carts up steep lanes, as though stuck in an earlier time. Ah Liam's best bet was to keep up his marks, qualify for the Youth League, and earn a place in Xiamen University. Then, finally, could he cross the channel and join in on the action.

He wondered if Comrade Ang had invited others to apply for the Youth League, or if he and Ping Ping would be their class's sole members. A smattering of raindrops tapped the crown of his head, and he peered into the sunlit sky. A knot of dark clouds gathered in the east, prompting him to hurry home and shut himself in his room with his application.

Ah Liam was an exemplary student: class monitor three years in a row, top marks in math and science, captain of the football team. Still, his application had to make up for his family's former wealth, his father's job, and even his mother's missionary-school education.

Pen poised over paper, Ah Liam let himself imagine what would happen if the Party learned of his grandmother's crime. His family was already under surveillance. Inspectors were routinely dispatched to the villa—neighbors and friends of his mother who questioned them about Pa's work in Hong Kong and when he would return to help rebuild the Fatherland. The inspectors were friendly, even apologetic, and Ah Liam didn't believe his family to be in serious trouble. No doubt his confession would change that, but perhaps he'd been wrong to hide what Grandma had done. Perhaps a little fear was precisely the push she needed to leave the past behind and change her ways, for how would she learn her lesson if she faced no punishment?

Five years earlier, when Ah Liam's last two cousins had moved away, he'd begged his mother to let him go with them, but of course she'd said no. Loneliness and boredom drove him to befriend the son of the assistant cook. The boy was a full head taller than he, and whenever they teamed up to play football against Ah Liam's neighborhood friends, they always won.

One day, while Ah Liam and his new friend were practicing drills in the courtyard, Grandma summoned him inside. "That boy should be helping out in the kitchen, but he can't if he spends all his time playing with you."

The injustice of it all crashed down on Ah Liam. His friend was also eight years old. Why didn't he go to school? Why did he wear Ah Liam's old clothes that were clearly too small for him? Why should he have to work in the kitchen with the adults?

Grandma's eyes lengthened into slits. "Because that's his fate," she said, "just as it is your fate to study hard so you can follow in the footsteps of your grandfather and father and bring prosperity to the family."

Everything Ah Liam had learned at school fell into place. He'd finally understood why the Chairman had declared, "Communism is a hammer that we use to crush the enemy." Suddenly Ah Liam saw the enemy all around him. It was the enemy who barred the servants from entering through the villa's front door, and reduced men to beggars who slunk around the marketplace back before the Party had rounded them up for rehabilitation, and caused his classmates to make fun of Pimple Face, his seatmate, whose mother was a widow and whose uniform was threadbare and ill fitting. Ah Liam knew he should take a hammer to his grandmother's callousness, but at that moment, he didn't dare. Instead, he let a few days pass and then returned to playing in the courtyard with his friend. Shortly after that, Grandma fired his friend's mother. She claimed the cook was no longer needed now that so few of the family remained. Ah Liam had cried and raged and kicked his bedroom door hard enough to crack the wood, but of course that changed nothing. Watching from his bedroom window as his friend and the assistant cook straggled down the street with meager knapsacks on their backs, Ah Liam vowed never again to stay silent in the face of the enemy.

Since then, his baser instincts—wasn't that Ping Ping's sophisticated term?—had wiped out the memory of that vow, driving him to swear himself and his sister to secrecy about what Grandma had done.

Now, however, this application presented an opportunity to reaffirm his dedication to the Party and make things right.

He lowered his pen and a stillness settled over him: the acceptance that what he was about to do could never be undone. He wrote, *Chairman Mao teaches that those who confess will be treated less harshly than those who refuse to admit their wrongdoings.* He went on to detail the horrific manner in which his grandmother had insulted the Great Helmsman, and why he had no choice but to expose her crime.

He didn't stop writing until he'd completed the entire application. When he finally raised his head, his hand and forearm ached. He was dizzy and famished. He walked through the dining room to the kitchen, where the sight of his grandmother made him freeze. He hadn't expected her to be up and about.

Leaning on her cane to shift the weight off her bound feet, she stabbed a finger in the pot on the stove and brought it to her lips. "No taste," she said. "Add more vinegar, more soy sauce, more everything!" This was his grandmother's refrain. Ma said her taste buds had grown numb with old age.

Grandma turned to Ah Liam. "I saved you the éclair," she said, pointing to the dining room.

Ah Liam made himself say, "I'm not hungry."

"If you say so," Grandma said, returning her attention to Cook.

Ah Liam went back to his desk and reread his application. Perhaps this line was too dismissive, that one too harsh. Perhaps he could tell Comrade Ang that he'd accidentally dropped his application in the spring by his house and request a fresh one.

From the kitchen, Grandma's strident voice rose. "Are you deaf? I said more vinegar! More!"

Did she have to scold Cook, a man with more white hairs on his head than black, as though he were a naughty child? If Ah Liam didn't hammer the enemy now, who knew what other crimes his grandmother would go on to commit. He smoothed the application between the pages of an exercise book so it wouldn't get rumpled in his satchel. Closing his eyes, he pictured himself with his fellow Youth League members on National Day. Arranged from shortest to tallest, they would parade through the town center in pairs, waving their red flags high in the air and singing "March of the Volunteers." The townsfolk lining the road beamed at them with pride and affection. The gold pins on their breastbones glinted in the sunlight. He and Ping Ping were almost the same height; there was a good chance they'd get paired together.

3

These days, Bee Kim rarely had reason to leave the villa, but someone had to sort through Hua's belongings and gather up the things
her daughters might want before the servants made off with them all.

For much of the morning, while Bee Kim separated Hua's good
jewelry from the eye-catching but worthless trinkets, she kept her tears
in check. In fact, she was too angry to cry. Fury, pure and white-hot,
had driven Bee Kim to hammer the portrait of that damned megaloma-
niac who'd made Hua suffer. Who'd made all of them suffer.

Four years earlier, the Party had seized the last factory, and her Ah
Lip had gone from boss to janitor in a matter of weeks. He'd died of a
heart attack shortly after. None of Bee Kim's sons returned home from
abroad for fear not only of getting trapped, but also of being made to
pay for their father's so-called crimes. She locked herself in her room
and refused all visitors, especially Hua.

Now, of course, she regretted those months she'd spent resenting
her closest friend. But back then, no one would have blamed her. Hua's
Thomas had been one of the lucky ones. His had been designated a
"showcase factory," through which the Party toured Western visitors
to demonstrate the harmonious collaboration that had blossomed
between capitalists and communists. Yes, they levied outrageous taxes
that threatened to bankrupt him; yes, they planted a Party secretary in

the office next door, which essentially reduced Thomas to a figurehead. But at least he wasn't despised and humiliated by his own workers. For the most part, Thomas and Hua held on to their old lives, with a few opulent Party banquets thrown in, and Bee Kim hated them for it.

With time, however, she saw how fortunate her Ah Lip was to have passed when he did. Earlier this year, the Party decided Thomas was no longer useful to them and turned on him, and his employees followed suit. Gray-haired men who'd worked at the factory since they'd first traded their shorts for long pants imprisoned Thomas in his own office. Every afternoon for two weeks straight, Bee Kim accompanied Hua to the factory in Xiamen with tins of soup and noodles and those flaky red bean pastries Thomas loved. The apologetic guard always turned them away.

The last time they showed up at the gate, the guard wouldn't meet Hua's gaze. Hua gripped the young man's brawny forearm until her knuckles whitened. "What's happened to Thomas?" He stared at his shoes as he spoke. "Boss left us this morning." Hua's sack crashed to the ground. She fell against the gate, pounding the steel bars and wailing. Bee Kim had to enlist the trishaw driver to help drag her friend away.

In the months following Thomas's death, Hua cancelled their biweekly lunch dates. When Bee Kim showed up unannounced at Hua's house on the pretext of wanting to drop off a poetry collection she thought she'd like, she found the servants crowded around a heap of Hua's favorite garments. One of them whispered that Madame had sworn off bright colors and had resigned herself to a widow's wardrobe of drab beige for the rest of her days. Letters from Hua's daughters in America arrived at Diamond Villa, begging Bee Kim for news of their mother. She advised them to give Hua time. After all, that was what Bee Kim had needed after she'd lost Ah Lip. Needless to say, she'd never expected Hua to down that fatal dose of sleeping pills.

"You could have come and lived with me," Bee Kim said aloud to the empty room. "We would have been all right together."

She folded Hua's mink stoles and muffs into a small suitcase for the American daughters and ran her fingers across the shelves, bare except for an old bag of fabric scraps. She tossed the bag in the junk pile for the servants to pick through, and as the bag sailed through the air, a square of floral silk drifted out. She held the small blue-and-yellow square to the light. She touched the cool silk to her cheek, inhaling its musty scent.

Bee Kim had been married for less than a month when her tyrannical mother-in-law ordered her to mend an armful of dresses, even though there were plenty of house girls up to the task. Determined to prove herself, she worked through the night by candlelight, only to discover in the morning that she'd pricked her finger with the needle and bled across the bodice of the old woman's favorite dress. Bee Kim ran to Hua in a panic, certain the old woman would make good on her threat to send her back to her parents in disgrace. But Hua was a gifted seamstress. She managed to hunt down a bolt of the same blue-and-yellow floral silk, and together, she and Bee Kim set about sewing an entire new dress. The next time the old woman asked a house girl to bring her the dress, the copy was hanging in her wardrobe, and when the frog closures gaped, she lamented she'd gained weight.

Bee Kim dropped the fabric square in the bag of scraps and wiped her eyes with her handkerchief, for what would Hua's servants think if they found her in this state?

Bee Kim was settling down for a nap before dinner when she heard a knock on the front door. Her daughter-in-law's residents association meeting had gone long again, so she'd have to see who it was.

The children had answered the door, and a pair of women clad in the cadre's drab uniform of dark-gray tunic and trousers peered in. Bee Kim recognized them both. The tall one, with the long face and large teeth of a horse, lived in the row of smaller houses two streets over.

The short, plump one was married to a good-for-nothing gambler who had grown up with Bee Kim's sons. The women would have been well aware that Seok Koon was at her meeting, so perhaps they'd planned to avoid her. Perhaps they'd come hoping to intimidate an old woman while she was all alone.

Ah Liam said, "I told them my ma was out."

The boy's grave expression made Bee Kim loosen her grip on her cane. Though small for twelve, he tried so hard to embody his role as man of the house. She smiled at him and said, "But of course these comrade aunties already knew that."

The cadres pretended not to hear this.

The horsey one bared her oversized teeth. "We're sorry to barge in like this, Mrs. Ong."

"Yes, please pardon the intrusion, Mrs. Ong," said the plump one.

Bee Kim frowned to make clear the imposition. "It's no trouble at all."

No one knew of the wrecked portrait except for Seok Koon, so what had brought these women here? Had Mui Ah been spying on them? The house girl had the sly aura of a fox fairy; Bee Kim had never trusted her.

She waited for the cadres to comment on how tall the children had grown, or on the *People's Daily*'s latest reports about the "Let a hundred flowers bloom" campaign. Inspections always began with small talk, as though the cadres had just dropped by for a chat.

This time, however, the horsey one hung her head and said, "This is a little embarrassing, but might we talk in private?" She gave Bee Kim a meaningful look.

So that was it. Mui Ah had betrayed her. Bee Kim willed herself to stay calm. "Of course. We'll have more privacy in the study."

She pulled back the sliding door and led the cadres into the room, never glancing at the new, pristine portrait hanging in the center of the wall. The cadres each took a stool around the marble-topped table, and the horsey one looked over at Ah Liam and San San, lingering in the doorway. "It would be better to talk without the children."

Bee Kim slowly lowered herself into her rocking chair, wincing as her anklebones cracked. "San San, don't you have a piano lesson tomorrow? Shouldn't you be practicing?"

Her granddaughter's disappointment was plain, but she trudged off without protest. Ah Liam turned to follow her, and Bee Kim said, "Grandson, you may stay."

Ah Liam's eyebrows shot up. The cadres frowned at each other.

Bee Kim directed him to the stool closest to her. "I'm an old lady who is a bit hard of hearing," she explained. "I need him here."

The boy stared down at his lap, refusing to meet Bee Kim's smile. Lately, she'd watched him pore over the propaganda in the papers; she'd overheard him quoting the Chairman to his sister. It would be good for him to see his beloved Party in action.

"Very well," the plump cadre said. "We don't want to unnecessarily take up any more of your time, so let me speak frankly. Your family has been reported for rightist behavior. We have orders to search your home."

"Rightist behavior" was a catchall phrase that encompassed everything from donning a blouse of too bright a hue all the way to writing an essay in criticism of the Party, but still Bee Kim's mouth went dry. Beads of sweat dotted her grandson's forehead, and she felt sorry for him. He was so sensitive, so anxious. Perhaps she shouldn't have made him stay. For his sake, she adopted a lighthearted tone. "You've troubled yourself to come all this way, so please, feel free to look around."

The women went straight to the bookcase. All of Seok Koon's English books and classical music scores had long been stashed in the attic in preparation for precisely this scenario. Even so, they found plenty of questionable titles: a mystery series her daughter-in-law enjoyed, the illustrated fables she and Seok Koon had read to both children, even a few translations of Russian authors, whom Bee Kim could have sworn were Party-sanctioned.

As the books piled up on the ground, Bee Kim feared the cadres' silence on the wrecked portrait meant she'd missed the chance to defend herself, that the Party had already accepted her alleged crime as fact and had turned their attention to collecting additional evidence. Days earlier, she and Seok Koon had concocted the best excuse they could: Enraged by her old friend's lack of Party loyalty and cowardly suicide, Bee Kim had taken a hammer to a photograph of Hua. In her heightened emotional state, the hammer flew from Bee Kim's grasp and shattered the glass on the Chairman's portrait.

Now Bee Kim blurted, "Comrades, I fear there's been a misunderstanding—"

The women turned to her, as did Ah Liam, who looked up for the first time. Bee Kim sensed she could be blundering down the wrong path. What if they knew nothing of the portrait? What if this were just another routine inspection, albeit conducted by particularly overzealous cadres?

"Go on," said the plump one.

Bee Kim wrung her hands. "I was wondering . . . what kind of rightist behavior?"

The cadres exchanged a look, and the horsey one said, "I'm afraid we're not at liberty to say."

This, Bee Kim knew, was the worst possible response. Her grandson must have known it, too, for his lower lip began to tremble.

"Whatever it is we've done," Bee Kim said, "we humbly ask for the chance to repent. We would, for instance, be grateful for the opportunity to show our gratitude to the Party by investing all foreign remittances from my sons in government bonds."

This time the women chuckled.

Bee Kim looked straight at the plump cadre. "My oldest son, Hong Zhai, you of course know well, because he was your husband's childhood playmate."

The women stopped laughing.

"We're just low-level cadres," the horsey one said.

The plump one added, "Those matters are too sophisticated for the likes of us."

Bee Kim felt the back of her neck tense. The family couldn't live like this, with members of their own household turning on them. If she hadn't taken in Mui Ah when she'd just hit puberty, the girl would have starved to death, or been sold to a brothel, and this was how she repaid her? Thank heavens Seok Koon had sent another letter to Hong Kong. Ah Zhai would find a way to get them out.

Less than an hour after they'd arrived, the cadres were standing by the front door with two large boxes.

"This is all we can take today," the horsey one said somewhat apologetically.

With their arms full, the pair struggled to open the door. Ah Liam lifted a hand to help, but a sharp glance from Bee Kim made him reconsider.

Once she and the boy were alone, he scrunched his face like he was about to cry. She shook her head and motioned him close. "Grandson, let this be a lesson. Trust no one except your own family."

4

As soon as San San heard the front door slam, she pulled her fingers from the keyboard. The music room shared a wall with the study, and she'd spent the last hour playing through her Bach Inventions as quietly as she could while attempting to eavesdrop. As far as she could tell, there'd been little talking, and the inspectors had spent most of the time pulling books off shelves.

She longed to go to Ah Liam, but out of guilt, her eyes lingered on the music score. Auntie Rose always knew when San San hadn't practiced enough, and she hated to disappoint her teacher, who often reported to her mother that she had plenty of talent and not enough discipline. It was true. What San San adored most was drawing glorious melodies from the piano without regard for tempo, dynamics, articulation. She had no use for scales and arpeggios, chords and cadences.

She flipped back to the beginning of the score, but the sounds of Grandma and Ah Liam muttering to each other were too enticing to bear. She waited for her brother to go to his room, and then she knocked and nudged open the door.

To her surprise, he was lying in bed with the covers pulled up to his chin. He took one look at her and yanked the blanket over his head. "Go away."

San San tugged on the blanket. "What did those aunties want?"

"Go away."

"What books did they take?"

"I said, 'go away.'"

She stared at the lump that was his body, at the tufts of hair sticking straight up like joss sticks. "I didn't tell," she said.

Ah Liam lowered the blanket to reveal his eyes. "I know."

"Then who did?"

Ah Liam sat up. "It might not have been about that. We've had inspections before."

San San held her brother's gaze. "Not like this one."

He picked at the blanket's fraying edge. "They didn't even mention the portrait."

San San thought about that. Could the timing of the inspection have been entirely coincidental?

"All they took were Ma's Russian books," Ah Liam said. "It's probably a new crackdown on foreign literature, or something."

The front door opened. Ma was back.

"We'd better tell her," San San said.

"Leave it to Grandma."

"No," San San said, and then lowered her voice. "We need to tell her what Grandma did."

Ah Liam kicked off the covers. "She already knows," he said. "Didn't you see the new portrait? Grandma wouldn't have been able to take care of that on her own."

San San supposed he was right. She was glad they no longer had to keep secrets from Ma.

Ah Liam went to his desk. "I need to do homework now."

San San had more questions, but she didn't want to give him a reason to make her leave. "I won't disturb you." She sat on his bed and reached for the comic book on his nightstand. Its title was *The White-Haired Girl*.

"Wipe your nose. I don't want your snot all over the pages."

As usual, her handkerchief had vanished from her pocket, so she rubbed her nose on her sleeve. She examined the book's flimsy cover, the black ink already smudging beneath her fingertips. The heroine had the beautiful face of a young maiden but the tresses of a crone.

Meanwhile, her brother expressed his irritation by noisily opening and closing various workbooks, rattling desk drawers, acting as if this whole thing were her fault.

Finally she said, "Ah Liam, you didn't, did you?"

He raised himself to his full height and spun around. San San shrank back, bracing for an explosion.

Mui Ah knocked and called through the door, "Dinnertime."

Neither of them acknowledged her.

Ah Liam spoke slowly and loudly, as though San San were dumb. "I just said the inspection wasn't about that. I swear, if you ask one more time . . ." His voice trailed off.

She clamped her lips together. If he'd simply answer the question, she wouldn't have to keep asking.

Ah Liam stormed off to the dining room, and she plodded behind, knowing better than to expect the grown-ups to be more forthcoming.

At first, the sight of Ma and Grandma at the table set San San at ease. But then she noticed their furrowed brows and downturned mouths. Even though Cook had made her favorite *popiah,* she made no move to fill her plate.

"What's wrong?" her brother asked.

The shadows beneath Ma's eyes were the shade of a bruise. In a weary voice she said, "Children, we have some bad news. A letter from your pa arrived. He is very, very ill."

San San's stomach churned. She tasted acid at the back of her throat. She hadn't seen her father in ages, but red envelopes of money arrived to mark each passing year, accompanied by sepia-toned portraits to remember him by. The latest portrait showed Pa's square-jawed face beneath glossy, slicked-back hair, his thin lips stretched into a knowing half smile. How could tragedy befall such a handsome, serene man?

"We must go to Hong Kong at once," said Ma. "The doctor fears there isn't much time." A single tear trickled down her cheek, causing San San's eyes to brim.

Ah Liam slumped forward on his elbows, nearly toppling his empty plate. San San's anger toward him faded. She felt sorry for her brother, who remembered much more about Pa than she. From time to time, she climbed in Ah Liam's bed and begged him to recount the tale of Pa's last visit to the villa, six years earlier, and the magical gifts he'd brought from the colony: freshwater pearls the size of marbles for Ma, fine embroidered silk shawls for Grandma, an electric train set with shiny forest-green cars for Ah Liam. "Each time we thought Pa was done, he'd call for the servants to bring the next trunk," her brother said, his voice filled with awe. For San San, Pa had brought an exquisite baby-girl doll with rosy cheeks and golden ringlets and eyes the pure blue of Ma's porcelain rice bowls. The doll had been handmade in Germany, so Ah Liam suggested the name "Hansel." Hansel had lost much of her luster and a good chunk of her hair, but continued to accompany San San to bed each night.

Now Ah Liam's voice emerged scratchy and reed thin. "What kind of sickness?"

Ma said, "The doctor doesn't know. No one knows."

Grandma added, "He's lost all strength in his legs. He hasn't left his bed in days."

Ma said that first thing in the morning, she would go to the safety bureau to request four exit permits.

In her head, San San transformed her father's flat, colorless portrait into a real man, someone who could tower over her and sweep her into his embrace and rub his stubbly chin against her cheek. Try as she might, she couldn't imagine him lying helplessly in bed. She didn't like to think about Pa in his home in Hong Kong, for if there were a concubine by his side, she knew there could be other children, too. Now, however, for the first time, she was grateful her father wasn't all alone in the colony, though she knew better than to voice this thought aloud.

5

S toked by sleeplessness and stress, Seok Koon's frustration boiled over. She pounded her fist into her pillow, again and again, savoring the ache that spread down her arm. The escape plan had been in the works for months, and now her mother-in-law's single, reckless act had ruined all their hard work. Earlier, when Bee Kim had told her about the cadres' visit, Seok Koon had drawn on every drop of self-control to hold her tongue.

She reached again for her husband's letter—as though she hadn't memorized every word—the cream-colored envelope and matching paper, luxuriously thick and pliable.

My beloved wife, the letter read. The greeting, a mere formality, was enough to make the muscles deep within her belly tighten. *Make haste and bring my mother and the children. My only desire is to see the faces of my family one final time.* Enclosed with the letter was a note from a Dr. Kwok, and she reread that, too. This Dr. Kwok had visited the patient, her husband, on May 8, 1957. The patient was extremely weak and was paralyzed from the waist down. The patient was unable to keep down food and had to be fed by IV. The cause of these symptoms was, for now, unknown, and the prognosis did not look good.

Even though Seok Koon knew it was all a ruse, the words surged through her with a power of their own, whipping her thoughts into a frenzy. Given this latest investigation, the prognosis of their escape did not look good either. How could her mother-in-law be so thoughtless? If not for dear Rose, Seok Koon would never have been able to find a replacement portrait so quickly and discretely. Rose had been the most talented pianist in their conservatory class. Upon graduation, while Seok Koon and the rest of her classmates had squelched any lingering professional ambitions and embraced new roles as wives and mothers, Rose had opened a piano school. Only when the school had established itself as one of the islet's most prestigious had she married Lee Chin Kong, a respected doctor who now treated the highest-ranking Party officials. Somehow Chin Kong had arranged for the new portrait to be delivered to the villa in secret, but even he could not procure the necessary exit permits. For those, Seok Koon would have to take her chances with the desperate, clamoring horde at the safety bureau.

Nowadays a special pass was needed even to board the ferry that crossed the five-hundred-meter channel to Xiamen. No matter the weather or the hour, a queue snaked around the side of the safety bureau, as on this gray, humid morning, thick with the smell of mildew and impending rain.

Around here, no one was a stranger. The bank manager and his wife stood at the head of the line, and Seok Koon wondered how early they'd arrived to claim that prized spot. Behind them was the assistant principal of the high school, whose youngest son had drowned in Flourishing Beauty Cove last year, and behind him, the widow who lived in opulent Sea and Sky Mansion, the first home on the islet to install a flush toilet—sent from Manila by her doting children. Seok Koon pretended not to notice any of them. Now was not the time to make small talk, for what could they possibly say to each other? "Fancy seeing you here! You're planning to flee, too? I'm trying for Hong Kong. You?"

Over a decade earlier, when this old but graceful ivy-covered Edwardian mansion had been not the safety bureau but the British consulate, her husband had been invited to take tea with the ambassador himself, and Seok Koon, the new bride, was brought along. The ivory ankle-length dress she had made still hung in the back of her armoire, waiting to be passed down to San San. The dress was light and airy, the antithesis of how she'd felt that day, prodded by Ah Zhai to speak the English she'd learned from American missionaries, displayed like a songbird in a cage. Ordinarily, Seok Koon loved the shapes and sounds of those foreign words. She'd dreamed her own children would learn English, and the three of them would have a secret language to themselves. But these days, the top students learned Russian, and anyone who spoke English knew better than to flaunt it.

The assistant principal complained to no one in particular that the line had barely budged. Several heads nodded, but none continued the conversation. To pass the time, Seok Koon studied the trickle of people emerging from the mansion's heavy doors, drawn men and women, dressed like her, in dark, conservative clothing, their faces as overcast as the sky. She worried the director was in a miserly mood, even as she reasoned that the fewer permits he'd given out thus far, the stronger her own chances.

Now the door swung back to reveal a tall man in a tailored Western suit. Unlike those who'd come before him, his complexion was bright, his manner upbeat. It was Chin Kong.

The sight of a friend lifted Seok Koon's spirits. She raised her hand and cried out, startling the doctor. Everyone in line stared.

Chin Kong bowed slightly, his manner surprisingly formal. "Mrs. Ong, how do you do?"

Seok Koon matched his tone. "I'm quite well, Dr. Lee. What brings you here this morning?"

"Just examining a few of my patients," he said.

Seok Koon realized he'd probably met with the director himself.

Chin Kong edged away from her. "I really must be going. I'll be sure to tell my wife I saw you."

"Yes," she said quickly. "Please send my regards to Rose." She wished there were a way to thank him for the new portrait, but he was already walking briskly down the lane.

His curtness unsettled her. Was her family in such deep trouble that the doctor could not be seen conversing with her? She scanned the now-averted faces of her fellow permit seekers. She'd believed the particular etiquette of the queue dictated one keep to oneself, but perhaps the rest of them were simply evading her. Had news of her family's troubles already spread across town?

Someone nudged her forward. It was her turn.

She tripped up the worn marble steps, greeted the bored youth manning the door, and followed his directions. The safety bureau's interior possessed none of the crumbling charm of its façade. The soot-darkened walls were the same dull shade of gray as the dirty concrete floors and the cadres' uniforms. Even the air, filled with the smoke of a hundred cigarettes all exhaled at once, was gray.

In this dingy, miserable world, the sole splash of color came from the brilliant, beaming portrait that greeted Seok Koon upon entering the director's office, as though she were here to see the Chairman himself.

Up close, the safety bureau director was shorter than she'd expected, with a round, almost jolly face that filled her with hope. This Comrade Koh, she'd heard, had recently relocated from Quanzhou. Apparently he refrained from socializing with the locals, preferring to spend his spare time entertaining important visitors who stepped off the ferry from Xiamen.

Seok Koon bid the director good morning and sat down on the hard wooden chair. When he responded with a short nod, she asked whether he was growing accustomed to the slow pace of life on the islet.

Comrade Koh located her file and flipped through the pages. "I go where the Party needs me. My personal desires and habits are insignificant."

Seok Koon dropped her head in dismay.

"Tell me why you're here."

Seok Koon slid Ah Zhai's letter across the desk. "It's my husband. He's dying, in Hong Kong, and we must go to his side."

Comrade Koh's fingers were fat as sausages, the knuckles covered with coarse black hairs. He opened the envelope roughly, ripping the flap. He gave the letter and the doctor's note a cursory glance before returning to her file. "It says here your family is currently under investigation."

"A simple accident," Seok Koon said. She launched into the explanation she and Bee Kim had prepared. "My mother-in-law—oh, she's so clumsy in her old age! She was aiming the hammer at a photograph of—"

Comrade Koh interrupted. "Exit permits take at least a month to process, maybe six weeks."

Seok Koon contorted her face to express deep sorrow. "My husband could leave us in a matter of days." She stared at a spot on the desk until her eyes watered. "There must be an exception you can make?"

The director frowned, his bushy eyebrows forming a V in the center of his forehead. "The Party is very sorry for your troubles, but four exit permits is simply impossible."

She flung herself across the table and grasped the director's clammy hands. He shrank back in surprise.

"My husband wants to see his children before he goes. Surely you can find it in your heart to help us."

And then, a miracle. The director's round face softened like a lump of uncooked dough. Seok Koon swore she caught a glimmer of warmth in those beady eyes.

"Two permits may be possible."

She sat up. "What good would that do?"

The director puffed his chest. "I'm going to say this one last time. Four exit permits is out of the question. I'm almost at my monthly quota and it's only"—he glanced at the calendar on his desk—"only May twenty-first."

"Forgive me," Seok Koon began in her most contrite tone.

He cut her off. "You're wasting my time. Come back when you've made up your mind." He shut her file and tossed it atop a towering pile. The file skidded off and landed on the grimy floor, spilling its contents in a graceful fan. The director scowled at the papers and then at Seok Koon.

Somehow her legs hauled the dead weight of her body out of the safety bureau, past the never-ending queue, and up the road. Just beyond the gates of the former Methodist Girls' School, renamed Dragon Head School after its street, two girls held a thick rope of interwoven rubber bands at shoulder height, while a third took a running start and scissored her legs across the rope with startling grace. The girls' cheers rang out like sirens. Seok Koon ducked her head and pushed on. In the leafy, bougainvillea-filled gardens of the sanitarium that was open only to high-level cadres, a nurse pushing an elderly gentleman in a wheelchair chattered on in a loud, cheerful voice. But Seok Koon saw the old man's face was blank as paper, that the nurse might as well have been talking to herself.

Outside the villa, Seok Koon's arms hung dumbly at her sides; she could barely lift them to open the heavy gate. Her mother-in-law loved to boast that Diamond Villa's gate was the islet's largest and most ornate—no mean feat in an area filled with lavish mansions, built by overseas Chinese who'd made vast fortunes in Southeast Asia. In truth, Seok Koon found the gate ridiculous in its opulence and in its irreverent mélange of Eastern and Western architectural styles. An archway of art deco sunbeams crowned the towering wrought-iron doors, which were lined with a dozen carved canaries holding coins in their beaks, supposedly bestowing blessings on four generations of Ongs. Now, more than ever, those canaries seemed to taunt Seok Koon as they reveled in their boundless good fortune.

On the front landing, the wives who'd taken over the villa's first floor squatted in a circle, scrubbing tubs of laundry while their half-clothed children splashed in the overflow. At the sight of Seok Koon, the women stopped talking and stared unabashedly, daring her to reprimand them, as she had the first time they'd commandeered the landing. She trudged up the stairs.

The following morning, Seok Koon marched into the safety bureau clutching a pink cardboard box of French pastries with a fat envelope of money tucked in the corner. She and Bee Kim had agreed there was nothing to lose.

She offered the director the pastry box with both hands. Comrade Koh lifted the flap, plucked out the envelope, and tossed it on the table in disgust. He whispered fiercely, "Are you trying to get both of us in trouble?"

From the other side of the thin wall came the clack-clack-clack of a typewriter. Seok Koon berated herself for heeding her mother-in-law's advice. Could she even convince the director to give her the two permits he'd initially offered? Maybe Ah Liam and Bee Kim could leave first. She'd stay behind with San San and wait for two more. But her mother-in-law was so frail, she could no longer walk without a cane. How could she get herself and the boy all the way to Hong Kong?

Meanwhile, the grim-faced director was shuffling the papers in Seok Koon's file. He glanced at the envelope, now lying contritely by Seok Koon's elbow, and shut the file. "You'll be pleased to know that Dr. Lee Chin Kong, my friend and physician, has encouraged me to reconsider your case."

Seok Koon gasped. Her gratitude to Chin Kong—and to Rose, who she knew must have pressed her husband to act—filled her entire being. She thought she might lift right into the air.

"I've managed to get you a third permit."

Her spirits plummeted back down to earth. She was ready to drop to her knees and beg, but the director held up his hand. "It's the best I can do."

The words spilled from her mouth. "Thank you, comrade, oh thank you." Now was not the time to worry about how to tell Bee Kim she would have to remain behind—just temporarily, of course.

A strange smile spread across Comrade Koh's face. "Good. Which child will you take?"

The muscles in Seok Koon's body went slack inch by inch. "What do you mean?"

"Well, Mrs. Ong, you cannot take them both."

A howl rose in her throat; she managed to force it down. "Their father is dying."

The director's doughy face twisted into a smirk. "And your mother-in-law? Does she not care to see her dying son?"

Seok Koon thought quickly. "My mother-in-law is old and weak. You know how it is—that generation and their lotus feet. She rarely even leaves the house."

Comrade Koh's eyes were opaque. "The children are probably too young to really know their father anyway. Hasn't he been abroad for quite some time?"

She pressed her forehead to the cold metal desk in a kind of kowtow. "Please," she said, unable to hold back tears. "It's my husband's last wish."

"Mrs. Ong, I really don't have time for this. Surely you've seen the queue outside."

Seok Koon pushed herself up on her elbows and met the director's gaze.

He tapped his desk drawer. "The permits are right here. If you don't want them, someone else will."

"Tell me what to do to get a fourth."

"It's out of the question," he said. And then his sausage fingers crept across the desk until they brushed the envelope of money.

Seok Koon watched the director tuck the envelope in his breast pocket. The typewriter dinged in the adjacent room.

"I see," she said.

He patted his pocket. "Still, things have a way of changing quickly around here. Why don't you send an associate back next week."

Seok Koon stared into the depths of the director's beady eyes, trying to discern if any bit of him could be trusted. She calculated how much money was left in the safe and said, "I will."

"Good," he said, clapping his hands. "You and two family members will leave right away. You may remain in Hong Kong for up to fourteen days. Seven is standard, but because Dr. Lee is a good friend, I'm giving you a little extra time."

"Thank you so much," she murmured automatically. She didn't trust Mui Ah, who Bee Kim was convinced had turned her in, so Cook would have to come back for the fourth pass.

Comrade Koh spread three permits on his desk. On the first, he printed Seok Koon's name. On the second, he printed Bee Kim's. When he got to the last one, he waited with his pen poised. "Well?" He was clearly enjoying himself.

Seok Koon's fingers twitched involuntarily. How she longed to strike the man squarely on his bulbous nose. She jammed her hands beneath her skirt. The director's gaze flicked up to the clock on the wall. The tick of the second hand thundered in her ears; she couldn't think amid this racket.

"Well, Mrs. Ong?"

She pulled herself together. "Comrade, I beg of you, don't make me do this."

He threw his pen on the desk and it clanged to the floor.

"Ong Wee Liam." She heard herself speak her son's full name and knew it could never have been otherwise.

She bent to retrieve the director's pen, and he wrote the characters with a flourish. She slid the permits into her pocketbook and staggered to the door, where, for what seemed like an eternity, she fumbled with the doorknob. Her palms were slick with sweat; she could not find purchase. Had the director somehow locked her in?

"Mrs. Ong," he said.

She turned to find that Comrade Koh had opened the pastry box and was biting into an almond tart.

With his mouth full, he said, "I forgot to say I hope your husband makes it."

"Thank you," she choked out, and then she found her voice. "My associate will be back next week for my daughter's permit."

Crumbs gathered wetly in the corners of the director's mouth. "We'll do our best."

She dried her palms on her skirt and yanked open the door.

How did one tell one's daughter that the entire family was going to leave her behind? By dinnertime, Seok Koon still had no answers. The only thing she and her mother-in-law could think to do was to deliver the news as matter-of-factly as possible, as though they could somehow lull San San into failing to notice what was about to take place.

"They gave me three permits," Seok Koon announced, taking her seat at the table. "Ah Liam, Grandma, and I will go first. San San will stay behind with Cook and Mui Ah—just for a few days—until her permit comes through."

The girl's chewing slowed. She lowered her chopsticks to her rice bowl.

Seok Koon rushed to fill the silence. "We'll leave on the very first ferry tomorrow morning so we can meet the train in Xiamen."

Bee Kim chimed in, "Did you hear that, Ah Liam? Make sure you get all your packing done tonight."

The girl stared into her bowl.

Seok Koon kept talking in that same relentlessly cheerful voice. "Auntie Rose will stop by every day, so don't even think of skipping piano practice. When you arrive, you can play your new piece for your pa. He'll be so impressed."

"Ah yes," said Bee Kim. "Your pa's loved classical music ever since he was a young boy."

San San's face gave away nothing. "How many days?"

"One or two," Seok Koon said. "Four at the most."

San San's eyes locked on to hers, and she read something like defiance in her daughter's steady gaze. If the girl refused to be placated, then couldn't she at least sob and shriek like other girls her age?

"It'll go by in no time. Cook can prepare all your favorite foods," said Seok Koon. Ridiculous words that would soothe only a younger, simpler child.

"That's a marvelous idea," Bee Kim said. "Girl, write down everything you want to eat, so Mui Ah will know what to buy at the market."

San San bit her lip. "I don't really care."

Seok Koon shot her mother-in-law a look of desperation.

"What about *popiah*? Or *kiam peng*?" asked Bee Kim.

Ah Liam said, "Give her my permit. I'll stay behind."

Seok Koon's pulse soared. "The permits have already been assigned."

Ah Liam's still-unchanged voice always rose in pitch when he was agitated. "But if someone has to travel alone, shouldn't it be me?"

Seok Koon's hand smacked the table. "I can't discuss this right now. I have enough to worry about as it is."

Ah Liam squinted and looked away, and Seok Koon regretted her tone.

"May I be excused?" San San asked.

Bee Kim leaned over. "Are you feeling ill? Do you have a fever?" She pressed the back of her hand to the girl's forehead.

Seok Koon motioned for her mother-in-law to retreat. "Go ahead."

Her daughter's footsteps blasted down the hallway. San San's bedroom door slammed shut, the noise as sharp as any rebuke. In the center of the table, a skin of fat had congealed on the brown sauce in the dish of braised pork.

"May I be excused, too?" said Ah Liam.

Seok Koon threw down her napkin. "Whatever you want," she said. "I have to give the servants their instructions." She stood and went to the kitchen.

Bee Kim tried to make up for Seok Koon's harshness. "Your father needs you by his side," she told the boy.

"I know," he said, "but I'm worried about San San."

From behind the kitchen door, Seok Koon watched her mother-in-law smooth the cowlick on the back of her son's head. The boy had grown several centimeters these past months but was still small for his age.

Bee Kim said, "Cook will take San San all the way to the border. She'll only be alone for the very last stretch, and then we'll meet her in Hong Kong." She released a strained laugh. "Have some faith in your sister."

Seok Koon turned to find Cook and Mui Ah waiting by the stove.

"Don't worry about Little Miss," Cook said solemnly. "We'll take good care of her while you're gone."

In two days, he was to go back to the safety bureau to try again. Seok Koon handed over an envelope for the director, fattened with even more money than the first, along with a promise to send twice that amount for Cook to keep once San San was safe in her arms.

Mui Ah wiped tears from her eyes, even though everyone supposedly believed the family would be gone for no more than two weeks. "Master will recover," she sniffed. "I know he will."

Seok Koon tried to remember if Mui Ah had met her husband more than once. She thanked them for their well wishes and retired to her room to finish packing, making sure to leave several valuables prominently displayed: a crystal vase of chrysanthemums that were just starting to wilt, perfume bottles with yellowed French labels.

When she was done, she went to her daughter's room.

The light was on, but San San lay on top of the covers with a pillow over her face. Her beloved doll was splayed on the rug.

Seok Koon picked up the doll and smoothed its sparse blonde mane. "What happened to Hansel?"

San San kept her face covered. "I'm too old for dolls."

Seok Koon set the doll on the nightstand. "Are you feeling a little better?"

"No."

Seok Koon sat down beside her daughter, who didn't make room on the bed. When she lifted the pillow off San San's face, the girl threw her forearm over her eyes.

Seok Koon said, "It's only a few days."

"You already said that." The girl rolled over to face the wall.

She stroked her daughter's back, her fingers lingering on the faint knobs of her spine. "I'll miss you, San San."

In a spiteful voice, the girl replied, "But it's only a few days."

When had her children grown so rancorous, so mean?

"All right, then." Seok Koon rose to her feet. Her daughter's shoulders trembled, ever so slightly, and she softened her tone. "Do you want me to turn out the light?"

"I don't care."

Seok Koon tugged on the chain, and, in the darkness, her daughter stirred.

"Mama."

Seok Koon held her breath. "Yes?"

"What if Pa dies before I get there?"

Seok Koon flew to the bed and enveloped San San. "He'll wait for you. I swear he will."

At first the girl's thin body held taut, but when Seok Koon tightened her embrace, San San melted in her arms. Tears streamed out of San San swiftly, silently, soaking Seok Koon's neck and chest. In that moment, Seok Koon believed she and her daughter could stay intertwined like this, that she would never have to let go.

6

Only because the steps were wet and slippery from a brief pre-dawn shower did Bee Kim concede to take Mui Ah's arm. The sedan chairs were waiting; the luggage, piled in a wheelbarrow. Passing through the gates, Bee Kim gazed up at the coin-bearing canaries and asked them to bless her family one last time. Four decades she'd spent in this villa, and now she was leaving everything behind: the priceless antique furniture that had been in the family for generations, the gold and jade she couldn't layer over the jewelry she already wore without inviting suspicion, Ah Lip's pewter cufflinks that lay nestled in a worn velvet box on her nightstand. And, of course, the girl.

There she was at the top of the stairs, still clad in her white night-gown, stoic as a sentinel. Even as an infant, San San had rarely cried, as if she'd understood from birth that there was no point in vying with her more demanding brother. Only once could Bee Kim recall her speaking up. One evening, a year or two earlier, Bee Kim had plucked the last slice of hard-boiled egg from the tofu stew and dropped it in Ah Liam's bowl, prompting San San to ask, "Why don't I ever get the last egg?" Bee Kim turned in surprise. Up until that moment, she hadn't quite realized what she'd been doing. She answered smoothly, "Because your brother is older and eats more than you." San San studied her for a beat and then whispered into her bowl, "I don't like eggs anyway."

"Come here, girl," Bee Kim called.

San San approached. A droplet of mucus threatened to spill from her nose. Bee Kim offered up her handkerchief, and the girl blew into the cloth and looked up with uncertainty.

"Keep it, silly gourd," said Bee Kim. She cupped San San's face in her hands and found herself at a loss for words. She gently pinched the girl's cheeks to hide her discomfort and then reached beneath her sleeve and forced a slender, filigreed gold bangle from her wrist, wincing as it constricted her fleshy hand. She slid the bangle up San San's thin arm, almost to the elbow. "So you'll think of your grandma while we're apart."

The girl looked doubtfully at the bangle. "Thank you."

Bee Kim signaled to Mui Ah. "Help me in the sedan chair."

Her grandson appeared by the luggage, his damp hair plastered across his forehead. The sleeves of his lightweight blazer grazed his wrist bones, and Bee Kim's chest tightened against the outpouring of tenderness she felt for the boy. For his sake, she would have given up ten times more.

Seok Koon came rushing down the stairs and knelt before San San. Bee Kim willed her daughter-in-law to stay strong. Seok Koon pressed the girl's head to her chest for a long while, and when they finally separated, San San blinked as though in a daze.

Seok Koon managed to smile and say, "See you soon, Daughter." Her eyes brimmed, but she did not cry.

Ah Liam came over and wrapped an arm around San San and whispered something in her ear that brought a grin to her face. Bee Kim wanted to scoop them both up and speed down the hill. It didn't make sense that they couldn't take the girl with them. She stared at the wheelbarrow of luggage, wondering how it hadn't occurred to her to at least attempt to hide her granddaughter in one of those cases. She closed her eyes and gripped her skull and waited for the madness to pass.

Meanwhile, Seok Koon and Ah Liam boarded the second sedan chair. They were about to set off when there was a clattering of footsteps on cobblestone. A man and a woman rounded the corner and ran toward them.

"Sorry we're late," Rose said breathlessly. She nodded at Bee Kim in greeting.

Seok Koon jumped down from the sedan chair and embraced her friend.

"We wanted to say goodbye," Chin Kong said, mopping the perspiration from his brow with his handkerchief.

Seok Koon shook Chin Kong's hand and thanked him for all he'd done.

Bee Kim scanned the windows of the first two floors of the villa for spying neighbors, but it was hard to see in the dim early-morning light. For heaven's sake, the family was only supposed to be gone for two weeks.

"Nonsense, it was nothing," Rose said, wiping her eyes.

In a low voice, Chin Kong added, "We only ask that you remember us later, when you're in a position to offer help."

Bee Kim looked over in alarm. Her ears weren't as sharp as they'd once been; she must have misheard. Chin Kong, the important doctor and Party member, was as red as they came. He had no reason to leave.

But the stunned expression on her daughter-in-law's face was unmistakable. "Anything you need," Seok Koon stammered. "Anything at all."

"Don't worry about San San," Rose said, going over to the girl.

San San let her piano teacher take her hand, and once again those crazed thoughts descended upon Bee Kim. If the girl had been an infant, she would have fed her rice liquor and bound her beneath her clothes. "All right then," she called out. "We mustn't miss the ferry."

Finally they were off.

The tall wrought-iron gates—the finest in all of Drum Wave Islet—receded. Rose and Chin Kong waved. Cook and Mui Ah shouted, "May the heavens protect you."

Only San San, ghostly in her billowing nightgown, watched in silence. The knowing expression on the girl's face slashed through Bee Kim, and she let out a moan. The front chair carrier stopped short, drawing curse words from his partner behind.

"Madame, do you need to turn back?"

Up ahead, the other sedan chair slowed.

Seok Koon called, "Did you forget something, Ma?"

Bee Kim shook her head. "Keep going. We mustn't miss the boat." For the rest of the way, she stared resolutely ahead.

Down by the ferry docks her sedan chair landed with a thud. Lifting her eyes, Bee Kim saw that on this, her last morning on Drum Wave Islet, the sky was flat, colorless, dull. Somehow, over the years, without her noticing, the sky, too, had grown weary with age.

At Xiamen harbor, they sent Ah Liam to flag two trishaws to take them and their luggage to the train station. Eight hours after boarding the train's soft-seat car, they arrived in the village of Gongbei, whose sole distinguishing feature appeared to be a rudimentary customhouse separating the mainland from the peninsula of Macau. A stream that was more mud than water marked the border. Bee Kim searched in vain for a bridge before concluding she would have to tramp right through the yellow mud on her already aching bound feet.

She couldn't fret for long because a mean-looking guard with a ruddy face and a thick neck barked through a bullhorn for all of them to line up and hold out their exit permits. Two younger guards trooped down the line in opposite directions, and Bee Kim panicked as the flimsy document was seized from her. What was to prevent them from tearing her family's permits to shreds, or dropping them in the stream, or claiming they'd never handed them over in the first place? She touched her grandson's arm, uncertain if she was requesting assurance or attempting to assure him, and he lifted his elbow for her hand to slip through.

Near the end of the line, one of the young guards addressed a man in a Western suit.

"Don't lie to me," the boy warned the much older man.

"It's the truth," the man pleaded.

The boy held the exit permit high in the air and ripped it in half.

Bee Kim and Ah Liam gasped in unison. She tightened her grip on his arm. A baby wailed and its mother tried desperately to hush it.

"You can't do that," the man sputtered. "I have permission to leave. Get me your superior."

The mean-looking guard strode over, crumpled the two halves of the man's exit permit in his large hand, and threw the paper ball onto the ground. The two young guards seized the man under his arms and half walked, half dragged him into the customhouse.

Even as Bee Kim clung to her grandson, she dared not look at him or Seok Koon. Instead she studied the intricate embroidery on her diminutive shoes. How absurd they appeared next to Ah Liam's sturdy, dirt-caked canvas pair, like a toy version trying to pass for the real thing. A few paces away, the baby whimpered but didn't cry.

After hauling away their luggage for inspection, the head guard ordered them to turn over their money. Her daughter-in-law dutifully held open her wallet, and at the sight of the thick stack of bills, Bee Kim tensed. The guard plucked out the stack and counted the bills, pausing every so often to look from Seok Koon to Ah Liam to Bee Kim. She pulled her sleeves over her fingers to hide her rings, and scanned her grandson and daughter-in-law for things that might catch the guard's eye. Her grandson's wrist bones peeking out of his too-small jacket looked so defenseless, so fragile. When the guard was done counting,

Bee Kim feared what he would say, but all he did was hand the bills to one of the younger guards and move down the line.

More time passed. Even leaning on her cane and on Ah Liam's arm, Bee Kim's thighs and calves ached desperately. Each time she shifted her weight, a searing pain shot down her shins to her feet. Finally their exit permits were returned to them, and another couple, a young man and woman, were dragged away. Ah Liam leaned in and opened his mouth, but Bee Kim warned him with her eyes to stay silent.

The head guard raised his bullhorn to his face. "You've all been cleared to exit China. Collect your luggage and go."

Bee Kim's exhale whooshed through the air. She hugged her grandson tightly and whispered, "Almost there."

Seok Koon and Ah Liam each took one of Bee Kim's arms and helped her down the steep bank and across the stream. With every slippery step, the mud sucked at her shoes, threatening to swallow them whole. More able-bodied passengers scrambled past, kicking up dirt in all directions. At the city walls, Bee Kim fell against the smooth, dark stones to wait while her daughter-in-law and grandson fetched the luggage. Each time they passed the guards, she held her breath and prayed.

At last they stepped through the city gates, and Bee Kim was dismayed to be greeted by another checkpoint. But this time, the Portuguese guard merely stamped their permits and waved them along to await the final leg of the journey.

Inside a small, clean waiting room with windows overlooking the water, Bee Kim explained to Ah Liam that all that remained was for them to be spirited into Hong Kong in the hold of a cruise ship.

When the boy looked shocked, Bee Kim hurried to add, "Everyone does it this way." She waved a hand at the other passengers in the room. "Even high-level cadres. You saw how difficult it was for your ma to get our exit permits? It's ten times harder to get an entry permit for Hong Kong."

"What if they catch us?"

"This isn't China," she said. "In Hong Kong, they want to help us, not arrest us." She pointed to a nearby rack of colorful glossy magazines and newspapers and urged her grandson to take one. "There, the press is free to publish whatever they want."

Her grandson went to the rack and examined a newspaper called the *Sing Tao Daily.* Bee Kim turned to her daughter-in-law. "It will be good for him to see the way people live outside our China."

But Seok Koon didn't respond. She stared out the window with her arms wrapped around herself.

"It's only a little bit longer now," Bee Kim said gingerly, because acknowledging what was truly on her daughter-in-law's mind would release a torrent of her own.

Seok Koon stared into the distance. "This was a mistake. I must turn back."

Bee Kim loosened one of the arms folded across Seok Koon's chest and pinned it to the armrest of her chair. "You can't."

Seok Koon twisted to face Bee Kim. "They have to let me back across. There's no rule against going the opposite way."

"Listen to me, Daughter-in-Law. San San's permit will come through, and if it doesn't, Zhai will know what to do." Words she'd repeated to herself throughout this daylong journey.

"All those people turned away with no explanation."

"That won't happen to San San."

Seok Koon's voice rose. "How can you be so sure?"

Ah Liam glanced up from his newspaper.

"There, there," Bee Kim said in a soothing tone. "We made it, didn't we? She will, too."

"But what if those despicable guards take her away?"

Bee Kim threw up her hands. What did Seok Koon want from her? Of course nothing was certain. The girl might never get her exit permit. The girl might make it all the way here, only to get turned back on a technicality, or because the guard was in a bad mood. The girl could fall ill tomorrow. People died in all sorts of freak accidents. Her own sister had died that way when she was only six. Bee Kim, too, yearned to cry and lament and let loose her frustrations, but she wasn't doing that, was she? No, she was focused on getting them to safety.

Seok Koon's tearful gaze bore down on Bee Kim, pleading for things she had no right to ask for and Bee Kim had no right to give.

7

The ship was supposed to have docked two hours ago. Ah Zhai paced the perimeter of the crowded arrival hall, chain-smoking cigarettes, stepping over sleeping vagrants, ignoring vendors hawking steamed meat buns and unshelled peanuts and sheets of dried cuttlefish on wooden skewers. In the sticky late-afternoon heat, his cream linen suit jacket felt as stifling as bandages. Above his head, a row of ceiling fans revolved so sluggishly he could see the thick layer of dust coating each blade. He removed his straw fedora and fanned his face, but there was little relief.

A pair of young women—sisters from the looks of it—hurried through the hall hand in hand. They were fashionably dressed in fitted cheongsams, one the shade of a ripe peach, and the other, the pale green of those sugared almonds Lulu lately craved. Ah Zhai's gaze lingered on the women, appreciating their sheer buoyancy on this oppressively hot day. Such garments had been banned in new China. He'd seen pictures in the paper of city ladies dressed like cadres in dull, shapeless uniforms, with severely bobbed hair. He hoped Seok Koon hadn't cut her hair, and then immediately reprimanded himself for allowing so superficial a thought to enter his mind. Six years had passed since he'd last seen his mother and wife and children. Six long years during which his guilt had accumulated, drop by indiscernible drop, until one day, not long ago, he'd looked down at the rising water and discovered he was about to drown.

Eight years earlier, when Ah Zhai first broached the topic of moving the family to Hong Kong, his father had adamantly refused. He'd put his whole life into his factories; he wasn't going to simply hand them over to the communists. Ah Zhai could tell Seok Koon disagreed, but she would never have defied her father-in-law. So Ah Zhai didn't push. Besides, his father had a point: it was too early to tell what the new ruling party was up to. Ah Zhai returned to Hong Kong and promptly purchased the townhouse so Lulu would have room to entertain. Two years later, the communists imposed restrictions so stringent, they essentially sealed the borders. And two years after that, his father was dead.

Across the arrival hall, people stirred. A cruise ship approached, as shiny and imposing as one of the new harbor-view hotels. Ah Zhai hung back and let the hordes surge past, envying every wide-eyed, open-faced man and woman who was no doubt meeting a legitimate passenger and not a refugee stowed below deck.

The ship dropped its gangplank, and the real passengers streamed out, cheerful and relaxed. Ah Zhai combed their faces for outliers, for those who looked harrowed or fatigued. His son was almost thirteen, his daughter nine. The latest photographs he had were several months old. He wondered if his son, small for his age, had grown at least as tall as his mother, if his daughter's masculine features—narrow eyes and an angular jaw inherited, they said, from his mother's dead sister—had softened with maturity. These children he barely knew. All these years, San San and Ah Liam's absence had been a dull, constant ache in his side—something that went unnoticed for long stretches of time, but, when pointed out, caused pangs of worry and regret.

A few paces away, a man hoisted a toddler high into the air, and the toddler burst into tears. A Western couple embraced so fiercely that Ah Zhai had to look away. "How old-fashioned you are," Lulu would have said with a clattering, bell-like laugh. These past weeks, aside from a few minor—and understandable—outbursts, she'd been thoughtful and generous, helping him prepare for his family's arrival. "Nothing will change, bunny," he'd vowed again the night before as they clung to each other in bed.

The stream of passengers thinned along with the crowd in the arrival hall. So many things could have gone wrong: Their permits had been stolen. They'd missed the boat, or train, or ferry. The border guards had turned them back, or worse, imprisoned them for some unknown offense. What a mistake to embark upon this foolhardy plan. Ah Zhai cursed himself for acting too late, or perhaps he'd been too hasty?

In the years following his father's death, the Party's moods had grown increasingly erratic and extreme, culminating in the torture and subsequent death of Uncle Thomas, his father's lifelong friend. This, coupled with the additional pressure the Ongs were facing, which Seok Koon hadn't been able to elaborate upon in her letter, had strengthened Ah Zhai's resolve to get his family across the border at any cost. But what if he'd miscalculated? What if he'd picked the wrong moment to act?

Someone tapped his shoulder. Ah Zhai turned to find a uniformed crewman clutching the most recent photograph of himself that he'd sent his family.

"Mr. Ong?" The crewman held up the photograph to Ah Zhai's face.

He followed the man to the far side of the hall, where a trio in rumpled, mud-stained clothing cowered in the corner with their luggage.

"Ma," Ah Zhai said, his voice breaking.

He embraced his mother, eager to prolong the moment before he had to face his wife and son. His mother's shoulder blades shifted against his arms; she was even frailer than he remembered. He pressed his lips to her thinning crown of hair, breathed in the musky scent of her scalp, and felt his doubts fade.

"Take off your hat, Son," his mother said. "Let me see your face. My, you've lost weight."

"It's stress," said Ah Zhai, running a hand through his hair. "That, and old age."

His wife hung back, holding on to the boy, who still only came up to her nose.

Ah Zhai must have pictured this reunion at least a hundred times. His wife would be shy at first. She would blush and duck her head to hide her smile, as she had fourteen years earlier, when she'd spotted him waiting by the conservatory gate on a scorching afternoon, much like this one.

But the weather was the only constant, for he could find no traces of the cheerful, soft-spoken schoolgirl in the woman standing beyond arm's reach. Her brow was pinched, her lips strained into a smile that was almost a grimace. Her once lustrous hair hung in two heavy wings by her chin. He wanted to hold her, not from desire, but from pity.

In the end, his hands remained by his sides. "My wife," he said.

"My husband."

"I hope the journey wasn't too difficult."

"It was fine."

His wife told the boy to greet his father, but Ah Liam stood there with his mouth agape.

"Don't you remember me?" Ah Zhai asked, clapping his son on the back.

The boy edged away from him, his eyes on his mother.

Ah Zhai hid his dismay by asking, "And where's the little one?"

Ah Liam kept staring at Seok Koon. "You said he was too ill to get out of bed."

So they hadn't told the boy. Ah Zhai would have done the same thing. "Where's the little one?" he asked again, but his wife and mother were fixated on the boy.

"Son, it was the only way for us to leave," Seok Koon said.

Bee Kim said, "You saw what happened during that inspection. We lied to keep you safe."

"Where's my daughter?" Ah Zhai asked.

Abruptly all three of them turned. There was a flash of terror in his wife's eyes. "They made us leave her behind."

Ah Zhai raised his voice as though the problem was that she'd misheard the question. "What are you talking about? Where is she?"

"Just for a few days."

"Who made you leave her?"

His mother said, "It's temporary. Her permit will come through next week."

"I tried everything," said Seok Koon. "They wouldn't let us bring her."

Bee Kim was talking on and on about Hua's suicide, a hammered portrait, a couple of vengeful inspectors. Seok Koon interrupted to describe the wretched director of the safety bureau. Ah Zhai's temples throbbed. He yanked his tie from his neck. This heat would kill them all.

His mother said, "Our own house girl spied on us and reported us to the authorities. Can you imagine such a thing?"

Ah Zhai pressed his fingers to his temples. Nine-year-old San San, alone in the villa with a couple of servants who'd revealed themselves to be traitors? It didn't make any sense. "How do you know her permit will come through?"

His wife's face fell, and Ah Zhai almost wished he hadn't asked.

Like a mantra his mother repeated, "We had no choice. It was the right thing to do."

"I wanted to stay behind," said the boy. "Why didn't you let me stay behind?"

Tiny fists pounded the inner walls of Ah Zhai's skull. "What did the safety bureau director say?"

All three of them talked at once.

"He all but promised us the permit."

"He's a good friend of Chin Kong's."

"I should have stayed instead of San San."

"All cadres are corrupt. He won't turn down the bribe."

Ah Zhai couldn't think straight. He had to get them out of this sweltering hall. He signaled for a porter to deal with the luggage and said, "Let's go. This isn't the place to discuss this." He took off, and his family hurried behind him, their voices a blur.

Outside the harbor, the bustle of the city seemed to chasten them. He helped his mother into the front seat of the car, while Ah Liam and Seok Koon settled into the back. He inserted the key in the ignition and turned up the air-conditioning as high as it would go.

In a determined voice, his mother said, "What a beautiful car, Zhai."

Seok Koon agreed. "Son, do you like your pa's car?"

At first the boy was silent, and then he said, "Mui Ah didn't turn Grandma in. I did."

The high pitch of Ah Liam's voice was the first thing that struck Ah Zhai. His son still sounded like a girl.

His wife inhaled sharply. "What are you saying? No, I won't believe it."

His mother said, "Whom did you tell? How could you do such a thing?"

Only then did Ah Zhai comprehend his son's confession. He adjusted his rearview mirror until it captured the boy's brazen gaze. Who was this stranger in his back seat? Where had he learned such evil, or was it somehow innate?

"I had to," Ah Liam said. Under his breath he recited, "Whoever sides with imperialism, feudalism, and bureaucrat-capitalism is—"

Ah Zhai swerved to the side of the road and stamped on the brakes. The boy slammed into the back of Ah Zhai's seat, which knocked the breath out of him. Ah Zhai twisted around to look his son full in the face. "Don't ever let me hear you quote that bastard again. You are too young and too stupid to understand anything."

The boy's lower lip trembled. He squeezed shut his eyes.

Ah Zhai felt his wife and mother silently urging him to keep talking, to say something reassuring and finite. He returned his hands to the steering wheel and released the brakes.

At the stoplight, he regarded his wife's and son's ashen faces in the rearview mirror. Beside him, his mother wrung her hands like she was determined to squeeze every drop of life from them. The specter of his daughter—that funny flat-faced little bundle who rarely cried, that agile toddler whose watchful eyes missed nothing—loomed over them all. When the light turned, he accelerated, fearful of what he'd done.

8

At last, a full four hours after San San and Cook had joined the queue outside the safety bureau, the door swung open. San San stood on her tiptoes to get a better look at the cadre who held a long rolled-up poster and a bucket of paste. Voices rose up and down the queue.

"Please, comrade, when will the director be taking meetings?"

"Comrade, I've been waiting since six this morning."

"So have we," San San cried.

"That's nothing! We've been waiting since four."

The cadre turned her back to them. She brushed long stripes of paste on the door and put up the poster. San San pushed forward to get a closer look, but she was too short to see over the grown-ups. "What does it say?" she asked, tugging on Cook's sleeve. "How much longer?"

Cook's lips moved as his eyes swept across the poster. San San had already noticed his poor reading skills. She elbowed her way to the front of the crowd.

No exit permits will be issued from now through the month of June. The safety bureau will reopen for requests on July 1, 1957.

It was only the end of May. Her father might not last that long. Surely the safety bureau would make an exception for her, if she could just explain everything. She weaved her way back to Cook.

He scratched his head. "We'll ask your ma what to do."

She wanted to smack him awake. "We don't have time for that."

A commotion rose from the side of the mansion. A short, stout man with a doughy face and beady eyes, flanked by two guards, hurried to a waiting car.

"Comrade Koh," several cried as they gave chase.

"My wife is ill!"

"My brother is dying!"

"I've been waiting five months, you have to help me!"

San San didn't join in. No exceptions, she realized, would be made for her.

The guards waved their batons to keep back the pursuers. The stout man slid into the car, which sped off.

"Your mother will know what to do," said Cook. Everything about him, from his nervous, shifting gaze to his hunched-over posture, signaled his helplessness.

San San's frustration turned to disdain. How could her mother have left her with this bumbling, useless man? How could he be expected to take charge of anything? If she were to have any chance of getting to Hong Kong in time to see her father, she would have to figure it out on her own.

The following day, right before the final bell, Teacher Lu wiped off her chalk-stained fingers on her handkerchief and announced, "You students have received a golden opportunity to thank the peasants who have sacrificed so much for our country."

San San knew what was coming. She sank in her seat.

"This weekend, we need volunteers to assist at a tea plantation in Anxi."

The last time San San and her classmates had volunteered at a textiles factory in the city, they'd spent hours washing floors and cleaning lavatories. For days afterward, San San had scrubbed her skin to rid it of the acrid smell of bleach.

"How lucky you are to be able to give back to the people who are the backbone of this great nation," said Teacher Lu, placing hand over heart as though overcome by emotion.

One by one, San San's classmates raised their hands, and Teacher Lu wrote their names on the blackboard. San San sat as still as a statue, hoping against all odds that Teacher Lu would overlook her. Soon, she and Stinky, the class troublemaker who also had a flatulence problem, were the only two who had yet to volunteer.

"Anyone else?" asked Teacher Lu.

San San's seatmate and best friend, Little Red, kicked her under their shared desk. Dropping her head, San San raised her hand. A second later, Stinky caved, too.

Teacher Lu clapped her hands. "One hundred percent volunteer participation yet again. As our Great Helmsman says, education and productive labor must go hand in hand. See you all tomorrow at five a.m. sharp."

San San smacked Little Red's knee under their desk, harder than she'd intended.

Little Red batted her lashes and muttered, "If I have to suffer, you do, too," at which San San couldn't help but smile.

The next morning, San San and her classmates rode the ferry to Xiamen where they boarded the bus that would take them to Anxi. The bus was hot and noisy and stank of diesel fumes, but San San took a strange comfort in all these bodies crammed in around her. She hadn't slept soundly in the three days since her family's departure, and now she leaned her head against the window and instantly fell asleep.

She awoke to find her hand in a softly snoring Little Red's. Outside her window, the wide paved road filled with swerving bicycles and honking pedicabs had given way to a winding mountain path and peasants on donkeys. In place of unfinished buildings shielded by scaffolding were verdant fields cut into the gently sloping hillside, all of it veiled by a vast curtain of fog. This strange, beautiful landscape filled her with hope. When Little Red yawned awake, San San said, "It won't be as bad as last time. You'll see."

The students were greeted by an old man with a leathery face and blackened fingernails that looked as though they were caked with blood, but which he explained were stained with tea. He led them across the dense, almost-black soil, past peasants bent low over tea bushes, like a scene out of a propaganda poster. One of the peasants grinned at San San, revealing a startling mouthful of twisted, brown teeth that was nothing like the bright white smiles of the poster peasants.

They stopped at a simple shed in front of which a few thin donkeys idled.

"Now for your assignment," the old man said. "You students are going to transport donkey manure to fertilize the bushes."

San San turned to Little Red in outrage, but the sight of her friend's quivering chin made her stop short. "Don't be sad," she whispered, and then she gifted Little Red a nugget of knowledge she hadn't known she possessed: "Donkey manure stinks much less than the human kind."

Little Red giggled through her tears, and San San joined in, drawing a stern look from Teacher Lu.

The old man took them around the side of the building to a deep pit. The stench hit them full in the face. San San switched to breathing through her mouth, and Little Red was kind enough not to point out her earlier error. They were told to line up to collect carrying poles that had a bucket attached to each end. Right away San San's pole chafed her shoulders. Within a few steps, she felt blisters forming on her skin. She attempted to shift the pole but only succeeded in tipping half a bucket of manure down the side of her pants. The clammy stickiness sickened her. She kept breathing through her mouth, but the stench coated her tongue and the insides of her throat until she could almost taste it. She set down her buckets in despair.

Her classmates tripped past her with considerably less difficulty. Even Little Red was already several paces ahead. San San gathered her strength and lifted the pole back over her shoulders, careful not to disturb the buckets' contents. A giant sneeze rose through her and she quickly set down the buckets. Once she started sneezing she could not stop. Her eyes itched and watered; it took all her willpower to avoid rubbing them with her filthy hands. With two fingers she pinched her grandmother's handkerchief out of her pocket, blew her nose, and then regarded the soiled fabric with remorse.

Teacher Lu was coming toward her with her hands on her hips.

"It's my immune system," San San explained, repeating the phrase her mother used. "I'm always catching cold."

"Your classmates are already on their second round." Teacher Lu lifted the pole back onto San San's shoulders and went to check on Stinky, who had also fallen behind.

Despite the ache that spread from her neck and shoulders to her lower back, San San somehow made it to the row of bushes. She emptied what remained in her buckets and returned to the pit to start all over again.

Through each round, her nose continued to run. She had to stop every few steps to blow into her grandmother's handkerchief. She pushed herself onward by imagining her father, lying on his deathbed, unable to eat or move. How could she complain when he was suffering so? She set down her buckets and sneezed three times.

Teacher Lu appeared beside San San and said in a surprisingly gentle tone, "It's almost lunchtime. Go and take a short rest." She pointed to the communal dining hall where they would take their afternoon meal.

San San trudged in the direction her teacher had pointed, fighting to hide her glee. By now the sun had summoned enough heat to burn through the fog, and she was parched. Inside the dining hall, a young woman with deep lines radiating from the corners of her eyes gave her a tin cup of water. She drank greedily and then went back outside and found a shady spot beneath an acacia tree.

Two short, sturdy men pushing a handcart piled high with pallets of tea leaves walked past.

"There?" one man asked, pointing to one of two trucks parked several meters ahead.

"Yeah," said the other. "The one going to Hong Kong."

San San flattened her back against the tree trunk and listened for the men to say more, but they only grunted and gestured as they loaded the pallets into the truck bed. The moratorium on exit permits, she saw, applied only to people, while goods passed freely across the border. She pictured a fancy tea shop in Hong Kong, stacked to the ceiling with tins of pungent leaves. Her mother would enter, pointing to the tin that held the very leaves that San San had labored to fertilize. Her mother would return to her father's bedside with that aromatic brew, blowing gently before tipping the cup to his pale, chapped lips, both of them oblivious to the chain that led back to their absent daughter.

San San knew she had to act. When the men wheeled away the empty cart, she made sure she was alone before scrambling into the truck bed. But the pallets were packed so snugly there was no place to hide. She jumped down from the truck bed and scurried through the passenger door into the cab, where she folded herself in the space beneath the dashboard.

Another man returned to count the pallets and make sure they were properly stacked, but she was well out of sight. Later—but hopefully not too much later—when the driver entered the truck, San San would have to convince him to take her along. She prayed he'd arrive soon, before anyone noticed she was missing. "Please just hear me out," she'd say quietly but firmly. "My father is dying in Hong Kong. My family had to leave without me. My father is rich and will reward you hand-somely for bringing me to him."

In the distance, her classmates called her name. She curled up tightly on the floor of the truck. She picked out Little Red's voice among the cries and wished she could have informed her of her plan, to spare her from worrying. And then San San thought of all the other people who would worry: Cook and Mui Ah. Auntie Rose. She'd have to send a letter the instant she reached Hong Kong. Perhaps the driver would have paper and a pen, so she could write the letter on the way there and give it to him to mail when he returned to Anxi. Did they have mail service in the countryside?

Shouts of her name grew louder. Her nose was running again, and she dabbed the edge of her handkerchief to her raw nostrils. A gust of wind blew in through the open window. She felt her insides constrict, and then the sneeze catapulted out of her. "Achoo! Achoo! Achoo!"

The passenger door of the truck swung open. San San smacked her head on the dashboard as she sat up. "Achoo!"

"She's here, I found her," someone cried. "The little scoundrel is right here."

A pair of rough, calloused hands dragged San San from the truck. When her feet hit the dirt, her legs crumpled; she clung to the stranger's arm.

The arm belonged to a stocky woman with a broad, flat face. "You lazy worm, you naughty girl. Everyone's been searching for you. Your teacher's worried sick."

San San twisted around to meet the woman's eyes. "Please just hear me out," she pleaded, but her teacher was already running over.

Sweat dripped down Teacher Lu's face. She doubled over and rested with her palms on her knees. When she'd caught her breath, she seized San San by the shirt collar and dragged her to the bus.

"I'm sorry, Teacher," San San said. "I felt so sick and so exhausted, I just wanted to rest for a little while." The last thing she wanted was to reveal her true motive.

"Wait here," said Teacher Lu. To the bus driver, she said, "Don't let her out of your sight."

The driver smoked and turned up the volume on his small radio and ignored San San except to ask, "Why would you do such a stupid thing?"

The bus's dirty windshield turned the clear sky the color of smog.

San San said, "I guess I'm stupid."

After a while, her classmates filed onto the bus. They laughed and pointed and made faces at San San, all except for Little Red, who stared straight ahead and marched past.

Teacher Lu got on last and sat down next to San San. She pinched her arm and said, loud enough for the whole bus to hear, "You bad, bad egg. You're in more trouble than you can even imagine."

San San's classmates tittered, and she hung her head.

"You're really shameless," said Teacher Lu, "shirking work while the rest of your classmates sweated through their shirts."

San San realized she'd managed to convince her teacher that laziness was her sole crime. "I'm sorry, Teacher. I see how my selfishness caused my friends to suffer. I promise to fix my bad attitude." She dared not peek to gauge her teacher's reaction.

9

E ach morning, Seok Koon hastily changed out of her nightgown and flew downstairs to check the mailbox, even though she knew it was too soon for a letter from Diamond Villa to arrive.

She told herself the director would keep his word, but just in case, she spent her days traversing Hong Kong Island and parts of Kowloon in search of anyone who might possibly increase San San's chances of making it safely across the border. At nine o'clock sharp, she arrived at the offices of the United Nations High Commissioner for Refugees on Queen Victoria Street, and when the aloof receptionist announced once again that she had no available appointments, Seok Koon parked herself on the lumpy sofa directly opposite the reception desk, in case of a cancellation. Afternoons, she braved stinking, chaotic streets to visit the community centers that were sprouting up all over the colony to cater to newly arrived immigrants and refugees. Evenings, she wrote her daughter breezy, light-hearted letters describing their seventh-floor flat in the stately building that was taller than any on Drum Wave Islet, the pale-pink curtains and canopy bed in San San's new room, the Broadwood baby grand piano that no one would touch until she arrived. She closed each letter with the promise that Pa would hang on until San San reached his bedside.

None of Seok Koon's efforts to devise an alternate plan panned out. She hadn't managed to see the UN High Commissioner or even a lesser staff member. The written appeals she'd left at the reception desk had been ignored—if the girl had even bothered to pass them on instead of chucking them in the wastebasket when Seok Koon turned her back. At her last visit to a community center clear across town, Seok Koon spoke to a wild-eyed man who'd swum six hours from Guangdong to Hong Kong, somehow avoiding the guards, with their vicious dogs, who patrolled Kowloon's rocky coast. But that information was of no use to Seok Koon. No matter how strong a swimmer San San was, she couldn't possibly complete such a feat.

And then, on day ten, a letter from Cook finally arrived. *No exit permits until July,* he'd written in his shaky childlike scrawl—a message so pressing, he hadn't wasted time seeking out a professional letter writer.

For the first time since she'd set foot in the colony, Seok Koon found herself at a complete and utter loss. She hurried down the hallway to her room to avoid the inevitable questions from her mother-in-law and her son. In four days, her own exit permit would expire and the Party would confirm what its cadres must have suspected all along but never said aloud: the Ong family had left for good. In four days, regardless of the lies Seok Koon would fold into another envelope bound for Diamond Villa, her clever daughter would march one step closer to the truth. Worst of all, Comrade Koh would be reprimanded for his poor judgment, and San San's chances of ever getting a permit would plummet to zero.

In the next room, Bee Kim expelled a string of coughs. Seok Koon reached for her pocketbook and straw hat and left the flat—anything to delay handing over the letter, anything to delay the ensuing conversation about the necessity of patience and of staying strong for her son.

On the street, Seok Koon lowered the brim of her hat and wondered where to go. Approaching the provision shop at the end of the block, she slowed and ducked inside. A noisy electric fan on the counter kept the store relatively cool. Her nostrils filled with the musty scent of dried sour plums in a large burlap sack on the concrete floor.

After greeting the proprietress behind the counter, Seok Koon spotted bins of sweets lining the back wall: fruit-flavored lozenges wrapped in multicolored cellophane, milk chocolates shaped like gold coins. She pictured her daughter slicing open a box, squealing with delight as the sweets rained onto her lap. Seok Koon filled two paper sacks and took them up to the counter.

"So many sweets," the proprietress said. "Are you having a party?"

Seok Koon smiled vaguely and handed over her money. The box she sent San San would be bursting with candies, so that even after the censors confiscated their share, there would be plenty left over. Then she saw her daughter digging through the box for the letter that contained news of the family's indefinite delay. She saw her daughter sniffling, too proud to cry. Repulsion poured through Seok Koon. She disgusted herself. How could she belittle her daughter with such a cheap and obvious ploy? How dare she even think to suggest that a couple of sweets could make up for what she'd done?

When Seok Koon first held her baby daughter in her arms, she'd kissed that silky, translucent cheek and made a silent vow: in her home, at least, her daughter and son would be treated the same, regardless of what the outside world would later bestow or withhold. As San San grew up, however, Seok Koon fretted over her plain appearance; she simply couldn't help herself. Her daughter was said to resemble Bee Kim's late sister—whose death had never fully been explained—while Seok Koon's fair skin and round eyes had been wasted on her son. She began to wonder if she were in fact limiting her daughter by failing to prepare her for life away from home. At the age of ten, Ah Liam stopped attending piano lessons, and seven-year-old San San, who up until then had been permitted to do everything her big brother did, declared she would stop, too. But her daughter had real talent, and when Seok Koon forbade her from giving up the piano, San San kicked over a vase of pussy willow branches and faced Seok Koon without remorse. In a fit of anger, Seok Koon said, "You aren't the least bit pretty, so your only hope is to cultivate other skills and pray someone marries you." Her daughter ran off in tears, and Seok Koon clapped her hands over her mouth, appalled at the ugliness that had poured out of her—an ugliness that continued to fester in her deepest, darkest place, regardless of her good intentions.

Out on the sidewalk she paused, sick to her stomach. Should she throw out the sweets or give them to the vagrant she sometimes saw napping in doorways?

"Mrs. Ong, how are you?" the owner of the corner newsstand called out.

She turned reluctantly. "Fine, thank you, Mr. Cheong. And how are you?"

"Not bad, not bad."

A tabloid newspaper lay open before the old man, and the headline at the top of the page caught Seok Koon's eye: "Businessman Escapes with Aid of Underground Christians." She took a step closer. "Do you have another one of those?"

He gestured to the rack beside him that held half a dozen copies.

Seok Koon stuck a copy under her arm and thrust a coin at him. After a moment's thought, she set the paper sacks on the counter. "For your grandkids," she said and hurried down the street, ignoring the old man's polite protests.

Outside her building, she tore through the newspaper in search of the headline. According to the article, underground Christians stationed in various locations across the mainland had worked closely with churches in Hong Kong to get this Shanghainese businessman across the border. The harrowing journey had taken nearly a month. When the businessman finally arrived at his family's doorstep in Hong Kong, he was so battered and weak they mistook him for a beggar.

Just one day earlier, before Cook's letter, Seok Koon would have dismissed the article. Now, however, her desperation took over. She searched the text for a name or a detail to latch on to, but the businessman was determined to protect the identities of all who'd aided him on the mainland.

Near the article's end, Seok Koon saw a quote from a Father Leung of St. John's Cathedral in Hong Kong's Central District. Although he wouldn't comment on his church's involvement in such rescue missions, he said, "It is our duty as followers of Christ to help the persecuted in any way we can."

Seok Koon spun around and flagged a taxi careening down the street.

Minutes later, she stood on the peaceful, shady grounds of the elegantly unadorned English Gothic church. She could hardly believe that the madness of downtown was just steps away.

Inside the church, the high-ceilinged nave was empty, unsurprising for a Monday. Up above, stained-glass windows glowed like precious jewels, far more ornate than the ones adorning the chapel of Seok Koon's missionary high school. She passed rows of bare pews, wondering how she would find this Father Leung.

Nearing the altar, she stopped short. Tucked into a second-row pew was a small woman on her knees, her bowed head shielded by an enormous wide-brimmed hat.

Seok Koon quietly backed away, but the woman turned and opened one eye. "Can I help you?"

In stilted Cantonese, Seok Koon explained why she had come.

"Priests never work on Mondays," the woman said. "You'll have to come back tomorrow."

Seok Koon's spirits plunged to the ground. She hadn't prayed since high school, and even then, the verses they'd intoned in unison at morning chapel had seemed a game, not unlike the singsong chants heard across playgrounds. Still she lifted her face and sent a plea into the heavens: *please, please, please.* Her many, many hopes and wants precluded her from elaborating.

The woman directed Seok Koon to the church office, where the secretary would be able to assist her. Seok Koon introduced herself to a young woman with cat-eye spectacles who flipped through a large, leather-bound book before declaring she'd have to come back at the end of the week.

First the UN High Commissioner's office, now this. "Please, I can't wait that long."

"I'm sorry, Madame," the young woman said. Unlike the UN receptionist, she looked genuinely apologetic. "Father Leung is extremely busy."

The door that Seok Koon had entered moments before swung open, and a tall, trim man walked in.

The young woman adjusted her spectacles. "Oh," she said, "it's you."

The only priests Seok Koon had encountered were ancient anachronisms in their funny headpieces and robes. This man, dressed in a blazer and pressed slacks, looked more like an accountant, or a teacher.

He said, "One of these days, I promise, I'll stay away for at least twenty-four hours."

Somehow Seok Koon's prayer had worked. "Father, sorry to push in here," she began, ruing her poor Cantonese. "I really need help. Truly. I saw you in the newspaper."

The smile slid off the priest's face.

"I told her the earliest appointment was at the end of the week," the young woman said.

"That's all right," said the priest. "Why don't we chat in my office, Madame—?" He gave Seok Koon a questioning glance.

"My husband's name is Ong."

"Come this way, Madame Ong." He ushered her into a tidy room, lined from floor to ceiling with books. When he removed his hat, she saw his close-cropped hair was silver though his face was boyishly smooth.

"My daughter is on the mainland," Seok Koon said. "I must rescue her."

To her relief, the priest switched to Mandarin. "Where on the mainland?"

"Drum Wave Islet, off the coast of Xiamen, and I'm running out of time." Seok Koon's story poured out of her, and as she recounted the details of San San's plight, the priest tented his fingertips and listened, never interrupting, never hurrying her along.

Still, Seok Koon suspected him of judging her. He was human, after all. "The director swore it'd only take a few days. I never would have left her otherwise."

Father Leung brought his tented fingertips to his lips. "And you say she's only nine." He did not look hopeful.

"But so intelligent and mature for her age."

"Doubtless," he said, "but this is a highly dangerous process, and we've never rescued a lone child."

"But you've rescued others?"

The priest nodded almost imperceptibly.

"You have to help me," Seok Koon said. "I have no one else to turn to."

The priest raised his palms and gestured for her to stay calm. "I'm not ruling it out."

Seok Koon fought the urge to throw herself at his feet in gratitude. "Tell me what we'll need to do."

Father Leung explained the plan: Seok Koon would put up a sum of money, which his contacts on the mainland would use to pay a trucker who routinely crossed the border with a truck bed filled with vegetables, medicinal roots, textiles, teas—bulky commodities that could hide a human form.

"I want to be very clear," the priest said. "There are no guarantees. If your daughter is discovered . . ." He didn't go on.

Seok Koon stared at him, simultaneously wanting him to drop the thought and to keep talking.

"If your daughter is discovered, the punishment will be severe."

"I understand," Seok Koon said, though she knew that if she let herself explore the possible dangers awaiting San San, she'd go insane.

His gaze met hers. "I've made the trip at least ten times, and I can tell you that if it were my daughter, I'm not sure I'd go through with this."

Seok Koon's fury roared up from within. How easy for him to say when his children were safe at home. "I appreciate your candor," she snapped.

He gave her a sad smile, and she regretted her outburst. She took a deep breath to steady herself and asked conversationally, "And how many children do you have?"

"None," he said simply. "My wife—my late wife—couldn't conceive."

Seok Koon longed to take back the question, but the priest didn't seem to hold it against her. He reached for a notepad and wrote something down. He tore off the sheet of paper, folded it in half, and gave it to Seok Koon. "All of it goes to the smugglers. The church pockets nothing. Talk it over with your husband."

Forgetting her manners, Seok Koon unfolded the sheet, and at the sight of the long row of numbers, her mouth went dry. She did the math, converting Hong Kong dollars to yuan, but the sum remained astronomical. She refolded the sheet, dragging her thumb across the crease, and placed it in her pocketbook. "I'll have an answer for you by tomorrow."

"Just ask my secretary to let me know you're here." The skin around his eyes crinkled when he smiled.

She wondered how Father Leung's late wife had felt about him risking his life on these cross-border missions. Had they rescued people together? Was it something he undertook after her death to fill the void in his heart?

"I can't thank you enough, Father," she said.

"And you'll be at service on Sunday?"

Seok Koon found herself nodding, unable to say no to the man who was her only hope.

10

His chauffeur approached the circular driveway of the apartment tower, and Ah Zhai peered out the passenger window. The meticulously restored Beaux-Arts structure, with its grand pediment and column-flanked door, recalled the entrance to an important university or government building.

When his family first arrived, a week and a half ago, they'd been understandably wary. The islet's wealthy did not live in high-rises. Compared to Diamond Villa's ornate—in his mind, overdone—architecture, this building must have appeared too plain, too hard, too cold.

His mother had craned to take in the full height of the building and asked, "How many floors belong to us?"

"Just one, Ma," Ah Zhai had replied, tamping down his irritation. "It'll be smaller than the villa, but you should still have plenty of room." In the corner of his eye, he saw his wife's face blanch, and he wished he'd simply answered the question.

When they entered the sweeping, wood-paneled lobby, however, and paused before the towering arrangement of stargazer lilies, lit like a piece of sculpture by the glimmering chandelier, he saw they were suitably impressed. They would never know how much they owed Lulu. She was the one who'd used her cousin's connections to secure a flat in this exclusive neighborhood. She'd chosen the furniture and hired the household staff.

And how did he express his gratitude? By begging out of social engagements and returning home late. An hour earlier, when he'd called to say he couldn't meet her at the Parisian Grill after all, she'd had every right to be upset.

"Go ahead and neglect me, I can take it," Lulu cried into the phone. "But what about when Marigold arrives? Are you going to pass her over for your *real* children?" Lulu was convinced she was expecting a girl. She'd already tested and discarded other fanciful English names like Gwendolyn and Isabella.

What could he say to that? He intended to fulfill his obligations to all of his children, but that wasn't the answer Lulu wanted. "You and the baby are my everything," he said. "Once my family has settled in, I promise, everything will go back to normal." Seok Koon hadn't given a reason for insisting he dine at the flat that evening, but she so rarely demanded anything of him, he couldn't refuse.

"Go. Mari and I will be just fine on our own."

He could see her waving her cigarette, its long tail of ash dangling perilously over her bulging belly.

"Tomorrow," he pleaded, "we'll go wherever you want."

But Lulu had hung up.

Inside the elevator, alone for the first time all day, Ah Zhai slumped against the plush padded velvet wall and closed his eyes. His body ached in places he hadn't known possible: the roots of his hair, the sockets of his eyes, the hinges of his jaw. Lulu wasn't the only person upset with him. There was Old Wu, senior vice president at the factory and his father's former right-hand man, who'd calmly threatened resignation if Ah Zhai continued to resist layoffs and other cost-cutting measures. There was Mr. Tam, the stingy, unreasonable landlord from whom Ah Zhai had rented this very flat. There were the ruthless Mong Kok loan sharks, who ruled the dark and deadly streets Ah Zhai would never have dreamed of traversing a few months earlier, but which he now navigated with ease. And finally there was his family, whose collective accusatory gaze bored through his back each time he left the flat for the townhouse. All of these people demanded more, more—except for his daughter, who perhaps didn't know it was her right. But he was already wrung dry. He had nothing left to give.

Instead of inserting his key in the lock, he raised his fist and knocked. The maid pulled back the door, and the fragrance of sizzling garlic and ginger enveloped him. He traded his stiff leather shoes for soft slippers. Before he could relax, just for a moment, and appreciate these simple comforts, his wife materialized before him.

"Not yet," Ah Zhai said automatically. "He hasn't written back." He'd recently written to a business associate, rumored to be the half brother of a high-ranking cadre in Shanghai who might hold sway over the islet's safety bureau.

His wife didn't sigh or drop her gaze. "Thank you for making time for us this evening," she said.

Here she was again, pointing out his shortcomings. But when she held out his tumbler of scotch, her smile was warm. Their fingertips brushed, and he yanked back his hand, splashing a few drops on the floor. "Clumsy me."

Seok Koon waved off his slipup and called for the maid to bring a rag.

"Come," she said, leading the way to the dining room. "The food's ready."

Ah Zhai took a long sip of his drink. The honeyed, smoky elixir slid over his tongue and down his throat.

"Are you coming, Zhai?" Seok Koon asked. "I had the cook make all your favorite dishes."

He gazed after his wife's still-willowy figure in astonishment and gratitude. A quiet home-cooked meal with his family was exactly what he needed. His nerves could not have handled the frenzied, overperfumed air of the Parisian Grill, the deceptively competitive small talk with men he secretly despised and their giddy, gossipy wives.

His son and mother waited at a table laden with the dishes from home Ah Zhai missed most: winter melon soup, fried oyster omelet, steamed grouper with scallions, glutinous rice dumplings plumpened with minced pork. At the very center stood the pièce de résistance: bamboo shoots of the earth suspended in a mound of clear, quivering jelly. How had Seok Koon tracked down those ingredients? His mouth watered in anticipation of the cool, silky vinegar aspic, the briny, toothsome "bamboo shoots" that were actually Fujian's prized marine mud worms.

"What a feast," he said. "Are we expecting guests?"

"Only you, the guest of honor," said his mother.

He smiled fondly at her and even at his brooding son. Seok Koon gestured for the maid to top off Ah Zhai's glass, and his gratitude toward his wife blossomed into a deep, sweet tenderness, a kind of mournful affection. He recalled an evening, many years ago, when she'd come to him, shyly, clad only in a filmy white slip he knew she'd had made especially for his visit home. He'd told Lulu that he and his wife were no longer intimate, but there, in the dim glow of the lamp, Seok Koon's resemblance to Shangguan Yunzhu in her celebrated film *Shanghai Nights* excited him. They made love once, and then again in the middle of the night, when she'd roused him with her hand, even though she knew he had to catch the first ferry off the islet. At dawn, he left without waking her, planting a shoe on the white slip and ripping the delicate fabric. He hadn't known then that he'd never return.

Heat settled on the back of his neck. He masked his unease by waving his chopsticks and saying, "Eat while it's hot."

He ladled soup into his mother's bowl and filled his own plate. He couldn't remember the last time he'd savored these flavors. Lulu thought Fujianese food too heavy, too coarse.

Only after he'd cleaned his plate did he notice the rest of the family picking at their food. His mother had barely touched her soup. Seok Koon removed the fine bones from her piece of fish and then passed it on to Ah Liam.

"The meal isn't to your liking?" asked Ah Zhai. "Have I been away too long to remember how Fujianese food should taste?"

His son studied his still full plate.

His mother said, "The older I get, the less I eat," but she was eyeing Seok Koon askance.

"I guess I don't have much appetite either," his wife said. Her smile stopped short of her eyes.

The tension crept back into him. "Is something the matter?"

Abruptly, his wife stood. "Actually, there's something I need to tell you. I don't know why I thought to put it off." She left the room.

Ah Zhai felt cheated. "Mother, does this have to do with the little one?"

His mother leaned in. "No permits until July."

He fingered his tumbler. July was over a month away; they couldn't wait that long.

Seok Koon returned. "There's a moratorium on exit permits, but I may have found a solution." She opened a copy of a tabloid newspaper before him.

"What's this?" He brushed the tabloid aside. "Someone had better start explaining."

Seok Koon smoothed the tabloid and pointed to a headline. She was telling him about some priest she'd sought out who'd convinced her to pay a couple of thugs to smuggle their daughter across the border in the back of a truck.

He watched her chapped lips move, spouting those absurd statements. He didn't understand how anyone could be so naïve.

His wife pressed a folded piece of paper into his hand and said, "All of it goes to the smugglers. The church pockets nothing."

Ah Zhai unfolded the paper and took in the preposterous row of numbers. Three pairs of eyes stared back at him. "My wife, have you gone mad? Do I need to have you committed?"

Seok Koon's face crumpled like the sheet of paper in his palm. He threw the paper ball on the floor. "Entrusting our daughter to smugglers? Hiding her in the back of a truck for hours? Maybe days?"

"Zhai, I fear there's no other way," said Seok Koon.

Ah Zhai turned to his mother. Surely she still had her wits about her; surely she agreed with him.

"I don't know what to do," his mother said. "I've gone over it a thousand times in my head. What do you think we should do?"

His gaze landed on his son, who sank into his chair.

"You," Ah Zhai said, shaking his finger at the boy. "You are the reason we're in this predicament in the first place."

The boy's eyes filled. He was almost thirteen and still behaved like a child. Ah Liam's features may have resembled Seok Koon's, but Ah Zhai knew his sensitive temperament was his own. "Don't cry."

Bee Kim reached out to comfort the boy, but Ah Zhai's look made her pull back. He turned to his wife, determined to make her understand. "This scheme of yours is out of the question. We have no idea who these thugs are. What if they panic and turn her in?" He fought to keep his tone measured. "Do you know what happens to people who are caught attempting to flee? Do you really think those monsters will spare her because of her age?"

The veins in his wife's neck stood out like tree roots, but her voice was just above a whisper. "And if we do nothing, what will happen to her then? The abandoned child of capitalist traitors. They'll make an example of her, treat her worse than a stray dog." She pressed her face in her hands.

His mother touched Seok Koon's shoulder. "Zhai has a point. Let's not be hasty."

Seok Koon jerked away. "Contrary to what you may believe, Ma, your son is as human and as fallible as the rest of us. Ask him why he didn't send for us sooner? Why didn't he move us to Hong Kong before the borders closed?"

Ah Zhai slammed a hand on the table and stood. "Yes, if only I were a soothsayer, then our family could avoid all misfortune. Too bad I'm just a businessman." He kicked the paper ball with all his might, and it bounced meekly off the wall. "San San may have to wait until July, but she will cross the border safely like you three did."

His wife's head curled toward her chest as though she were trying to shrink into herself. His mother worked her napkin between her fingers like prayer beads. His son wept silently into his plate.

Ah Zhai's hands clenched into fists. "I told you not to cry." He looked about for something to hurl and then swept the half-full tumbler off the table. Amber droplets hit his face as crystal shattered against marble. He swiped his shirt cuff across his forehead. "Get someone to clean up this mess." He strode out the door without waiting for the maid to bring his hat.

Inside the elevator, his back found the soft quilted wall. He shut his eyes against the glare of the light and against that dizzying string of numbers no reasonable person would think to pay.

11

Day after day, San San sat in an empty classroom, laboring over her self-criticism essay. In the course of a week, she'd completed five different drafts—enough pages to paper a wall—but each time Comrade Ang came to inspect what she'd written, he rejected her work.

"You barely sound sorry," he said, ripping her pages in half as she held back tears. "Humble yourself before the Party and confess the full extent of your wrongdoings."

How do I do that? What does that mean? she longed to ask. *Tell me what to write, and I'll do it.* She couldn't understand why her brother spoke so admiringly of this cold, cruel man.

She started over, criticizing her family background in even harsher language.

My bourgeois upbringing is like a demon that seizes control of my body and mind, commanding me to give in to my selfish, lazy nature.

She thought of her grandmother's story about the neighbor girl who'd been possessed. Was it only a few weeks ago that she'd genuinely feared that her family's tainted blood had driven her grandmother to hammer the Chairman's portrait? Gazing up at the beaming face atop the blackboard, she was filled with spite toward her slightly younger but so much more naïve self. Who was the real deviant party here? She who wanted only to see her father one last time before he died, or the officials who refused to hear her out? If someone handed her a hammer right now, who was to say she wouldn't take out her anger in the only way available to her?

The tip of her pencil snapped. She'd marred her paper with a thick black cloud. Flipping her exercise book to a fresh page, she pushed these thoughts from her mind. She'd never get out of this prison if she allowed such distractions.

I am deeply grateful to the Party and to our Great Helmsman for showing me the error of my ways. Chairman Mao is the exorcist who has freed me from the demon and brought me back into the light.

"Not only did you shirk work," said Comrade Ang, "but you increased the workload for everyone else." He suggested she open with a paragraph about how she, the descendant of generations of landlords, had once again exploited the labor of the peasantry, perpetuating the very system the Party toiled to destroy.

As far as San San could tell, the only people who'd been affected by her actions were her classmates: the children, if not of capitalists and industrialists, then of powerful cadres. Still, she started at the beginning, writing until her hand cramped and her neck ached and the words no longer made sense.

By the time she was allowed to go home, the sun hung low in the sky. She was too exhausted to do more than swallow a few mouthfuls of dinner before retreating to her room. Lying in bed, she read her mother's most recent letter—which reported that Pa, though weak, was still hanging on—and drifted off to sleep. At some point in the night, she was awoken by Auntie Rose peeking through the doorway, and she managed to lift her impossibly heavy head and acknowledge her piano teacher before plummeting back down the tunnel of her slumber.

Sunday afternoon, back in that empty classroom, San San was considering whether mentioning her father's illness in her essay would garner a little sympathy from Comrade Ang, or, instead, accusations that she was making excuses for her behavior. If she decided to mention the illness, how would she convincingly describe Pa's precarious condition when her mother had been so vague? Why had her mother said so little? Was it because she didn't want San San to worry? Or because she'd sent the letter before she'd learned of the safety bureau's hiatus and had expected to give San San the details in person?

Her mother's letter had arrived the day before, but had been dated a week before that. San San's pencil clattered to the floor. She realized she had no idea whether her father was alive or dead. In the time it took for the letter to land on the islet and get past the censors and arrive at the villa, Pa's condition could have changed. For all San San knew, he'd miraculously recovered, or was already gone.

Her eyes fell on the calendar tacked on the wall. Somehow, without her quite noticing, the end of May had come and gone, and it was June. She walked up to the calendar to make sure she'd read the correct date. Could her family really be due back in three days? San San knew then that she would never set foot in Hong Kong. Never bid her father farewell. Never sleep beneath the gauzy pink curtains of her canopy bed. Never run her fingers across the smooth ivory keyboard of her Broadwood baby grand. The question of why her family had amassed such luxuries for so short a trip rose and then quickly faded, replaced by the knowledge that none of this mattered. No longer did she have to shoulder the responsibility of getting herself to Hong Kong. From here on out, all she had to do was await her family's return.

She picked up her pencil and sat back down. The knots and tangles that had strangled her mind instantly loosened their grip. She tore up the pages she'd already written and started over once again, determined to criticize herself so ruthlessly that Comrade Ang would have no choice but to accept her essay.

Indeed, upon reading the ten pages that had poured out of her in less than three hours, Comrade Ang gave her a stiff nod. "Tomorrow, you'll join your classmates."

She was too depleted to rejoice.

The following morning, she skipped down Tranquil Seas Road and detoured past Little Red's house so she wouldn't have to enter the classroom alone. But when she rang the bell, the house girl informed her that Little Red had left an hour earlier.

Minutes before the first bell, San San arrived to find her classmates already seated. Even more worrisome was the sight of Comrade Ang standing at the blackboard with his arms folded across his chest while Teacher Lu sat meekly in the back.

In a booming voice, Comrade Ang said, "Ong San San, take your seat," as though addressing the entire class.

She sat down beside Little Red and grinned furtively at her friend, who seemed preoccupied by her own fingernails. The rest of her classmates were focused on the political discussion leader, even Stinky, who typically pulled grotesque monkey faces whenever anyone inadvertently glanced his way.

The opening bell rang high and shrill.

"Now the self-criticism session can begin," said Comrade Ang.

San San's limbs grew heavy. Her hands and feet tingled. He hadn't mentioned this part. "Come to the front, Ong San San."

She pushed back her chair and walked slowly to the discussion leader. He handed her the ten sheets of paper she'd written the day before and told her to share her essay with the class.

"All of it?" Her voice squeaked.

"Of course."

A thousand pins pricked the backs of her eyes. Along with her last letter, Ma had sent a story called "The Little Match Girl," hand copied on lined paper to increase its chances of slipping past censors. The tale of the impoverished, unloved little girl who'd burned through her matches and frozen to death had made San San dizzy with rage. Now she channeled that rage toward Comrade Ang. No matter what, she would not let him see her cry.

She began to read.

"Louder," said the discussion leader.

She raised her voice.

"I said louder. Start over."

The words on the page blurred. She blinked hard and returned to the beginning. She dared not look at her classmates for fear of seeing in their faces even a sliver of Comrade Ang's contempt.

And then a strange thing happened. By the end of the first page, San San discovered she'd spent so many hours rearranging those same few phrases about her own unworthiness and the Party's magnanimity that she could detach herself from the meaning of the words and simply push air through her vocal chords and move her lips. Sound waves drifted through her ear canal without penetrating her brain.

When she'd read all ten pages, Comrade Ang let her take her seat.

This time, Little Red gave her a small, worried smile, and San San accepted the conciliatory gesture by squeezing her friend's clammy hand beneath their shared desk.

Comrade Ang said, "Now it's time for you students to participate in the criticism of Ong San San. Each and every one of you has a responsibility to help Ong San San correct her ways."

A cord tightened across San San's chest. How stupid of her to think that turning in that essay would make everything right. Her brother had once mentioned three boys who'd been forced onstage to have their heads shaved in front of the entire middle school. She couldn't remember their crimes.

Comrade Ang continued. "No stone must be left unturned if we truly want to help Ong San San grasp her faults." He looked around the room. "Who's first?"

Little Red raised her hand and leapt up without waiting to be called on. San San recoiled like she'd been slapped.

"Ong San San is always the last to volunteer for class labor trips," her friend said. "It's no surprise that she hid in the truck to get out of work. From now on, she must labor twice as hard as the rest of us to prove her loyalty to the Party."

Little Red took her seat. San San reached beneath their desk and pinched her friend's arm as hard as she could, but Little Red neither flinched nor turned her head.

Precious, a girl San San had never spoken to, was next. "Ong San San lives in a villa full of servants who wait on her hand and foot. No wonder she doesn't know the value of productive labor."

"Yes!" cried the typically stoic Comrade Ang, punching a fist into the air. "Laziness is a disease that must be eradicated before it contaminates us all."

Then came Stinky. "One time I asked Ong San San to help me with my homework, and she refused. Not only is she lazy, but she is selfish and arrogant, too."

San San was furious. How dare he spout such lies! Stinky never asked for help; he only begged to copy her assignments. The truth threatened to burst out of her, but she clamped her back teeth. She thought of the little match girl, lighting one match after another to block out a heartless, unforgiving world.

One by one, her classmates accused her of lacking empathy, of putting on airs, of disrespecting her teachers.

"Yes, yes, yes!" said Comrade Ang. "Here in new China we will stamp out arrogance, insubordination, and most of all, capitalistic deviance."

The classroom erupted in applause. San San's classmates jumped up and shouted over one another, desperate to add another transgression to the sprawling list. Their voices blended together until she could no longer make out what she was supposed to be guilty of. The accusations passed over her like a blade over a whetstone. None of them could widen the gash that Little Red had made with that first contribution.

After a long, long while, Comrade Ang held up his hand, and the classroom quieted. His face and neck were streaked with sweat. "Ong San San," he said, beckoning her to the front of the room.

With this last pronouncement, San San knew that the discussion leader had successfully appropriated her name. Never again would she be able to hear those three characters spoken in succession without filling with dread.

She heeded his instruction.

"Detach yourself from your ego," he said. "Confess your undesirable behaviors and incorrect thoughts once and for all."

San San knew there was only one way to bring the session to its end. Her teacher's desk and chair stood in the corner. She stepped on the chair and climbed atop the desk.

"What do you think you're doing?" asked Comrade Ang.

Her classmates sputtered to each other. Teacher Lu's hand covered her mouth.

Towering over all of them, her classmates, her teacher, and even the discussion leader, San San filled her lungs with air and announced, "I, Ong San San, am the child of capitalist, bourgeois landlords. My parents are the running dogs of the Americans and the British. My selfish, deviant behavior has harmed everyone around me, but most especially the peasantry."

From there she repeated her entire essay, virtually word for word, except this time at a screaming pitch. And when she finished with that, she pushed ahead, confessing to the litany of crimes her classmates had put forth. As she yelled, she watched her classmates watch her, enraptured, as though they were taking in a masterful film or opera. She waved her arms and shook her fists. She yelled until her throat grew dry and her voice went hoarse and her legs quivered with fatigue. And when she ran out of things to say, she borrowed crimes she'd seen in Ah Liam's comic books, crimes of hubris and backstabbing and betrayal, words she barely understood.

At last, when her voice was about to give way altogether, she croaked out, "I, Ong San San, do not deserve even one drop of mercy bestowed by the Party and by our great Chairman. I will spend the rest of my life striving to be worthy of their compassion."

In the back of the room, her teacher's face was shiny with tears. San San stepped down from the desk, clinging to the back of the chair to steady her wobbling legs.

Comrade Ang took one step toward her, and she cowered, fearing she'd misjudged the situation yet again.

The discussion leader turned to face the class. "The session is over. You are all dismissed."

San San staggered to her seat. She longed to sit awhile and rest, but not if it meant giving Comrade Ang a chance to change his mind. She shouldered her satchel and followed her classmates through the door.

Outside the school gates, someone tugged on San San's arm.

"You don't look well. I'll walk you home," Little Red said, trying to take San San's satchel.

"Don't touch me. You're not my friend." San San set off toward her house, and when she glanced over her shoulder, Little Red was following a few paces behind.

San San kept walking. Her shoes felt like they were filled with lead, but her head was empty, weightless, as though the slightest breeze would topple it from the stem of her neck. She was halfway up the hill to the villa when the brick wall lining the road began to sway. She pressed her back to the wall and lowered her satchel to the ground. She closed her eyes. How thirsty she was. When was the last time she'd had something to drink?

When she opened her eyes, Little Red was hurrying to her. Little Red's hand dug in her pocket and surfaced with a few peanuts, which she rushed to shell. "Eat something. You need energy."

San San's mouth flooded with saliva. Roughly, she pushed away her friend's hand, and the peanuts fell to the ground. Without thinking,

San San bent over to retrieve them. The path shifted beneath her feet, and she found herself lying prone in the dirt.

"San San!" Little Red cried. "Help! Help! My friend's fainted."

San San's chin ached, and her palms and kneecaps smarted, but aside from that she felt fine. She wanted to tell Little Red to stop causing a commotion, but she could not release her jaw.

Little Red continued to scream until someone said, "Run to the doctor's house. It's just down there."

San San let her cheek rest on the dirt path. She would get up soon, once she gathered her strength.

An authoritative voice roused her. "Can you hear me, San San? It's Dr. Lee."

The doctor's strong arms lifted her into the air. He carried her all the way to his house. There, in the cozy living room adjacent to the room where San San had her piano lessons, Auntie Rose cleaned off her limbs with a cool washcloth and fed her sips of water until she was able to sit up.

Dr. Lee hovered over them. "How did you get so dehydrated? Don't they give you anything to drink at school?" He held out two tablets for San San to swallow.

"We've been worried about you," Auntie Rose said. "The cook told us what happened."

Heat flamed across San San's cheeks. Her hands began to shake. She managed to set down the glass before it slipped from her grasp. "It's my fault," she said. "I'm a giant stupid egg."

She told Dr. Lee and Auntie Rose everything, from her failure to get an exit permit to the scheme she'd concocted at the tea plantation to the endless chain of punishments. How good it felt to share all this.

"The worst part is," San San said, "I brought all this suffering upon myself for nothing. When my ma gets home and finds out, she's going to be furious."

San San caught the glance that passed between Dr. Lee and Auntie Rose. Neither spoke.

"Have you heard from my ma?" she asked.

This time, Auntie Rose knitted her brow and stared long and hard at Dr. Lee.

"San San," he said, "there's something you ought to know."

Taking in their sober faces, any relief she felt from talking to these trusted grown-ups disappeared. She wished she were strong enough to dart away.

"Your family may have to stay in Hong Kong for longer than they thought."

"Why?" she asked. "How much longer?"

"To be honest, I don't know exactly," said Dr. Lee.

What else had her mother shared with them but not with her? "When did my ma write to you?"

Auntie Rose said, "We haven't heard from her since she left."

San San took comfort in this. "Then how do you have any idea what's going on in Hong Kong?"

Auntie Rose touched San San's cheek. "You're right. We don't know much, but your pa's illness is very complicated. There's a good chance they'll be delayed, and we don't want you to worry unnecessarily."

San San planted her feet on the floor. "My ma writes me almost every day. If she's going to be late, I'll hear it from her."

"You're right," Auntie Rose said. "Your ma loves you so much."

"No mother wants to be separated from her child," said Dr. Lee.

San San grew impatient. "I already know that." She reached for her water glass, threw back her head, and drank to avoid having to look at them.

12

Ah Liam dragged his suitcase from beneath the bed and removed the books and papers hidden inside: hastily printed pamphlets containing the Chairman's most important speeches and essays such as "On the People's Democratic Dictatorship" and "Cast Away Illusions, Prepare for Struggle"; Comrade Ang's personal copy of a slim, hardbound volume of the Chairman's poetry, which he no doubt regretted having lent him; and an exercise book in which he recorded those of the Chairman's quotations that most touched him.

He opened the exercise book and tore out a blank page.

> *Dear San San,*
> *I'm sorry it's taken me so long to write. Are you all right over there? Are you lonely? By now you've probably put two and two together. It's true. We aren't coming home. Pa was never ill. They lied to make us follow their orders.*

He crushed the paper into a ball, threw it in the wastebasket, and tore out a fresh sheet.

Dear San San,
I hate it here. Pa is always in a bad mood. When he
comes over, he and Ma fight. Grandma tries to calm them
down, which only angers them more.

He paused, not wanting to imply that his situation was worse than his sister's, even though he often daydreamed of switching places with her. He could have been the one left on the islet with no one to pester him—aside from the servants, whom he was not afraid to stand up to. His Youth League application would have surely cleared once he'd demonstrated his devotion to the Party by rejecting his family and their poisonous ways.

He tore out a fresh sheet of paper.

Dear San San,
I've decided to return to the mainland once I've found a
way to buy my ticket. Don't worry, I'll come for you soon.

A sharp knock made him jump. He shielded the letter with his arms.

The maid's voice came through the door. "Young Master, your father's here."

"Don't come in. I have to change," Ah Liam called back.

His father hadn't been by the flat since that disastrous dinner. Had he come to apologize to Ma? Ah Liam hoped the maid had known better than to reveal that she was at church again. Before today, he hadn't even known that churches were open on weekdays.

He tore the third draft of his letter into long strips. He smoothed out the other discarded sheets and tore them into strips, too. Then he returned the books to the suitcase and kicked it under his bed.

He wondered if his father had come specifically to see him, to point out, yet again, what a disappointment he was. If so, this time, he was ready. This time, no matter what, he would not cry. Gazing in the mirror on the armoire, Ah Liam spat in his palm and smoothed down his cowlick. He assured his reflection that, if given a chance to do it all over again, he would make the same decision to turn in his grandmother.

Since they'd arrived in Hong Kong, his grandmother had brought up his so-called betrayal only once. With no preamble, she'd put down her needlepoint canvas and said, "Grandson, I forgive you. You only did what you were taught to do." He was so surprised, he knelt before her and bowed his head before he realized he didn't want her forgiveness.

Now he tucked his shirttails into the waistband of his trousers and went to the sitting room. His father stood before the picture window, with its view of the lush, jade-green mountainside. From this distance, the rudimentary huts dotting the landscape, which his mother said housed refugees less fortunate than they, appeared almost quaint.

"Pa? You wanted to see me?"

His father turned. "I can't stay," he said, although no one had asked him to. "I just came to deliver some news. I pulled strings to get you enrolled at St. Mark's. You'll start Monday. We're very lucky they've agreed to take you so late in the school year."

"It's almost summer," Ah Liam said tentatively. He didn't want to set him off.

His father held up his hands. "You'll do a month now and then take summer classes. It's the only way you'll catch up. You have to learn English, and schools here are much more advanced."

I couldn't care less about English, he thought but did not say. After all he'd been through, didn't he deserve a summer vacation? And then he realized that school would give him a reason to leave the flat. He could sneak down to the train station to research ticket schedules and prices. He could ask for money to buy textbooks and supplies. If he was focused and efficient, he could be on his way home in a matter of weeks.

"I suppose you're right," he said.

"Excellent," said his father. He was already striding out of the room. "Tell your ma you start Monday. She can call my office if she has questions."

St. Mark's secondary school was a tall, cylindrical building at least three times as large as Ah Liam's simple, box-shaped schoolhouse on the islet. All in all, he counted five stories, stacked one on top of the other, like tiers of the odd, Western wedding cake he'd spotted in what were called the "society pages" of the *Sing Tao Daily*.

The school grounds were eerily quiet. Classes had already begun. Ma had made them both late by shutting herself in the study with the telephone, and when Ah Liam knocked again to hurry her, she burst from the room saying, "Contrary to what your pa believes, there are more important things to worry about than you learning English."

Now his mother paused before the circular courtyard, bisected by a flagstone path lined with hedges of magenta bougainvillea. "Isn't this lovely?"

"It's fine," said Ah Liam.

At the main office, a receptionist wrote down Ah Liam's classroom number on a slip of paper. His mother offered to walk him upstairs, but he insisted he'd be all right on his own.

He climbed the cool, dark stairwell to the third floor and arrived at a room equipped with enough overhead lights and ceiling fans to service his entire school at home. At the front of the room, a tall, color-less woman rapped a wooden pointer on a giant map of the world. The woman's skin was a dull beige, her eyes the lightest shade of gray—so pale that Ah Liam wondered if she might be blind. He couldn't remember the last time he'd seen a foreigner up close.

But the teacher was not blind, for before Ah Liam could knock, she caught sight of him and gestured for him to enter. Her thin lips parted and let loose a stream of strange, clipped sounds.

In Mandarin he said, "I'm sorry. I don't speak English."

Snickers rose around the room. Save for a half-breed boy in the front row, his new classmates were all Chinese, but not one of them came to his aid.

The teacher kept talking. She waved her arms at the rows of occupied desks and pointed to the back of the room, where Ah Liam gathered he was supposed to stand. Eager to end this one-sided conversation, he hurried down the aisle, tripping over a satchel, or maybe a foot, which earned him more laughs.

The lesson resumed. Ah Liam adopted what he hoped resembled a relaxed stance by leaning on the wall and crossing his arms over his chest. He studied the backs of the heads of his classmates, trying to figure out what made them seem older, more sophisticated than his classmates back home. Was it the way they wore their uniforms loose and casually rumpled? Their long, styled hair? On the islet, all the boys had cropped military-style cuts; the girls were not allowed to grow their hair past their chins. Here the boys wore their hair slicked back and wet looking. The girls had plaits down their backs, festooned with ribbons as colorful as butterflies. Ah Liam thought this display of vanity vulgar, indecent. Students were supposed to dress simply and modestly. He pictured the pale curve of Ping Ping's neck beneath her neat curtain of hair.

A janitor arrived with a spare desk, which he placed at the very back of the room in a row of its own. Ah Liam sat in his hard wooden chair and watched the teacher's lips, straining to pick out words he recognized. He quickly gave up. None of his classmates glanced his way. Even the teacher seemed to have forgotten he was there. How had his father come up with such a terrible plan? He was one of the top students in his entire grade back home, and now he would probably fail every assignment simply because he spoke no English. He didn't blame his mother for going along with his father's wishes; she only had room in her head for San San.

By the time the recess bell rang, Ah Liam's boredom and frustration had hardened into anger. He blamed his parents and his grandmother. He blamed his indifferent teacher, his sneering classmates. He blamed this entire hateful city, filled with people who called themselves Chinese yet lived to emulate their Western colonizers.

He reached in his satchel for Comrade Ang's poetry book. Clutching it to his chest with the cover facing inward, Ah Liam followed the swarm of students down to the courtyard and found an empty bench in a patch of shade. Shouts rose in the nearby field, punctuated by the satisfying thunk of feet connecting with a football. It hadn't occurred to him that they played football here, too. He longed to at least size up the players, if not join them. He wondered if he could try out for the team so late in the year, and then reminded himself he had no time to waste.

A few paces away, a trio of younger girls played a game that involved hopping across squares chalked on the ground. Back on the islet, the lower-school students had recess before the middle school. Occasionally, Ah Liam would pass his sister filing back to class. He'd trained San San never to call out to him, but if he was in a generous mood, he'd grin and tap the crown of her head, waiting for the cry of mock indignation that hid her pleasure.

He opened the book in his lap and tried to block out the girls' gay shrieks. The fragrance of deep-fried snacks wafted over from the canteen, making his stomach rumble. He fingered the coins his mother had given him, all of which he'd pledged toward his train ticket.

He turned the pages to his favorite poem, "The Long March." The day before, his grandmother had spotted the book sticking out from beneath his pillow and warned him not to let his father see it. "In fact," she'd said, "don't take it out of your room at all."

Now he lifted the book out of his lap, displaying the red cloth-bound cover for these students who were too ignorant to think of anything but their playground games.

The Red Army fears not the trials of the Long March
Holding light ten thousand crags and torrents.
The Five Ridges wind like gentle ripples
And the majestic Wumeng roll by, globules of clay.
Warm the steep cliffs lapped by the waters of Golden Sand,
Cold the iron chains spanning the Tatu River.
Minshan's thousand li *of snow joyously crossed,*
The three armies march on, each face glowing.

Shouts and laughter went on around him. Who would take any notice of a boy in an overstarched uniform with too-short hair, sitting all alone? He shut the book and dug in his pocket for his money. Just this once, he would splurge on a fruit ice.

He was counting out the strange shiny coins when a tall boy in the long pants of the upper-middle school stalked by. Without breaking his stride, the boy seized Ah Liam's forearm with one hand and snatched up the book with the other. In Cantonese he muttered, "Come with me."

Ah Liam's coins tumbled to the ground. "Let go," he said in Mandarin, fighting to break free. "I dropped my money."

The boy let Ah Liam pick up his coins, and then he half walked, half dragged him into a stairwell.

"You're hurting me," Ah Liam cried, his voice echoing off the walls.

"Shut up," said the tall boy, finally releasing him. "You'll get us all in trouble."

In the dark, cool space beneath the stairs, a girl and a second boy who was shorter and fatter than the first sat cross-legged on the concrete floor.

The tall boy waved Comrade Ang's book in Ah Liam's face. "Are you crazy? Going around with this in public?"

He couldn't believe his grandmother had been right after all. "Give it back," Ah Liam said, but the boy easily held the book out of his reach.

The girl rolled her eyes. "Give it back to him, Tek. His shrieks are driving me nuts."

The boy tossed the book at Ah Liam, hitting him squarely in the chest.

"Ai." Ah Liam stooped to pick up the book and carefully dusted it off.

The girl switched to Mandarin. "So, what's your name? When did you arrive in Hong Kong?" She stood and stretched her legs. She was very tall—almost as tall as the boy—and so thin that her arms swam in the ample sleeves of her blouse. Unlike the other girls with their elaborate plaits and waves, this girl's hair was a shiny black cap that curled beneath each of her small ears. Ah Liam had never seen anyone so odd looking yet so attractive.

He told them his name and where he was from.

"I'm Li An," said the girl. She pointed to the tall boy. "The bully over there is Ah Tek."

Ah Tek contorted his pockmarked face into a grotesque grin. He tilted his head toward the other boy, still seated on the ground. "That's Fatty."

Fatty pushed his spectacles up his bulbous nose and nodded. Ah Liam had to admit the nickname was appropriate.

"Where did you get that book anyway?" Li An asked.

"The political discussion leader at my school back home lent me his personal copy."

When the girl failed to look impressed, Ah Liam added, "I was in the process of applying to join the Youth League right before my ma made me leave."

"Is that so?" Ah Tek said, curling his upper lip.

Ah Liam sensed he was being made fun of. "Yes, the Youth League. The first major step toward Party membership. In fact, I'm saving up for my ticket home."

Ah Tek continued to smirk. "All by yourself?"

Ah Liam squared his shoulders and faced that horrid boy straight on. "How long have you been away? Or were you born here? Don't you know the Party welcomes all students home with open arms?"

Ah Tek raised his eyebrows at Li An, who in turn exchanged looks with Fatty.

"I've saved up almost enough money for my ticket," Ah Liam lied. "I don't plan to be at this school for long."

Li An stepped forward and placed a hand on Ah Liam's shoulder. Her fingertips seemed to sink though the thin fabric of his shirt, beyond the surface of his skin and deep into his flesh, leaving what he was sure would be an indelible mark, like a cattle brand.

"So," she said, "you're one of us."

13

The day her family was due home, San San dragged a stool to the window overlooking the front gate and knelt there until her kneecaps were red and sore. Mui Ah tried to lure her away with a mug of tea, a red bean bun, a bowl of spare-rib soup, but San San would not budge.

She knelt until it was too dark to make out the faces of the figures on the street below. She knelt until an hour after the last ferry was scheduled to dock. She knelt until her worries and fears and excuses jumbled together in her head in a cacophonous roar. When she heard Mui Ah shut the door to her room beyond the kitchen, she climbed down and hobbled, stiff legged to her own room.

She didn't know why she wasn't angrier, why a part of her already felt resigned. She was changing out of her school uniform when the heavy brass knocker struck the front door. She tore her blouse over her head and shimmied into her nightgown. She was halfway out of her room when Auntie Rose's voice drifted down the hallway. "How is she?"

Mui Ah clicked her tongue against her upper teeth. "She waited by the window for hours. She refused to eat all day."

San San silently shut the door to her room, switched off the light, and dove into bed.

Mui Ah knocked softly. "San San? Auntie Rose is here."

She lay very still. The door cracked open. She'd seen neither her piano teacher nor the doctor since the day she'd fainted by the side of the road. She'd been too angry to visit them; she'd even pretended to be sick to skip her piano lesson.

"Don't wake her. I'll come back tomorrow," Auntie Rose whispered. When the door shut, she added, "The poor thing."

Hot tears sprang to San San's eyes and she was filled with shame. Everyone, even the servants, had anticipated her family's delay. Only she had persisted in clinging to her mother's flimsy promises. She buried her face in the softness of her pillow to muffle her sobs.

In the morning, Cook announced he was moving into her grandmother's bedroom. "The bed will be better for my back," was all he offered by way of explanation.

San San was incensed. "You can't do that. My grandma won't allow it."

Cook looked at Mui Ah. "I really don't think she'll care," he said.

San San dashed off a letter to her mother reporting Cook's outrageous behavior, but when she realized she'd have to give it to Cook to mail, she hid the sheet of paper in a textbook.

Each day she accumulated new grievances, which she added to the letter. The way Cook and Mui Ah spent hours playing cards in the drawing room with the downstairs tenants. How they made a racket well into the night. How they lounged with their feet on the mother-of-pearl-inlaid rosewood chairs. How Cook left San San's supper in a pot on the stove and told her to serve herself and rinse off her dish in the washbasin. As soon as San San could steal a stamp, she'd take the letter to the post office herself.

At school, San San was allowed to attend regular classes, but Little Red had been moved to another desk, and she now sat alone.

One afternoon, outside the school gates, San San watched as Little Red trooped off with her new seatmate, a timid girl they called Steamed Bun because of her fair skin and round cheeks. She heard Little Red suggest she and Steamed Bun walk down to the beach. "I'll show you where to find the best seashells."

When Little Red took Steamed Bun's hand, San San bent over and scratched the mosquito bite on her ankle so she wouldn't have to watch them.

"San San," a familiar voice said.

At the sight of the doctor, San San's face reddened. "What are you doing here?"

"I came to pick you up from school," he said lightly.

She wondered what Auntie Rose had told him, if he'd come to gloat and demand an apology. "Since my brother's been gone I walk home by myself."

Dr. Lee squinted up at the hot afternoon sun. "But isn't it a pleasant day? Let's go for a stroll."

San San shifted her satchel to her other shoulder. "Don't you have to work?"

"Just a short stroll."

She finally agreed, simply to get away from her gawking classmates. She and Dr. Lee walked down Forever Spring Road, and she waited for him to point out that he'd been right about her mother.

In a low voice, the doctor said, "I have something important to discuss with you."

San San looked up in surprise. Did he have news from Hong Kong?

A pretty girl whom San San recognized as one of Ah Liam's class-mates and another of Auntie Rose's piano students skipped past. "Hello, Dr. Lee," the girl called out.

The doctor waved. "How are you, Ping Ping?" He waited for the girl to move out of hearing range and said, "Let's find a quiet place to talk."

The road swerved sharply to the west, and when the imposing granite statue of Koxinga came into view, they turned in to the entrance for Bright Moon Garden.

It was the hottest time of day. The grounds were empty except for a lone grandfather, practicing tai chi beneath the shade of a maple tree. The heady scent of honeysuckle tickled San San's nostrils, and her sneeze punctured the silence.

She followed Dr. Lee down the path to a stone bench, partially shielded by the thick, gnarled trunk of an Indian rubber tree. He craned to make sure no one had followed them.

She couldn't hold back any longer. "Did my ma write you? What did she say?"

He shook his head, and her heart dropped.

But then the doctor leaned in close. "Listen very carefully. Tonight, at two a.m. sharp, get out of bed and come straight to my house. Bring nothing. Make sure no one sees you."

"What?" she asked.

He repeated his instructions.

"But why?"

He held up his index finger. "I'll leave the side entrance open. Do not go to the front door, and do not ring the bell. Is that clear? Under no circumstances are you to ring the bell."

The doctor's intensity frightened her. She'd never seen him like this.

"Is that clear?" he asked again.

She nodded.

"Show me your watch."

San San stuck out the wrist that bore the watch her father had sent for her last birthday.

Dr. Lee checked her watch against his. "Don't fall asleep. Don't be late."

"I won't," she said. "But why?"

He stretched to check the other side of the tree before he spoke again—this time so quietly that San San thought she might have imagined the words: "We're taking you to your mother."

Her body went hot and cold all at once. She was dizzy with euphoria.

The doctor made her repeat his instructions back to him twice before he was satisfied, but San San needed more answers. "Did my ma send for me? Are you coming along? And Auntie Rose, too?"

Dr. Lee's lips smiled but his eyes were somber. "You're the one who's coming with us."

San San didn't understand why Dr. Lee and Auntie Rose would need to go to Hong Kong, but there were other, more pressing questions on her mind. "How is my father? How will I cross the border without an exit permit?"

Dr. Lee took her face in his hands and said, "Enough. Just make sure you heed my instructions." He rose and started down the garden path, and she had no choice but to follow.

When they passed the old man practicing tai chi, Dr. Lee called out, "Beautiful day, isn't it?" And the man flashed a toothless grin.

At the park entrance, Dr. Lee and San San stood in the long shadow of the statue of Koxinga.

"I have to go back to the hospital," said Dr. Lee. "Can you get home on your own?"

"Of course," San San said, trying to mirror his composure.

He patted her head and strode off. She leaned against the stone base of the statue and gazed up at the legendary local hero, admiring the determined jut of his chin, his fierce, unwavering gaze.

Grandma had told her the story of the brave warrior who'd lived on Drum Wave Islet hundreds of years earlier, back when the greedy Dutch had seized control of the neighboring island of Taiwan. With the goal of liberating his neighbors, Koxinga recruited and trained twenty-five thousand men. One fog-shrouded morning, near the end of the north monsoon, he and his men crossed the Taiwan Strait. The Dutch awoke to a swarm of masts so thick they couldn't make out the ocean below, but they remained calm. After all, they'd helped to perpetuate the rumor that Chinese soldiers were cowards who dropped their bows and arrows and fled at the first whiff of gunpowder. They went so far as to boast that twenty-five Chinese could not match the strength of a single Dutch soldier.

Bolstered by these beliefs, the Dutch captain marched his few hundred men straight at the fully armored Chinese soldiers. The Chinese unleashed a storm of arrows so great, they turned day into night. In response, the Dutch confidently fired three volleys in a row. To their great surprise, however, the Chinese showed no signs of panic and continued their attack. The Dutch dropped their weapons and retreated, but the Chinese did not rest until they'd slain 118 Dutchmen, as well as their cocksure captain.

Following his victory, Koxinga gave the Dutch a choice: surrender the region, or force him and his men to storm their fort. The Dutch saw no point in delaying the inevitable, and after thirty-eight years of forced rule, they relinquished Taiwan.

When San San and her brother were younger, they'd spent hours in the villa courtyard reenacting the epic battle with their imaginary armies. The game typically began with the two of them arguing over who would get to play Koxinga, and San San always lost.

Now, looking back, San San knew her brother had been right. She was too small, too weak, just a girl. In no way did she embody the courage and ferocity of Koxinga. She didn't even deserve to rest in this patch of shade beneath the hero's monument. Taking two steps forward, she surrendered to the sun's blaze. She hated her family for leaving her behind, for delaying their return without so much as an apology, but she hated herself more—her inability to stay mad at them, her overwhelming, helpless desire to rush to her mother's side.

14

Ah Zhai flicked the abacus beads up and down, up and down, as though by just doing the math one more time, the numbers would add up and he could pay his workers. Over the past month, he'd let go of a third of his seamstresses. He'd replaced some of the most loyal and skilled among them with recent refugees from the mainland who'd work for half the salary. Still, Old Wu insisted he do more, never mind that technically he reported to Ah Zhai. Because Old Wu had been sent by Ah Zhai's father to guide him through setting up the Hong Kong operation, he'd appointed himself the keeper of the late boss's wisdom. Every sentence that left his lips began with, "If Boss Ong were still with us, may he rest in peace . . ." But even the venerated Boss Ong couldn't have anticipated what would become of the once steady uniform trade as mainland garment factories relocated to Hong Kong in droves.

The telephone at Ah Zhai's elbow sprang to life. He lifted the receiver and heard his secretary's voice. "It's Mr. Tam again, sir."

He knocked the receiver against his skull, and for a brief moment his attention coalesced around that single spot of pain. He relaxed.

"Sir? Are you there?" Wendy's voice sounded not only through the telephone but also through the door, and the doubling effect was disorienting, like seeing one's reflection multiplied in a house of mirrors.

"Sir?"

He exhaled long and slow to smooth all traces of strain from his voice. "Tell him I'm in a meeting and will call him back as soon as I can."

"You told him that last time, sir."

He gritted his teeth. "I appreciate the reminder."

He was about to hang up when his secretary said, "It's just that Mr. Tam said to tell you that he'll be forced to call your home and talk to Miss Lulu if you can't take his call right now."

Slumped over his desk, Ah Zhai imagined gathering all the strength in his weary, aching, aging body and hurling the telephone straight through the wall. "Put him through," he said.

The line clicked over.

"Mr. Tam," Ah Zhai cried, his jovialness exaggerated to the point of absurdity. "How may I be of service?"

The landlord made a guttural sound of disgust. "Come now, Mr. Ong. Let's not waste each other's time."

Ah Zhai adopted a cool, reasonable tone. "You and I are both businessmen. We understand the ebbs and flows of the market. The uniform business has been tough lately." He was talking quickly, afraid of being interrupted—and of what the landlord might say next. "And getting my family over from the mainland wasn't cheap. But once my finances are back in order, I'd be happy to pay you the next six months' rent up front to make up for the delay."

"You have until the end of the month," said the landlord. "I hate to have to say this, but if I don't get the money, your family will have to make other living arrangements."

Ah Zhai stared down at the receiver in disbelief. He was a respected businessman from a distinguished family, active and well liked in the community. How dare this man treat him like some pathetic, defenseless debtor.

"Mr. Ong? Have I made myself clear?"

"You'll get your money." Ah Zhai slammed down the receiver with enough force to shake his desk. He caught the crystal ashtray before it toppled off the edge.

He lit a cigarette and replayed the conversation in his head. His free hand flexed as he imagined ringing the landlord's scrawny, sinewy neck, and what riled him most was something Tam hadn't even said directly to him: the threat to call his mistress.

Orphaned at age two, Lulu had been raised by a wealthy, doting uncle as one of his own. When the uncle discovered Lulu and Ah Zhai's budding affair, he threatened to disown her, and who could blame him? Ah Zhai was a married man, and Lulu had been all but promised to the middle son of the Low family, powerful property developers who'd be useful allies. But even back then, Lulu was stubborn and fiercely independent. She told her uncle that unlike her meek and docile cousins, she couldn't be bought with his dirty money. She packed up her belongings and moved in with Ah Zhai, who was simultaneously awe-struck and dismayed by his young mistress's behavior. He knew her courage was enabled by the ignorance of youth. Just seventeen, she didn't comprehend what she'd given up: the cousins she'd considered her brothers and sisters, the friends who'd no longer think her their equal, the financial security she'd never gone without. But Ah Zhai was touched all the same. Their first night together, he swaddled his hands in her wiry reddish-brown tresses—inherited from her French great-grandmother—and vowed he'd always take care of her, no matter what. She'd mocked his solemnity, saying, "Well, it really is the least you can do."

With time, people got used to seeing Ah Zhai and Lulu together, and the scandal faded. Lulu's old friends forgot what they'd been so incensed about and started inviting her to their luncheons and tea parties again. After her uncle passed away, Cousin Cynthia, whom Lulu had been closest to, got back in touch. Lulu had inherited nothing, but what did it matter when Ah Zhai had more than enough for both of them?

Now, he wondered how his finances could have possibly gotten so out of control. He was the sharpest of all his brothers, the one his father had trusted most. He'd been charged with modernizing and growing the family business, and no one had doubted that he'd succeed. So when had he lost his acumen, his golden touch?

He'd heard the gossip, of course. He knew those friends of Lulu's claimed Boss Ong had made all the decisions and Ah Zhai had merely implemented them. And maybe there was a shred of truth to that. His father had been a formidable and controlling presence who always got his way. Following his death, Ah Zhai made a few uncharacteristically risky investments that failed to pan out—the luxury hotel in Macau that went under before opening its doors, for instance. In retrospect, he saw those gross lapses in judgment for what they were: a delayed rebellion against his father's staunchly conservative approach. But all that was behind him. With a little time, he would turn things around.

Still, he needed money now, and there wasn't a loan shark in all of Mong Kok who would give him another cent. A wild thought entered his mind: what if he preempted Tam and told Lulu himself? Perhaps she could ask her cousin Cynthia for a loan. Already he could hear Lulu's perplexed response. "What do you mean?" she'd ask, furrowing her brow. "What did you do with all of yours?" As though his money were a hat, or a pair of spectacles, something portable and easily misplaced. Even greater than his desire to spare her from worrying was his unwillingness to face her disappointment, her dismay.

Last night Lulu had reminded him about the upcoming Red Cross Ball, one of the biggest social events of the year. Ah Zhai had made the mistake of voicing his ambivalence, and her reaction was unsparing.

"I don't know what's come over you," she said. "Do you even care for me anymore? For us?" She seized her pregnant belly with both hands.

He tried to calm her down. This late in her pregnancy, Lulu remained sylphlike aside from her swollen abdomen. She needed to gain weight and the doctor had advised her to eliminate all sources of stress from her life.

"Ignore me, bunny. I was spouting nonsense," he said. "Of course I'll pay for our usual table."

But Lulu had already moved on. "Go back to them if that's what you really want. I don't need your pity."

That was the last thing he wanted. He tried to make himself heard.

"I'll sleep in the guest room," she said.

When he followed, helplessly, she looked over her shoulder and said sharply, "No."

Again came the relentless ringing of the telephone. Ah Zhai snatched up the receiver. "For God's sake, Wendy, tell him I've left the office."

His secretary's voice wavered. "Sir, it's your—your—it's Miss Lulu's cousin. She says it's an emergency."

Cynthia had never called the office before. "What's the matter, Cynthia?" he asked. "Are you with Lulu?"

"We're at Mount Sinai," Cynthia said evenly.

A chill seeped through him. "Why? What happened? Is Lulu all right?"

A strange, strangled noise came through the telephone. It took Ah Zhai a second to realize that Lulu's stoic, imperious cousin was crying.

"Cynthia, please tell me what happened."

She choked out, "She started bleeding. They couldn't make it stop."

His forehead hit his palm. Why had he upset Lulu over such trivialities? He'd find a way to pay for ten tables if it would make this whole thing disappear.

Cynthia spoke again. "It's gone, Zhai."

And even though he'd known, he wished she hadn't said the words. "I'll be right there. Stay with Lulu. Don't go anywhere."

"Where would I go?" Cynthia asked, contemptuous even in her grief.

The fifth floor of Mount Sinai Hospital was actually the fourth, but the builders had simply skipped over the unlucky number that was a homonym of the character for "death." Ordinarily Ah Zhai would have scoffed at yet another example of Cantonese superstition, but on this particular afternoon, he needed every scrap of luck he could get.

Cynthia was pacing outside Lulu's room. "She's sleeping," she said by way of greeting. Her stony expression showed no traces of her earlier breakdown.

Ah Zhai peered through the small window into the colorless room. There Lulu lay, her complexion as wan as the bedclothes draped over her still-bulging belly.

Cynthia said, "You'll both want to be alone, so I'll be on my way. Just telephone if you need anything."

"Thank you, Cynthia, for your help."

She gave him a brisk nod and headed for the elevators.

Ah Zhai entered Lulu's room as stealthily as he could.

Her eyes darted open. "It's you."

He went to her side and gently clasped her hand. "How are you feeling, bunny?"

Lulu released a hollow laugh.

She was still young; they could have another baby. This did not at all seem like the right thing to say. In truth Ah Zhai had felt only a vague affection for the unborn child. It had been the same way with his son, up until the moment someone plopped the sleeping bundle in his arms and the sob surged up his throat, catching him completely unaware. Now, however, in this sterile room, his love for Lulu swelled to encompass everything she loved, and his heart ached. He longed to rest his palms on the hill of her abdomen, to cradle the space that their baby had filled. Instead he squeezed her hand, which sat limply in his like a cold, dead thing.

Finally he said, "Is there anything you need? Anything at all?"

Lulu pulled back her hand. "A divorce."

He squinted at her. Was she threatening to leave him?

She lowered her eyelids in exasperation. "Divorce your wife and marry me."

In all their years together, never once had Ah Zhai and Lulu discussed marriage. Lulu could not fault him for circumstances that had ossified long before her eyes met his across the ballroom of her uncle's mansion—she a teenage beauty with that mesmerizing hair, he the oldest and most accomplished son of the Ongs of Southern Fujian. And for his part, Ah Zhai would not insult Lulu by offering to take her as his second wife.

Now he fell to his knees so they were eye to eye. "You are the one I love. But she's a good woman. None of this is her fault."

Lulu looked resolutely away from him. "You and I can be husband and wife, or we can return to being strangers. Those are our only options."

His tie was slowly strangling him. He tore at the knot. "Please, Lulu, be reasonable." She was the one breaking promises; she was the one betraying him.

"I've been reasonable for ten years, and I'm sick and tired of it." She pulled the covers up to her chin and rolled over. "Go now," she said into her pillow. "Cynthia will come for me tomorrow. I'll stay with her until you've made a decision."

He stared at the curve of her back in disbelief. "Are you searching for a reason to leave me? Because you know I can't divorce Seok Koon." Never before had he spoken his wife's name to his mistress.

"So, you've made up your mind?"

He took her shoulders and tried to make her face him, but her entire body winced, and he let go. "I love you. I love our life together. I will love our children. That's what I've decided."

"Then you know what you need to do."

"Lulu, please," he cried.

She reached out and tapped a bell on the nightstand, which emitted a cheerful *ding*.

A large, capable nurse bustled into the room. "How can I help you, Miss Lulu?"

"Please see Mr. Ong out. I'm exhausted."

"Wait," he said. "We're not done yet."

"Come along now," the nurse said, taking Ah Zhai's elbow. "Miss Lulu needs her rest."

In the doorway he shook off the nurse's hand. "Rest well, Lulu. I'll be back in the morning."

"Don't come until you've made up your mind."

His face flushed in shame. To the nurse he said, "Make sure she has everything she needs."

"We take good care of our patients. You have nothing to worry about."

As the door swung shut, Lulu said, as though to herself. "He never even asked if it was a boy or a girl."

Anger coursed through Ah Zhai's veins. He stood there, seething, with his palm flat on the door, wanting to charge back in and shake Lulu until she came to her senses, wanting to flee down the corridor and never return.

15

San San clutched Hansel to her chest and inhaled the smell of the doll's candy-scented hair before tucking her in bed. She shed her nightgown to reveal her travel clothes, a lightweight cotton blouse and drawstring trousers, and pulled on her canvas shoes. She felt beneath her sleeves for her grandmother's bangle and her father's watch. Dr. Lee had said to pack nothing, and aside from her mother's letters—bundled in a tea towel and bound with a pink grosgrain ribbon torn from the waist of her favorite dress—she'd obeyed.

Outside a sharp cry sliced through the quiet. Across the courtyard, the windows of the maternity clinic that had been the servants' quarters blazed. A pair of nurses helped a woman with a belly the size of a sack of rice through the door. The woman moaned and cursed her husband, the heavens, even her unborn child. This was one thing San San wouldn't miss—the tormented screams that sailed through the courtyard at all hours of the day. How strange that giving birth could be so tortuous and yet so completely mundane.

Gazing around her room, San San bid a silent farewell to the bookcase lined with colorful volumes, the armoire brimming with party frocks and soft sweaters, the pale nightgown pooled on the floor like the wavy reflection of the moon in water. After a moment's thought, she kicked the nightgown under the bed and out of sight. At last she tiptoed through the dark flat to the front door, cringing as the latch clicked in place behind her.

The night was humid and warm. A couple of the streetlamps had burned out, and she was grateful for the added darkness. With her back pressed to the high stone wall lining the street, she crab stepped down the hill. From a distance came the sound of leather soles clapping against cobblestone. She dashed into an alley just in time to watch a woman, whose white nurse's uniform glowed in the moonlight, pass inches away from her, so close she could place her: the clinic's head nurse, no doubt rushing to assist in the cursing woman's delivery.

At the bottom of the hill San San rounded the bend and her piano teacher's home came into view. The villa was dark, the whole compound blanketed in a silence marred only by the blood pounding in her ears. Had they left without her? Had her watch stopped? She held the watch face to her ear, and the steady tick of the second hand helped ease her fears.

As Dr. Lee had promised, the side gate was unlocked, and she skirted around the back of the house to wait. Clouds drifted past the paper-fan moon. She imagined the scene that would erupt when she appeared at her family's Hong Kong flat. The tears and screams, the smothering embraces. They would beg her forgiveness; they would treat her like a princess.

Soon she grew tired of standing and dropped to a crouch, shredding blades of grass about her feet to distract from the doubts hovering at the edge of her consciousness. At half past two, she stood and stretched her legs and strained to pick out any signs of life in the villa. The backs of her eyes ached from fatigue. Why had she thought to depend on Dr. Lee and Auntie Rose after what her own mother had done? If she hurried home now and got back in bed, the servants would suspect nothing. Suddenly San San missed Mui Ah, who fussed over her when she had no appetite, who threatened but had never actually made her wash her own clothes.

The back door of the house creaked open, and the doctor's head popped out. San San was so elated, she would have cried out if he hadn't held a finger to his lips. Dr. Lee stepped back to let Auntie Rose pass. San San ran to her and hugged her fiercely, but Dr. Lee was already beckoning for them to follow him.

He led them out the side gate into the narrow lane. Two figures emerged from the shadows and waved them over to a large wooden handcart like the ones lugged back and forth from construction sites. San San wondered how they'd managed to transport the cart without being stopped by nosy neighbors.

The two men wore rough work clothes, but they were young and clean-cut and looked more like university students than laborers. They shook hands with Dr. Lee and spoke to him in low voices. Then they helped San San and Auntie Rose into the cart, and Dr. Lee climbed in after them.

"Everything's in place," one of the men told Dr. Lee. "At the Xiamen harbor, look for the ship flying the green flag. Our guy will be there to get you on board."

The other man hovered by San San's head, and her eyes lingered on the shiny gold cross dangling in the opening of his shirt. Impaled on the cross was the slender, sinewy figure of a foreign man, naked but for a small cloth tied around his waist. San San couldn't remember whom the figure was supposed to represent, nor why the cross was a discouraged symbol, but putting all that aside, she wondered why anyone would want to sport something so gruesome.

"What if the ship leaves without us?" Auntie Rose asked.

San San froze. It hadn't occurred to her that such a thing could happen.

"It won't," said Dr. Lee.

"But if it does?"

"We'll reach Xiamen with plenty of time."

"But if it leaves early?"

The man with the cross pendant leaned in. "The ship won't return for another two weeks."

Dr. Lee reached for Auntie Rose, but she turned away. San San wondered what business the doctor and her teacher had in Hong Kong. Surely they couldn't be embarking on this journey simply to escort her to her family.

The university students told them to lie down and stay very quiet. A dusty tarp was drawn over the cart, and San San cupped her hands over her nose and mouth and prayed she wouldn't sneeze. They set off down the lane, and then over a brief stretch of cobblestones so bumpy that she reluctantly freed one hand to cling to a handle on the side of the cart.

Beneath the tarp the air grew hot and stuffy.

"We're not the first people they've helped," Dr. Lee said to Auntie Rose.

The cart bumped over a pothole. San San let go of the handle in surprise and was flung straight into her teacher.

"Sorry," she whispered, but Auntie Rose pulled her close. Her teacher smelled of sandalwood soap and, not unpleasantly, of sweat.

Shyly, San San said, "I'm glad we're together."

Auntie Rose pressed her lips to the crown of San San's head and spoke into her hair. "We couldn't leave without you."

Her words thudded into San San's innermost place, kicking up a cloudy profusion of gratitude and bitterness, joy and anguish.

The cart rolled to a halt, and the students lowered the tarp. They were on a cliff overlooking the water, on the opposite end of the islet from the ferry terminal. In place of the broad paved road that led down to the docks was a punishingly steep slope covered with waist-high grasses, dotted here and there with jagged boulders.

San San's face must have shown her trepidation because the man with the cross pendant said apologetically, "This is the only place we could tie a boat without being seen."

Sure enough, down in the water, a rickety fishing boat was lashed to a boulder. San San reminded herself that the Xiamen harbor was only a few hundred meters away, a distance she could probably swim, if it came down to that.

Once again all the men shook hands, and then Dr. Lee rolled up the sleeves of his jacket and said, "Let's go."

San San felt a twinge between her legs.

Auntie Rose stopped short. "What's the matter, San San?"

Dr. Lee turned around.

San San shook her head but the sensation intensified. She squeaked out, "I think I have to pee."

Her teacher smiled, which only made San San more embarrassed.

"It's all right," said Auntie Rose. "Go behind those bushes. No one will see you."

San San hurried off, paying no heed to the grass blades that pricked her calves through the thin fabric of her trousers. She removed the bundle of letters from her waistband and placed it on a rock before lowering her trousers. A few moments passed before she relaxed enough to urinate, and when she was done, she cast about for an appropriately sized leaf.

She was glad she hadn't tried to hold it in. She felt considerably calmer, yet her heart seemed to beat louder and louder, until she realized the rhythmic pounding was coming from far away, as though from a parade or a political rally, though nothing like that could be occurring at this hour. The ground beneath her feet shook slightly, then more violently, and then the pounding transformed into galloping horses' hooves.

"Hands over your heads," a man yelled.

A horse neighed as if to reiterate the command.

Falling back on her bare haunches, San San yanked up her trousers and rolled into a tight ball.

"Walk toward us."

She could smell the pungent, brackish scent coming off the bodies of the riders and their beasts. There had to be at least a half-dozen men.

"Comrades," Dr. Lee said, his voice shockingly calm, "put down your batons. This is all a misunderstanding."

"Shut up. You can't talk your way out of this," the man who was clearly the leader said. "Bind their wrists."

Dr. Lee continued slowly, "You all know I'm a doctor, not a bandit. My wife here teaches piano."

One of the students said shakily, "We attend the university."

The strike of a baton silenced the student, and Auntie Rose shrieked.

"Shut up all of you," the leader said. "Take the three of them back to headquarters. I'll take her."

"No, please, no!" she cried.

Dr. Lee's voice lost all composure. "I won't go anywhere without my wife."

Again, the sickening sound of a baton connecting with a body. San San was shaking so hard, she feared they could hear her teeth chatter through the wall of bushes concealing her.

"Doctor, look around. Does this appear to be a hospital? You aren't in charge anymore."

San San bit down on her lower lip, afraid of what would spill out of her.

The second student said, "Comrades, please have mercy," which earned him a strike, too.

"Enough," said the leader. "We're wasting time. Let's go."

San San tasted blood where her teeth had shredded her lip. She waited until the galloping faded, and then she waited some more.

Later, much later, when she finally dared open her eyes and emerge from her hiding spot, the sun was rising over the water. The once menacing prickly grasses swayed benignly in the breeze. The wooden handcart lay toppled on its side, with the dusty tarp tangled in the spokes of its wheels.

Shielding her eyes with the flat of her hand, San San gazed down the steep slope at the rickety boat. It was too risky to attempt to row herself to Xiamen in broad daylight, and even if she somehow made it across the channel unseen, the ship with the green flag could have already set sail. If that were the case, how would she survive on her own in the city for two whole weeks?

But returning home was unthinkable. By now the servants would have reported her disappearance. Perhaps the authorities had already figured out her plan to flee with Dr. Lee and Auntie Rose. San San didn't know if children could be sent to the labor camps, and she had no intention of finding out.

Her only choice would be to hide out on the islet until Dr. Lee and Auntie Rose were released. Despite what the evil leader had said, San San believed Dr. Lee could convince the authorities to release him and Auntie Rose. He knew all the highest-ranking party officials. He'd probably saved some of their lives. They wouldn't keep him locked up for more than a few days. In fact, the Party would probably punish those bad men for what they'd done. Once Dr. Lee and Auntie Rose were set free, San San would go to them, and they could figure out their next move. Until then, she would fish for yellow croaker at Flourishing Beauty Cove, the way she and her brother had done last summer. She'd roast the small fishes over a fire. Perhaps she'd sleep right on the beach.

Her stomach growled; she hadn't eaten in a long while. This side of the islet was all but unpopulated, save for the arts college on Chicken Hill Road. She seemed to recall a longan tree that flanked the school gates. When no one was looking, she'd climb up and steal fruit.

En route to the college, a gust of wind lifted her shirttails. She reached back and brushed the waistband of her trousers. Her mother's letters were gone. Hurrying in the direction she'd come, she prayed those men hadn't returned. But when she darted behind the bushes, her bundle was exactly where she'd left it, lying on a rock like a lizard in the sun.

16

At long last, a letter from San San arrived in Hong Kong.

Dear Ma,

It pains me to report that Cook is behaving very badly. Can you believe he took over Grandma's bedroom? He actually sleeps in her bed! I told him Grandma would get mad, but he just laughed! I think you need to come home, although Auntie Rose said that my pa is still sick and that you may have to stay in Hong Kong for longer. How is my pa? Why didn't you tell me you'd be delayed? When can you come home?

Your loving daughter,
San San
PS. Cook and Mui Ah invite the downstairs tenants to play cards in our drawing room. They make a lot of noise! Even late at night!
PPS. I saw them put their dirty feet on our chairs!
PPPS. The kitchen is a mess! Piled high with dirty dishes that Mui Ah rarely washes.
PPPPS. Please come home soon.

Seok Koon stared at the last line until the characters blurred together. It was no use fretting about the servants' unruliness, not when there were so many other things to worry about. All that mattered was that they were good to San San. But how was she to ensure that from all the way over here? Should she tear off a letter to the servants, vowing to find a way to punish them if they mistreated her daughter? Should she ask Rose to intervene? But Seok Koon knew that if she angered Cook and Mui Ah, they would simply turn around and vent their wrath on San San. Should she send money, then? Enough to buy their kindness, but not so much that they grew greedy and hard-hearted. How much, exactly, would that be?

Her mother-in-law was playing mahjong at the Fujian Association. Seok Koon alternately envied and resented her each time she left the flat. And even if she'd been home, what advice could she have offered? The once opinionated Bee Kim was as lost as she, deferring to Ah Zhai at every turn. The other night, as Seok Koon had sat at the dining table, copying out another fairy tale for San San, her mother-in-law had intoned, "Better to raise geese than girls." It was a tired old saying, but Seok Koon had spun around, hot with rage, and caught the single tear wending its way down her mother-in-law's creased cheek.

Seok Koon glanced at the clock on the wall. For now she'd have to set aside the letter. Her haggard reflection gazed back at her in the vanity mirror. She dragged a hairbrush through her hair, slapped powder on her forehead and nose, and smoothed the wrinkles from the skirt of her new floral cheongsam.

Why the priest had sent for her today, she didn't know. On the telephone, all his secretary had said was that Father Leung had requested a meeting—the sooner the better. Seok Koon leaned in to the mirror and prodded her pallid, flaking skin before uncapping the tarnished gold tube of lipstick she'd discovered in the depths of her suitcase. It had been years since she'd worn lipstick, and when she slicked on the crimson shade, she couldn't deny her resemblance to a Peking opera singer. She snatched up a tissue and wiped off the garish paint.

She planned to slip out unnoticed, but when she pulled back the front door, there was Bee Kim, along with the maid who accompanied her everywhere.

"Going out?" her mother-in-law asked.

Seok Koon fingered a lock of her hair. "I have an appointment."

"Where at?"

"The church." Seok Koon steeled herself for Bee Kim's usual lecture on how she needed to listen to Ah Zhai, how those Christians only cared about converting you. She peeked at her watch.

Bee Kim scanned the length of Seok Koon's body. "New dress?"

Seok Koon blushed. "I thought I should get some clothes made for this humidity." She hadn't anticipated that the colors would turn out so bright. "You don't like it?" She hated herself for asking.

"What do I know of current fashions?" said Bee Kim.

The maid discreetly lowered her eyes.

For an instant Seok Koon considered changing, and then she took hold of herself. "I won't be long," she said and marched past her mother-in-law.

In the taxi, on the way to the cathedral, she ran through all possible reasons for this meeting. Maybe the priest had learned of forthcoming changes to the border policies; maybe he had formed a new connection on the mainland. Each time hope surged through Seok Koon, she sternly warned herself to expect nothing. More likely the priest just wanted her to reconsider his proposal that she put her piano skills to use by accompanying the children's choir—but why would that require an urgent in-person meeting?

When Seok Koon entered the church offices, the secretary said, "What a pretty dress."

She felt her cheeks grow warm. How could she waste money and time on something as unimportant as clothing when her daughter was suffering so?

"Father Leung is expecting you. Go right in."

Seok Koon wiped her damp palms on her seat, realizing too late she'd stain the silk, and knocked on Father Leung's door.

"Come in."

The priest was retrieving a book on a high shelf, and when he turned, she was once again jarred by the juxtaposition of his silver hair and smooth face.

"Good afternoon, Father," she said.

"Madame Ong, thank you for coming in on such short notice." The priest shook her hand. His palm was cool and dry against her clammy skin.

"I should thank you for making time for me."

He gestured for her to take a seat. "I wanted to discuss your daughter's situation."

She nodded, too tense to speak.

"I consulted a friend who works at the UN refugee agency. There might be another way to get your daughter out—a less risky way that your husband could accept."

Seok Koon had to stop herself from lunging across the desk and clasping Father Leung's slender, fine-boned hands. "How? When? Please tell me everything."

Father Leung elaborated. Seok Koon would have to send a letter to San San and her guardian. A seemingly ordinary letter. A letter explaining that all attempts to treat her husband's illness had failed, and that now the family was simply waiting for him to expire. (Obviously this would require another doctor's note, which was easy enough to obtain.) Once her husband passed away, Seok Koon would write, the family would wrap up business in Hong Kong and return to the islet.

Seok Koon didn't see how this letter would accomplish anything. "But why—"

Father Leung held up an index finger. The letter, he said, would go on to state that only one thing held up the family's return: San San. The girl needed to be in Hong Kong to collect her share of the inheritance. If she failed to appear, the capitalist pigs in the Hong Kong government would confiscate the money for their own use.

Seok Koon blinked, still confused. "Is that true?"

"It's an exaggeration, but that's beside the point." Father Leung said that Seok Koon must add that once the full inheritance had been collected, the whole family would board the train back to Xiamen, at which point they looked forward to investing the family wealth in government bonds. "Work that part in subtly, of course."

Seok Koon combed through the priest's words. What was she missing? Why would the communists fall for such an obvious scheme?

"I know what you're thinking," the priest said.

"Then, why?"

He chose his words carefully. "If the plan were to work—and I need to stress the word 'if'—it would be for several reasons. First, the communists desperately need the foreign currency that you're so generously offering to bring back."

One of the Chairman's famous sayings came to Seok Koon. "'One cent of foreign exchange—'"

Father Leung joined in. "'—is equal to one drop of human blood.' Exactly. If they're desperate enough, they'll take their chances. All they stand to lose is a nine-year-old girl."

Even as the river of hope swelled inside her, Seok Koon couldn't shrug off her doubts. "It seems too easy."

Father Leung stretched his lips into a half smile. "You know as well as I that all of China is wrapped up in the biggest charade the world has ever seen."

She tilted her head, unsure of where he was going.

"The charade that this impoverished, backward nation is in the midst of a new golden age, that it's only a matter of time before they surpass the corrupt and wicked West. The communists want to believe that you want to return. Indeed, they must believe it."

This confused Seok Koon more than ever. "I don't follow."

"Every single official at the safety bureau knew your family was fleeing for good, so why didn't they stop you? Why did they let you leave?"

"Because my friend, the Party doctor, intervened on our behalf?"

"Wrong," the priest said gently. "They let you go to sustain the charade. If new China is the paradise the Party claims it is, then no one in his right mind would ever leave. For those officials, acknowledging your family's scheme to escape would be tantamount to admitting that their entire lives—and the whole nation—are built on lies."

Seok Koon mulled this over. "So, in order for them to continue deluding themselves, they might actually send San San to us?"

Father Leung turned his palms skyward.

She asked, "How much money will we need?"

"Not too much—we don't want to raise suspicion. Just enough to make this worth their while."

The number he quoted was a good deal more than the amount he'd asked her to come up with before. But, as he pointed out, all Seok Koon had to do was make sure the funds were in her husband's bank account in case the Party decided to check.

"Just in case," she repeated. Despite her lingering doubts, the plan was truly risk-free. She could think of no reason for Ah Zhai to reject it. San San could cross the border in a matter of weeks. Days, even.

"Thank you so much, Father." Words she'd uttered so many times, they'd all but lost their meaning. How could she express the depth of her gratitude? In all of Hong Kong, this man was the only one who'd come to her aid.

"It's nothing," Father Leung said. "'Let each of us look not only to his own interests, but also to the interest of others.'"

It took her a moment to realize he must be quoting the Bible. "Indeed," she said.

He rose to his feet, and she did, too.

"You and your family will be in my prayers," he said. "In fact, why don't you bring them to church on Sunday? I'd love to meet your husband."

A bitter laugh slipped out of her. "My husband? I barely see him myself."

The priest's eyebrows inched up his forehead, and she hurried to explain. "My husband is a busy businessman with many, many obligations."

His face relaxed. "I see."

Suddenly, she wanted him to know the truth. "That's how my husband views me and his children, as another one of his obligations. Another of his burdens."

Father Leung averted his eyes, and Seok Koon knew she'd said too much.

"Every marriage has its ups and downs," he murmured.

"Indeed," she said, hurrying to the door. "Forgive me for taking up so much of your time."

Father Leung closed the distance between them. "Madame Ong."

Her hand slid from the doorknob and she turned to him. "Yes?"

"Do you know what I do when I feel lost?" His eyes were filled with such sadness, such compassion, that she felt guilty for making him share in her pain.

"What?" she whispered. "Tell me."

"Well, Madame Ong, I pray. I get down on my knees and ask the Lord for guidance."

The tension drained from her. "Of course."

"'He is our refuge and our strength, an ever-present help in trouble.'"

"That's good advice."

"Promise me you'll pray," the priest said. "Promise me you won't try to face this on your own."

And because she wanted nothing more than to leave the room, she vowed she would.

17

Standing before the half-open window of the Lin villa, San San stared into the kitchen at the platter of soft, rotting fruit. Her plan to climb the longan tree at the arts college and stuff her pockets full of the sweet, luscious orbs had been foiled by the guard stationed directly beside the tree. Now it was dusk, a full twenty-four hours since she'd last eaten. The cavernous space in her belly threatened to somehow swallow her whole from the inside out.

The sky had deepened to a dusty violet, yet the lights in the villa remained dark. Surely no one was home. In fact, judging from the state of the fruit on the platter, no one had been home in days.

The Lin villa, a sprawling redbrick structure veiled by overgrown palm and banyan trees, was the only home on this isolated stretch of Chicken Hill Road. San San had heard her mother and grandmother gossip about the villa's original owner, a famously reclusive and effeminate businessman who was said to have been waited on exclusively by young male servants. Later, San San looked up the word "effeminate" in the big dictionary in the study, but the definition made little sense. Men were brash and loud and tough; women, the opposite. She could no sooner picture a man adopting the mannerisms of a woman than a cat imitating a fish.

Grandma had said that this effeminate man had built his home far from town to avoid the prying eyes of neighbors. Even so, San San looked around to ensure she was alone before hoisting herself up on the window ledge and diving headfirst through the open window. She crashed upon the cold, tiled floor, too focused on her goal to notice the pain. She lunged for the platter, filling her mouth with mushy blackened bananas and pulpy persimmons that gave off a heady, alcohol-laden scent. She devoured the entire platter of fruit before she thought to scour the rest of the kitchen, where she discovered straw baskets of dried fish and meat, earthenware jugs of rice grains and sugar and flour, and, in the old-fashioned icebox, a bottle of sour soybean milk, the repulsive smell of which did little to dampen her spirits. Here was enough food to sustain her for weeks. She stuffed her cheeks with *bak kwa,* sucking on the juicy sheets of cured pork to draw out every drop of salty sweetness before consenting to chew and swallow.

With her appetite tamed, San San explored the rest of the house. Through the kitchen door was the dining room, furnished with a long teak table and an enormous chandelier. The tall windows were flanked by heavy velvet drapes, held back by lengths of silk rope as thick as her wrists. By now the sun had set completely, but she dared not turn on the lights.

Dragging a finger across the dusty sideboard, San San guessed the villa's current owners, Old Mrs. Lin and her spinster daughter, would not be returning anytime soon. All of Drum Wave Islet was rife with rumors of those who'd disappeared across the border, abandoning family heirlooms and other treasures to fend off suspicion for as long as possible. She wandered into the sitting room and collapsed on a round sheepskin rug, large enough for her to stretch out on. Spinster Lin was tall and mannish with a stiff helmet of hair. San San was trying to remember the last time she'd seen the woman in the shops along Dragon Head Road when the realization exploded inside her like a burst of National Day fireworks. She darted upright, recalling all the valuables left behind in the flat: the pearls and gemstones in Ma's lacquered jewelry box, her perfume bottles and crystal vase, even this gold bangle beneath her sleeve, foisted upon her by Grandma.

San San had never been surer of anything than she was of this: No one was coming back for her. Ma, Grandma, and Ah Liam had left for good. Was her father even ill, or was this yet another of her mother's lies? The shattered portrait, the inspection, the rushed procuring of exit permits—all these events crashed into place, and she understood what her brother had done. Her heart clenched at the injustice of it all.

She seized a heavy blue-and-white vase and hurled it on the wood floor, but only succeeded in chipping its lip before it rolled halfheartedly into the wall. She kicked the vase with all her might and stubbed her toe. Shuddering in pain, she wrapped the sheepskin rug about her shoulders, stirring up a cloud of dust that made her eyes itch and relinquish fat, salty tears.

The next time she opened her eyes, she was blinded by sunbeams shooting through the tall windows. The sheepskin rug was rolled snugly around her like a *popiah* wrapper. Her throat burned and her tailbone ached. When she tried to lift her head, the room spun, forcing her back onto the floor. Her gaze landed on the grandfather clock in the corner of the room. It was too bright to be five in the morning, but could she really have slept until five in the afternoon?

She rushed to the windows and freed the velvet curtains from their slings, and then ran through both floors of the house, sealing all the drapes, liberating more swirls of dust that made her sneeze. Her vision blurred, but she pinched her arm until the tears subsided, determined not to waste any more time feeling sorry for herself. She had to find a way to reunite with Dr. Lee and Auntie Rose. For all she knew, they'd already been released. First thing in the morning, she would head to town to uncover news of them, and to do so she needed a suitable disguise.

She climbed the stairs to Spinster Lin's spacious dressing room and rifled through drawers and closets. If she tied a scarf over her head and donned a pair of threadbare pajamas, could she pass for someone's house girl? In her youth, Spinster Lin must have been slender, judging from the row of pastel dresses, the fabric yellowed with age and emitting a faintly rancid odor. Tucked behind the dresses was a leather portfolio of letters that revealed that Spinster Lin had once had a lover, a married Nationalist colonel who had fled with his wife and child to Taiwan. Perhaps that was where Spinster Lin and her mother had gone.

When night fell, San San decided to sleep right there in the dressing room, for if a former servant or suspicious household registration officer suddenly entered, it would be a while before he thought to look in there.

She was gathering up the bedclothes from Spinster Lin's bed when moonlight streaming through a gap in the curtains drew her to the window. The Lins' still-manicured tennis court lay dormant beneath the pale globe in the sky. How she longed to stick her head through the window and breathe in the cool, fresh air; how she longed to skip across the smooth, unblemished surface of the court.

Muffled giggles pierced the stillness. San San cracked open the window and squinted into the darkness. Two figures squeezed through a hole in the fence. From their heights, San San guessed they were kids, and then, as they moved out of the shadows and into the court, she recognized the broad forehead and sharp chin of Little Red. San San almost pushed open the window and called out, so excited was she to see her friend. What had drawn Little Red all the way to this side of the islet? Had she heard of San San's disappearance? Was she worried? Did she miss her?

But the sight of Steamed Bun, Little Red's new seatmate, silenced San San. She watched Steamed Bun pick a tennis ball off the ground and hurl it in the center of the sagging net. Their laughter rang out like bells as they tossed the ball back and forth, urging each other to go higher, farther. They must have heard the rumors and come to investigate the abandoned house.

Little Red found a tennis racket lying in the grass. She positioned herself behind the white line, tossed the ball in the air, and reared back her arm. The racket strings struck the ball with a satisfying *thunk*, followed swiftly by the sound of smashing glass. Little Red dropped the racket and sprinted to the hole in the fence, with Steamed Bun following close behind. Their shouts were wild and shrill.

San San went downstairs to the kitchen but dared not go toward the shattered window in bare feet. A burst of wind lifted the muslin curtain, and the tennis ball rolled languidly across the shard-littered tiles. The next time it rained, there would be a big mess.

That night, San San dreamed that Auntie Rose and Dr. Lee knelt before her and asked her to be their daughter. They completed the adoption paperwork. The official was poised to lower his seal on the final document when the drumbeat of horses' hooves and the pungent, brackish scent of evil men overpowered them all. The leader of the riders was a slender and sinewy foreigner, naked except for a cloth tied around his waist. He ordered his men to bind Auntie Rose's and Dr. Lee's wrists and drag them away. And through it all, they ignored San San's pleas; in fact, they showed no signs of even having heard her.

She awoke drenched in sweat, determined to reunite with her piano teacher and the doctor. For the first time since she'd left home, she bathed in very hot water, combed back her hair, and covered her head with Spinster Lin's rust-colored scarf. She tugged on a pair of worn, earth-toned pajamas, rolling up the pant legs so they wouldn't trail on the ground. Her reeking cotton blouse and trousers she let soak in the leftover bathwater before finally setting off for town.

It was midmorning, but here on the islet's outskirts, the road was all but empty. Occasionally she spied a student hurrying to the arts college or a laborer with a cart of building materials, and she hid behind a tree or shrub until they went by. She passed the islet's only inn, which housed all visiting dignitaries, and the adjacent seafood restaurant, which, so early in the day, already gave off the intoxicating fragrance of fish tossed on an open grill.

At the mouth of town, she slowed before the entrance to the cemetery and went inside. Two months had passed since the Clear and Bright Festival, when she and her family had come to clean her grandfather's grave, and his headstone was now stained with soot. She knelt on the grass and rubbed at the headstone with the heel of her hand.

Back when Grandpa was still alive, Ma would send San San to his bedroom to call him to dinner. He always beckoned her in, winking as he withdrew a silver-colored cardboard box from a desk drawer. The box was filled with wafer-thin squares of milk chocolate that melted the instant they touched your tongue. San San and Grandpa would each have one, and he'd hold his index finger over his lips to remind her to keep their ritual a secret. Her grandfather would never have let the family leave without her. San San tried to remember if her brother ever went to her grandfather's room. Could they have had their own secret ritual? Could Grandpa have given Ah Liam something even better than those weightless chocolate squares?

She was dragging her thumb over her grandfather's name when something brushed her shoulder. At the sight of the old gravedigger crouched beside her, she cried out.

"I didn't mean to startle you, little sister."

She scrambled to her feet. The gravedigger had always kept his distance, and she'd never seen his skeletal face up close, his large sunken eyes and scraggly white beard.

"Don't be afraid. Why are you here by yourself?" He grimaced, or maybe smiled, and his toothless maw sent San San running for the cemetery gates.

"Where are you rushing off to?" he called. "I won't bite." He cackled at his own joke.

San San ran until she could hear the bustling hum of the marketplace, and then she slipped into an alley to catch her breath. She began to question her plan. What if her disguise wasn't good enough? What if she was recognized? She wished she'd thought to smudge her face with dirt and wondered why she'd bothered to bathe.

The loudspeaker attached to the wall above her head crackled to life and "The East Is Red" spewed forth in tinny streams. The music was soon replaced by the town announcer's supple voice. "Attention, attention, revolutionary comrades of Drum Wave Islet. Please assemble at the high school basketball courts. The denunciation session will start momentarily."

San San's head teemed with the jeers of her classmates. She felt a new pang of sympathy for the criminals who were about to be escorted onto the basketball court's makeshift stage. But the timing of the session worked to her advantage: once everyone had gathered at the high school, she'd be free to roam the marketplace and study the latest news posters.

"The East Is Red" resumed playing, urging the townsfolk onward.

"Who's being denounced this time?" San San heard a man ask.

"Who in heaven's name can keep track?"

"I think it's those students. Troublemakers, all of them."

When the streets had emptied, San San headed to the marketplace. The wall by the main entrance was plastered with the usual propaganda images of rosy-cheeked peasants and brave soldiers waving their fists in the air. Passing over the slogans urging her to "Be a Sputnik, Not an Oxcart!" and to "Stop American Aggression, Liberate Taiwan!" she searched the news reports and found herself staring at her very own face, rendered in thick black brushstrokes below the words, "Missing Girl, Big Reward." She ripped down her portrait and tore it into long strips, and then her eyes focused on the poster directly beside the blank space she'd just created. The balled-up strips of paper fell from her hand. On the morning of June 17, this poster declared—tomorrow—the denunciation session and subsequent execution of Lee Chin Kong and Rose Lee would take place. The pair had been found guilty of betrayal, capitalistic deviance, and the kidnapping of a young girl, who remained at large.

From across town came the faint claps and cheers of those gathered at the high school. Only then did it dawn on San San that the students being denounced must have been the pair who'd attempted to help her escape.

"Struggle, struggle against the rightists!" the townsfolk chanted.

For the second time San San ripped the poster off the wall and hurled it on the ground, and then she walked briskly in the direction she'd come, back to the Lin villa.

Her thoughts tumbled around in her head. She had to turn herself in; it was the right thing to do. But Dr. Lee and Auntie Rose had already been sentenced, and she'd gone through enough with Comrade Ang to know that nothing could change the Party's mind. Only one thing mattered to those people: to make an example of the criminals. The truth was irrelevant. She had no choice, then, but to leave the islet at once. But the city of Xiamen was vast and inscrutable. How would she survive there? She was just a child; she must seek help—from Cook and Mui Ah? From Little Red? The answers eluded her. She was at a loss.

As she approached the cemetery, she ducked her head and quickened her pace. She was hurrying past the gates when a cold, rough hand seized her arm.

She screamed and pulled away, but the gravedigger tightened his grip. "Don't be afraid. I just want to talk."

"Let me go! Help! Help!" Her cries dissipated in the air. Everyone was too busy denouncing criminals to come to her aid.

"I won't hurt you," he said. The stale odor of his breath repulsed her. The skin around his purplish lips was bursting with sores.

San San screamed again and again.

The gravedigger slapped a hand over her mouth. "Shut up. I said I won't hurt you. You're the Ong girl aren't you? The one they're searching for?"

She bit down on his knobby finger as hard she could.

He shook out his hand and snarled, "Fuck your mother."

San San wriggled from his grip.

"Wait," the gravedigger said. "Come back!"

She raced off, pumping her arms and raising her knees, and when she felt the thin fabric of Spinster Lin's pajamas rip at the seams, she widened her strides and ran for her life.

18

Night after night, Ah Zhai tossed and turned in the newly vast four-poster bed, tangling himself in the bedding, darting awake before dawn. Each evening after work, his chauffeur delivered him to Cousin Cynthia's, where he cajoled and begged the housekeeper to let him see Lulu. But the skinny, sullen servant barred the door, and once, when he'd pushed past her, she'd screamed for the kitchen boy to help. Cynthia herself had appeared at the top of the stairs with her arms crossed over her chest. "Really, Zhai," she'd said, condescending as a headmistress, "you can't force her to see you."

Like any other couple, Ah Zhai and Lulu of course had their rows. He'd accuse her of behaving like a spoiled child, and she'd fire back that he was ungrateful, hard-hearted, and worse. A few years into their romance, after a particularly ferocious argument, she'd even packed her bags and returned to her uncle's house. Ah Zhai had fumed and then wept and then resolved to honor Lulu's decision. She was so beautiful and vivacious and young—he must have been an imbecile to think she'd settle for being his mistress. But less than twenty-four hours later, Lulu had marched through the front door and ordered the maid to unpack her luggage. Ah Zhai gingerly approached, and she melted into his arms, heaving with sobs. He showered her with kisses and held her until she quieted. He would never ask what made her change her mind, and she'd never offer to tell him, but he suspected her uncle had turned her away, that Lulu had realized then that Ah Zhai was all she had.

In the six years since the border had closed, Lulu and Ah Zhai had never spent a night apart—until now.

Bleary with fatigue, Ah Zhai made it through the morning by gulping down a steady stream of strong red tea. He pushed aside the documents he'd been struggling to read for the past hour, dialed his secretary's line, and asked her to bring him a fresh pot.

"Of course, sir," Wendy said.

He heard her move down the hallway in her sensible flat shoes. Unlike the other secretaries, she wore minimal makeup, boxy blouses, and skirts that covered her calves. He appreciated that about her. He disliked people who tried too hard to be something they were not.

Several minutes later, his secretary returned to her desk outside his office, but instead of bringing him the pot, she fell into conversation with someone who must have been waiting to see him.

"Please take a seat," she said. "I'll let Mr. Ong know you're here."

He glanced at the clock. There were no meetings on the calendar. When the phone rang, he asked, "What's holding you up, Wendy?"

"Your wife is here, sir."

He very nearly dropped the phone. "What in heaven's name for?"

Wendy answered evenly, "Well, sir, she didn't say."

Ah Zhai could think of no one he wanted to see less. Dazed with longing for his mistress, he felt, in some strange way, that seeing his wife right then would be a violation of his and Lulu's love. "She can't just show up like this."

His secretary dropped her voice. "Is that what you want me to tell her?"

Ah Zhai hung up the phone and trudged to the door. Seok Koon sat in a low leather armchair with her knees held together and her elbows pinned to her sides, as if she were trying to take up as little space as possible.

Mustering every ounce of energy within him, Ah Zhai said, "Why, Seok Koon, what a pleasant surprise. Do come in."

In her bright floral dress, Seok Koon looked almost like a local. Was she wearing lipstick? Had she dressed up just to come to his office? He realized he had no idea how his wife spent her days.

"Forgive me for barging in like this." She was careful not to touch him as she entered his office.

"No need to apologize." Ah Zhai signaled for his secretary to bring a second teacup with the teapot.

Once Wendy had shut the door behind her, he poured the tea and said, "So, what brings you by today? How is the boy liking school?"

Seok Koon batted away his pleasantries. "I must talk to you about San San. Please, Zhai hear me out."

He set down the teapot. The air in the room grew suddenly stifling. He stripped off his suit jacket, and she waited for him to drape the garment over the back of his chair before beginning.

So she'd gone to see that priest of hers again, and together they'd hatched another scheme. He should have guessed as much. This time, though, he had to admit it wasn't such a crazy plan. Everyone knew the communists were desperate for foreign currency—so much so that they just might take a chance and let his daughter cross the border.

"All we have to do is make sure the money is in your bank account," Seok Koon said.

Ah Zhai forced himself to nod. The loan sharks were out of the question. He'd have to let go of the servants, sell the cars, maybe some of Lulu's designer furniture. He'd be lucky if all that netted half of what was needed.

His wife was waiting for a response.

"It's not unreasonable," he said.

Seok Koon's eyes welled. She reached in her pocketbook for her handkerchief and dabbed her eyes. "I think this will work, Zhai. I really do."

"It's certainly worth a try."

She daintily blew her nose.

"Now," he said, "about the funds."

She lowered her handkerchief. "Yes?"

"I'll just need a few days to get everything in place. A week or two at most."

The color drained from Seok Koon's face. "We can't prolong this any longer. Our permits have already expired. The servants have taken over the flat. Do you know that the cook has moved into your mother's bedroom?"

The words washed over Ah Zhai without sinking in. "You don't understand the first thing about money."

Instead of recoiling, his wife leaned in and pressed both palms flat on his desk, as though ready to reach out and slap him if provoked. He felt himself duck.

"I'm begging you, Zhai. We must act now. We may already be too late."

His fingernails dug into the flesh of his thighs and the pain made him exhale. "My wife, we're both in agreement here. I'm simply asking for your patience."

"We can't keep spouting the same old lies. Do you think the Party will accept you've been 'clinging to your deathbed' forever?" She covered her face with her handkerchief.

He swiveled his chair to face the window, unable to watch her cry. He'd finally pulled together enough money to pay the landlord, but if he didn't hand that over right away, Tam would evict his family. He wondered, crazily, if he could move his mother and wife and son into his soon-to-be-bare townhouse. To do so would be to accept that Lulu had left for good. Was this the sacrifice demanded of him by his family and his late father and the rest of his long string of illustrious ancestors?

Ah Zhai felt his chair spin around. His wife fell to her knees before him. "My husband, I know you barely know our daughter. I know she's only a girl child, as loathsome as a cowbird."

"Get up," he said.

"But she's bright and obedient. She's a good girl."

"Please, my wife, get up."

Seok Koon flung her torso to the floor, pressing her forehead to the carpet. "If you can't do this for the girl, do it for me. I swear I will never again ask anything of you."

What was she implying? That she would grant him a divorce? "Stop this nonsense. Get up right now." He no longer cared if his secretary overheard them.

Seok Koon's voice was muffled by the carpet. "I won't until you agree."

Curled up on the floor, she was as helpless as a child, but, without money, he was helpless, too. "I just need a little time."

Seok Koon said into the carpet, "There is no time."

For a split second, he considered blurting out his financial woes. Instead, he seized the heaviest thing on his desk—a glass paperweight shaped like a swan—and raised it above his head. His wife's shoulder blades shuddered beneath the lustrous silk of her dress. He heaved the swan onto the carpet in disgust, and it bounced up and dove headfirst into the thick weave before landing on its side.

Startled, Seok Koon raised her head.

"Write the letter," Ah Zhai said. "The funds will be in my account." He fell into his chair, overcome with exhaustion.

At last his stubborn wife rose. She crawled over and nestled her face in his lap, her tears moistening his trousers. He stiffened, unsure of whether to nudge her away or comfort her.

Aside from the occasional cursory embrace, or the dry sweep of his lips across her cheek, they'd barely touched. Now, however, her forehead pressed his inner thigh and he felt himself stir.

"Thank you, my husband," she whispered.

The brief flicker of arousal immediately gave way to repulsion. He feared she might kiss him through his trousers. He gingerly rolled an inch backward in his chair. He didn't know if his wife's face expressed disappointment or relief.

Gruffly, he said, "I have work to do."

"Of course."

At the door, Seok Koon murmured her thanks once more.

Ah Zhai gazed down at his gold watch, which had been his father's, and his grandfather's before that, and wondered how much it would fetch at the pawnshop.

19

A deafening crash jolted San San awake. She raised herself on her elbows and gazed out the sole window in Spinster Lin's dressing room, round and high like a ship's porthole. Rain poured down in sheets. The sky was so dark she could barely make out the hands on her watch.

And then she remembered what day it was. She clambered up the step stool to press her face to the windowpane. Surely the denunciation session would be postponed. The whole town couldn't be expected to assemble outdoors in this storm.

A flash of lightning evoked the jagged edges of the hole in the kitchen window. San San ran down the back stairs. Water spilled into the kitchen, drenching the straw baskets of dried goods and the earthenware jugs lined up against the wall. She wrapped her arms around a jug and strained to lift it, managing to clear the ground by no more than an inch. Changing course, she shuttled the much lighter straw baskets into the dining room, where the sight of the long teak table gave her an idea. She pulled open sideboard doors and drawers until she found a bright red tablecloth made from stiff, coated cotton. The fabric wasn't waterproof, but it was better than nothing.

By now the pool of rainwater had crept halfway across the kitchen's tiled floor. Water soaked through San San's canvas shoes and the hems of her borrowed pajamas as she worked to tack the tablecloth over the broken window. Using all of her body weight, she heaved the jugs, one by one, to the opposite side of the kitchen. Rain continued to pummel the tablecloth. At this rate, the cloth would soon grow too wet to be of any use, but she'd worry about that when the time came.

She shut the kitchen door and retreated to the living room to dry her feet on the sheepskin rug. It was then that the announcement came through the street-corner loudspeakers, informing the revolutionary comrades of Drum Wave Islet that due to inclement weather, the denunciation session and subsequent execution of Lee Chin Kong and Rose Lee would be pushed back to the following day. San San fell onto the stiff-backed sofa and stretched out her sore arms in relief.

She must have dozed off because the next thing she knew, a watery ray of sunlight shone through a crack in the curtains and angry fists hammered the door.

"Open up! Housing Registration Board. Open up right now!"

She leapt up.

"If you don't open the door, we'll have no choice but to kick it down."

She grabbed her shoes and sprinted to the stairs.

"We saw the cloth over the kitchen window. We know you're in there."

In the dressing room, San San retrieved her mother's letters, now stashed in Spinster Lin's leather portfolio. She ran down the back stairs into the kitchen, splashed through the rainwater pool, and slipped out the door just before the blast of splintering wood. She stuffed the portfolio in the waistband of her pants, knotted the drawstring as tight as it would go, and ran toward the sea.

Thanks to the storm, Flourishing Beauty Cove was deserted. The summer before, San San and her brother had begged Ma to let them sleep right on the beach after a lazy day of swimming and fishing, but to no avail.

That night, however, San San learned that the sand that was so soft and inviting against her feet made a poor mattress, that palm fronds were no substitute for a blanket, that upon sunset, the balmy ocean breeze grew relentless, harsh.

The next day she combed the rocky shore in search of the oyster bed that a friendly fisherman had once led her and her brother to, but either the bed had somehow vanished, or she'd misremembered the spot.

Lightheaded with hunger, she ventured back to the arts college on Chicken Hill Road. An enormous padlock hung from the gate. The summer holidays, she realized, had just begun, which meant there was no one to keep her from climbing the longan tree. She gorged herself on the succulent fruits until her stomach ached, and spent the rest of the afternoon recovering on the floor of an empty classroom.

The following morning, the town announcer's voice, transmitted by the many campus loudspeakers, echoed across the college. Due to an impromptu visit from important city officials, the denunciation session would be postponed by yet another day. And by the time *that* day rolled around, San San was convinced that Dr. Lee and Auntie Rose's denunciation session would never take place. The Party was most likely trying to save face. Once the townspeople lost interest in the case—or found a new case to focus on—the Party would quietly release the captives.

In one corner of the classroom blackboard, San San marked another passing day. The ship with the green flag would return to Xiamen in a week. If the doctor and her teacher could not leave with her, she trusted they'd know how to get her on board.

Roaming the vacant grounds, she waited and waited for the announcement that would postpone the denunciation session yet again. This time, however, none came.

When she could put off leaving no longer, San San climbed over the college gate and hurried to town, taking the long way to avoid passing the cemetery. Perhaps the Party would save face by going forward with the session, after which they would let Dr. Lee and Auntie Rose return home. San San would have to sneak over to their house before the session ended. She pictured her teacher's face lighting up when she saw her.

She reached the town square as the last few stragglers, tiny-footed crones leaning on walking sticks, made their way to the high school basketball courts. Instead of following them through the gates, she circled the perimeter of the school. About fifty meters away from the basketball courts stood an old oak tree. She scrambled onto a low, sturdy branch behind a thick veil of leaves. She only had to peek through the leaves to gain a clear view of the stage that had been erected in the front of the courts.

Students arranged according to grade sat cross-legged on the already sun-scorched concrete, while the townsfolk filled in behind them. Some of the townsfolk sat on stools they'd brought from home, cooling their faces with paper fans. San San scanned the rows of elementary school students. It was hard to tell, given their identical white shirts and navy-blue shorts or skirts, but wasn't that Little Red right there in the third row? The girl with the pointy chin turned slightly, confirming San San's suspicion. Little Red pulled a loop of string from her pocket and engaged the girl next to her—Steamed Bun, of course—in a game of cat's cradle. The thumb-sized lump in San San's throat welled to a fist.

A man with Cook's round belly and head of gray hair caught her attention, but this time she was mistaken. The man was a stranger. She'd spent the past week in total solitude, and yet she'd never felt more alone than she did at this moment, sitting on her tree branch, close enough to shout her presence to the entire town. She searched in vain for Cook and Mui Ah, wondering how hard they'd looked for her. She hoped they'd told her mother she'd gone missing; she hoped the news had devastated her.

The town announcer, an attractive woman whose tunic and trousers were somehow sleeker and less drab than everyone else's, strode onstage and led the townsfolk through a rousing rendition of "Socialism Is Good." San San had always admired the announcer's mellifluous singing voice, and despite her distress, she found herself humming along.

Once the song was over, the hateful Comrade Ang bounded onstage with a bullhorn. San San hadn't seen him since her self-criticism session, and she hoped he'd trip on a loose plank and fall flat on his face.

But Comrade Ang moved with grace and ease.

"Serve the people!" he yelled into the bullhorn.

"Serve the people!" the crowd yelled back.

And, "Dare to struggle, dare to win!"

And, "Fight, fight to the finish!"

The crowd clapped their hands and stamped their feet. Comrade Ang's face turned bright red as he continued to shout and wave.

San San typically enjoyed chanting sessions—all these voices in unison, like an immense chorus or orchestra, something she never experienced in her own musical life. "The piano is a lonely instrument," her mother had warned when San San first started lessons. Auntie Rose had countered, "Self-sufficient—one needn't ever depend on an accompanist."

This morning, however, San San drew no pleasure from the crowd's wanton, almost hysterical display. Their eyes bulged and their jaws flexed, turning their faces into ghoulish masks. How had she never noticed before?

Above the furious chanting soared the wail of a siren. A police van sped past San San's tree and halted at the edge of the basketball courts. Comrade Ang signaled for the crowd to quiet down and ceded the stage to the announcer.

"The prisoners have arrived," she said.

The crowd erupted. If San San hadn't been holding on to her branch with both hands, she would have covered her ears.

The van door opened, and two policemen clad in crisp olive-green uniforms stepped out. They saluted the assembled before leading out their charges. Soiled pillowcases masked the prisoners' faces. Baggy jumpsuits hung off them like burlap sacks.

A low hum of approval rose from the crowd. It was impossible to tell if the prisoners were male or female, young or old, but San San was certain they could not be Auntie Rose and Dr. Lee. These figures were emaciated, shrunken, nothing like her plump, pretty teacher and the tall, broad-shouldered doctor. In fact, now that she stopped to think about it, she hadn't heard their names mentioned all morning. Had she mistaken the date? Was she at the wrong denunciation session?

The policemen prodded the prisoners with the butts of their nightsticks, as though they were too squalid to be touched. Blinded by the pillowcases, wrists bound behind them, the pair gingerly edged forward.

The crowd jeered.

"Show those turtle eggs who's in charge now!"

"Make that son of a dog pay!"

By now San San was sure she'd somehow attended the wrong session, and she laughed along, her voice foreign and rasping in her ears.

After the prisoners had shuffled along for a little while, the policemen grew impatient. They seized their bound arms and half pushed, half dragged them onstage. The prisoners stood there dumbly, their covered faces jerking toward each insult that flew through the air.

"Let the denunciation session begin!" cried the announcer.

On cue the policemen rammed their nightsticks into the prisoners' backs. They crumpled to the ground as if made of cardboard. If either, or both, cried out, the sound was lost in the crowd's cheers.

San San's throat constricted. She clung so tightly to her branch that she wouldn't have been surprised if her palms began to bleed.

The announcer unfurled a long scroll and began to recite the prisoners' crimes, but the chanting crowd drowned her out. Only after Comrade Ang sprang onstage and waved his arms wildly did everyone finally calm down.

When the announcer declared it time to reveal the faces of the counterrevolutionaries, a hush fell over the basketball courts. The seated townsfolk rose from their stools. The kindergarten teachers quieted the smallest students. Every muscle in San San's body tensed with dread and hope and fear.

The policemen took their places behind the kneeling prisoners.

"Here we go," said the announcer. "One . . . two . . . three!"

The dirty pillowcases flew off. A strangled wail left San San's lips, a strange, animal sound she'd never made before.

There, onstage, was the doctor, barely recognizable beneath the foul, blood-soaked bandages encircling his head and one eye. His other eye was swollen shut.

Someone in the crowd yelled, "Scoundrel! Pervert!"

Dr. Lee's head jerked, seemingly involuntarily, in the heckler's direction, drawing more taunts.

But it was the sight of Auntie Rose that made San San let go of the branch and lose her balance and very nearly crash to the ground.

Auntie Rose's thick, luxuriant hair had been shorn to the scalp, revealing the tender, bony knobs of her skull. Her skin had lost all color, aside from a brilliant crimson slash down the side of her face from temple to chin. She knelt with her head cocked to one side, half-open eyes blinking slowly as though she were barely awake.

A line of children trooped onstage.

"Please welcome our little friends," the announcer said.

The children filed past Dr. Lee and Auntie Rose with their eyes trained straight ahead. There was Kong Ping Ping, a classmate of Ah Liam's, and little Tan Huat of Sea and Sky Mansion, and the Gao brothers, who were identical twins. It dawned on San San that like her, all of them were Auntie Rose's piano students.

"Go on, little friends," the announcer urged. "Tell everyone how Rose Lee polluted your bright young minds."

Ping Ping took the microphone and gave the crowd a dazzling smile, as if competing in a talent show. "Rose Lee only teaches her students Western music. Rose Lee idolizes Mozart and Chopin and Bach. She believes Chinese music to be inferior to Western music. She has poisoned the minds of our islet's next generation of musicians, and she must be punished."

The crowd applauded, and Ping Ping passed the microphone to the next child in line, but San San was no longer listening. She watched the way Auntie Rose hung her head, her eyes milky, her face blank. She wondered if her teacher was feigning stupor in hopes of garnering pity. They're just words, she longed to tell her teacher. Let them pass over you, and soon it will all be over.

When the last child had spoken, the announcer retrieved the microphone. "We have assembled all of Rose Lee's former students except for one," she said to the enraptured crowd. "One student did not get to speak. One student's voice has been silenced forever."

The announcer turned and pointed first at Dr. Lee and then at Auntie Rose. "Where is Ong San San? Confess to the masses before you meet your end."

The crowd erupted once more.

"Confess! Confess! Where is Ong San San?"

San San dropped down from her branch and hid behind the thick tree trunk.

Onstage, Dr. Lee raised his face to the sky and contorted his features in agony. The announcer passed the microphone to one of the policemen, who held it to Dr. Lee's lips. His voice was hollow and hoarse. "I don't know where she is. I swear on my father's grave."

An icy current poured through San San. She wrapped her arms around herself and pressed her forehead to the rough tree bark.

"Confess!" yelled the crowd. "Worthless traitors! Heartless kidnappers!"

If San San turned herself in, was there any chance that Dr. Lee and Auntie Rose would be released, or would she be shot alongside them for trying to flee? Had her disappearance caused their sentence, or was it part of an auxiliary crime, wielded by the Party to rile up the masses?

Egged on by the crowd, one of the policemen reared back his leg and kicked the doctor with his heavy black boot. The doctor groaned and toppled onto his side. This finally shook Auntie Rose awake. She tried to crawl to him, but the other policeman restrained her by the collar like a dog.

"Take them away to be executed," the announcer said.

San San wiped her tears. If she turned herself in, might she be allowed to see Dr. Lee and Auntie Rose one final time? The van door shut. The crowd began to disperse. She blew her nose on her sleeve and jogged toward the town square. She had to make it back to the arts college without being seen.

"San San," a deep voice cried. "San San, is that you?"

She didn't need to turn to know exactly who it was. Cook, along with Mui Ah, hurried toward her. Her mind screamed, "Run!" but her feet lagged. The storm within her lifted, making way for a long-overlooked memory: her Hansel clad in a tiny striped nightgown that Mui Ah had sewn from old drapes.

"I told you it was her in that tree," Mui Ah screeched. "Didn't I tell you?"

Mui Ah's mouth was a gaping hole. Cook's face was purple with exertion. But they looked overjoyed to have found her. Maybe, just maybe, they would hide her; maybe they would help her escape.

"Call the police," Cook gasped.

San San snapped out of her trance and sped up.

"That'll slow us down more," said Mui Ah. "Catch her first and then we'll call the police."

San San's thighs and calves blazed, her lungs threatened to burst, but she knew now to keep running, to never let herself get caught. If there was one lesson she'd learned over the past month, one lesson her family's betrayal had taught her, it was this: the only person she could depend on was herself. The corollary to that lesson was clear: she would never again put herself in jeopardy for anyone else. She would never turn herself in.

At the top of the hill, she glanced back and spotted the old gravedigger two steps behind Cook. "I told you I saw her the other day. No one ever listens to me."

San San veered off the main road, leapt over the low gate of the postmaster's house, and crouched behind a hedge. She cupped her hands over her nose and mouth to muffle her panting and peeked through the leaves.

"Which way did she go?" Cook wheezed, his belly heaving with each breath.

Mui Ah said, "You go that way, I'll go this way. She can't be far."

Cook bent over and rested with his hands on his knees. "If her mother finds out, she'll have me killed," he said to the gravedigger, who said, "Worry about that later."

San San's fingers brushed the portfolio of letters tucked in her waistband, her grandmother's filigreed gold bangle, the red-leather strap of her silver-faced watch. She had to get off the islet. There was nothing left for her here.

20

S eok Koon was so furious she could barely choke out the words, "Thank you for your help," before hanging up the phone.

Although it was the middle of the day, the sky outside her window was evening dark. Lightning slashed the dense clouds, followed by booming thunder, as though Nature herself shared Seok Koon's rage.

Another doctor's note had been procured. The letter had been carefully crafted to get past censors and would arrive in Diamond Villa in days. Father Leung had included San San's name in Sunday's prayer bulletin and assured Seok Koon that he was personally praying for the girl's safe arrival.

But when Seok Koon had telephoned her husband's banker, just to confirm the funds were in place, she discovered that less than half the needed sum had been deposited into Ah Zhai's account.

"Your husband did indeed pay us a visit yesterday," the banker had said. "No, I don't believe he mentioned anything about another deposit."

"That can't be right," Seok Koon said. "Please check again."

But the banker had returned with the same number, and when Seok Koon pressed him to check one more time, he said curtly, "Mrs. Ong, I suggest you take this up with your husband. Clearly there's been some kind of misunderstanding."

According to his secretary, Zhai was currently in a very important meeting and could not be disturbed. And even if he had come to the phone, what would Seok Koon have said? How much harder could she beg? How could she make him care?

She wondered if her husband had always been this selfish, this coldhearted. The first time Zhai had waited outside the conservatory gates, Rose had spotted him before Seok Koon had: a trim, confident figure in a straw boater that had struck them as the height of sophistication. What had Seok Koon known of her suitor? She'd admired his impeccable manners, his self-assuredness coupled with that irresistible impish grin. She'd been flattered by his attention. She'd felt pride when family and friends congratulated her on forming such a good match. Beyond that, however, she drew a blank. She could not remember if she'd thought him kind or upstanding. She could not even remember if she'd enjoyed his company, so focused was she on ensuring he enjoyed hers.

That afternoon, they'd meandered through Bright Moon Garden on the way back to the home where she boarded during the school year. She'd asked him to tell her about Hong Kong, which even back then he'd visited regularly for business.

"It's dirty, crowded, a real mess of a city. The only good thing about Hong Kong is it reminds me how lucky we are to live here, on Drum Wave Islet. I would never raise my family there."

She'd blushed and looked down to avoid appearing presumptuous. Three weeks later, he and his family traveled to her parents' house in Fuzhou for the betrothal, and they were married two months after that.

Ah Zhai maintained his promise, keeping his family on the islet while he braved frequent trips to the colony. He returned home exhausted and relieved, brimming with tales of the things he'd seen—a whole street of shops that served only snake soup, which the Cantonese believed to be medicinal; the fortune-teller who chased him down to warn of impending financial ruin, that crazy old hag. Back then, Seok

Koon had imagined a bleak, licentious land of fog and shadows. Now, however, she saw that Hong Kong was like any other city in prerevolutionary China: gritty, noisy, chaotic.

One day, right around Ah Liam's third birthday, Zhai burst into the villa with a trunk full of presents, not just for the birthday boy, but for Seok Koon and Bee Kim, too: jade and silks and a lacquered jewelry box inlaid with a pair of mother-of-pearl cranes. Even as she swooned over the treasures, Seok Koon's delight was tinged with doubt.

Ah Zhai's trips to Hong Kong grew longer, but his stories faded away. He came home distracted and impatient and always, always with presents, each more extravagant than the last, as though the luster of a jade pendant in the rare shade of apple green could somehow blind a wife from seeing into her husband's heart.

When Seok Koon went into labor again, Zhai didn't come home for the birth, and when the baby turned out to be a girl, everyone praised him for having the foresight to prioritize his work.

That, Seok Koon knew now, was the moment when she'd lost him for good. And by letting go without a fight, she would have to shoulder part of the blame for his indifference toward San San.

Another crash of thunder. Thick ropes of rain plunged from the sky. She wondered what the weather was like on the islet. Summer holidays had begun, and if the day were fine, her daughter would be at Flourishing Beauty Cove with Little Red, swimming, fishing for yellow croaker, harvesting wild oysters.

Suddenly the room was too dark, too claustrophobic. Seok Koon could not breathe. She needed to go outside, see the ocean, inhale the brisk, briny air. She saw herself dipping a toe in the swirling, rain-pocked waters of Repulse Bay, the waves spiriting her longing across the South China Sea to her daughter, who splashed in the surf beneath a cloudless blue sky. Seok Koon imagined diving beneath the surface, knifing her limbs through the water, propelling herself straight into her daughter's arms.

Beneath a large umbrella, Seok Koon stood by the side of the road until her skirt and the back of her blouse were soaked, but no taxi would stop. All of Hong Kong, it seemed, was out on these stormy streets, trying to get from one place to another.

An empty taxi careened down the road, its wipers working furiously. Seok Koon waved and waved, but it refused to slow. The taxi was followed closely by a capacious silver Jaguar. By the time Seok Koon registered the need to jump back, it was too late. The Jaguar's fat tires rolled through a puddle, drenching her in filthy water. She cried out, filled with the crazed urge to fold her umbrella and hurl it like a javelin at that ridiculous boat-sized car.

To her surprise, instead of speeding away, the car pulled to a stop. The driver's door opened, and a uniformed chauffeur, toting an umbrella of his own, came toward her.

It took Seok Koon a second to recognize her husband's chauffeur. But when did he buy this ridiculous car? Anger roiled inside her. Could Zhai really be throwing away money at a time like this?

The chauffeur bowed deeply. "Please accept my sincere apologies, Madame Ong. I didn't see you."

"It's my fault for standing so close to the edge." She glanced down at her mud-streaked skirt and then strained to see in to the back seat of the car. What was Ah Zhai doing in this part of town? She wondered if his important meeting was over, or if his secretary had simply lied.

"Come, we'll give you a lift to wherever you're going."

Seok Koon marched over to the Jaguar, the chauffeur hurrying to keep up. She yanked back the passenger door and was greeted not by her husband but by a very pale young woman with a wiry, reddish-brown mane and eyes the color of weak tea—rare for a Chinese.

"Hurry up and get in before we both get drenched," the young woman said in a tone so commanding that Seok Koon immediately folded her umbrella and complied.

The young woman held out her hand. "Nice to finally meet you, Mrs. Ong, I'm—"

"Lulu," Seok Koon said.

The woman pressed her lips into a grim line. "Indeed."

Of course Seok Koon had expected her to be beautiful, but the young woman was like none she'd ever seen. From this angle, Lulu was all limbs and bones, like an adolescent boy in the midst of a growth spurt. From another, the light brought out the flecks of gold in her weak-tea eyes, the vertiginous slope of her cheekbones, the sensuous curve of her lower lip.

"Where to?" the chauffeur called back.

The absurdity of Seok Koon's plan to go to Repulse Bay in the middle of a storm grew clear. All she wanted was to talk to this strange young woman, the only person who might have insight into her husband's opaque mind.

"Well?" asked Lulu.

"I need your help," said Seok Koon.

Lulu's face softened. "And, I suppose, in a way, I need yours."

So, this meeting was no grand coincidence. Lulu had come looking for her.

"You first," said Lulu.

"It's my daughter." Seok Koon felt her tears forcing their way out. "Forgive me," she said, fishing in her pocketbook for her handkerchief.

Lulu held out her own handkerchief, and when Seok Koon brought the ivory, lace-edged cloth to her face, she smelled roses in full bloom.

"The daughter you had to leave behind."

Seok Koon was taken aback by this near stranger's bluntness, but then she realized it freed her from having to explain. "I have a plan to rescue my daughter, a good, solid plan, but—" her voice trailed off. She could not speak her husband's name.

"But?"

"You're the only one who can change his mind."

Lulu made a sound that was part scoff, part laugh. "That may have been true in the past, but I've lost any sway I once held. He's made his choice, after all."

Seok Koon frowned. "What do you mean?"

Lulu arched an eyebrow. "He put the townhouse up for sale. He's moved in with you. How much clearer could it be?"

This was the first Seok Koon had heard about the sale of the house, though, of course, her husband never told her anything. "He hasn't been by the flat in weeks."

Lulu's eyes narrowed. She had the chauffeur turn around and ferry them to her cousin's home where she was staying—very temporarily, she added darkly.

Seok Koon dared not ask her to elaborate. She didn't know what to make of Lulu's brusque yet beguiling manner. She felt a begrudging respect for her husband, who had managed to capture the attention of this odd creature.

In Lulu's cousin's drawing room, over cups of English tea, which Seok Koon found too bitter black and too bland with cream, the women pieced together all they knew.

Abruptly Lulu set down her cup. She rose to her feet and went to the window to watch the falling rain. "It appears our Mr. Ong Hong Zhai is broke."

"I don't understand," said Seok Koon.

"Ruined, bankrupt, penniless."

But how could that be true? What of Zhai's lavish lifestyle? The generous monthly allowance? Ah Liam's private school fees?

Lulu returned to her seat opposite Seok Koon. "He fired all the servants and sold the cars. The chauffeur, the housekeeper, they all showed up here, begging me to talk some sense into him. I persuaded my cousin to take them on."

Seok Koon tried to absorb this new information. "I see."

"After I heard he'd put the townhouse on the market, I figured he'd moved in with you. I drove by your flat today to confirm my suspicion. But I see now that he was just trying to raise money as quickly as possible."

Seok Koon knew she should feel sorry for her husband—for how long had he kept this tremendous secret?—but her thoughts were consumed by San San. Her bright, determined daughter had taken her first steps early, earlier even than Ah Liam. That long-ago summer day, Seok Koon had looked up from her mystery novel to see her baby toddling toward her, chubby arms outstretched for balance, face beaming, mouth a joyful O. Seok Koon fell to her knees and reached for San San, who took two more steps and tumbled into her lap, all softness and laughter and squeals.

Without money, all was lost.

"What will you do now?" Lulu asked.

"I don't know," said Seok Koon. Any remaining threads of self-righteousness, of indignation, vanished, leaving her empty and slack. She saw no way to rescue her daughter. She watched Lulu drain the last of her tea as though observing a museum exhibit. "And you?" she asked.

Lulu shrugged her thin shoulders. "I can't impose on Cynthia for much longer. I've overstayed my welcome."

Seok Koon looked around the immaculate room at the rose-and-pearl–striped wallpaper and the vase of robin's-egg-blue hydrangeas atop the fireplace. An oil painting hung above the upright piano, a still life of waxy-looking apples. She wanted to ask where Lulu's parents were. Surely someone like her had other family and friends to lean on.

Lulu returned her cup to its saucer with particular care. "I had a daughter once."

Seok Koon studied the young woman's smooth face. "Oh?"

"Her name was Marigold."

"A beautiful flower," said Seok Koon. "A beautiful name."

21

To play the East Wind or the 7 Bamboo—to go for the quick, easy point, or to wait, bide one's time, try to win it all, but, of course, risk losing everything in the process? Wasn't that the eternal dilemma, in mahjong as well as in life?

The game was going poorly. Bee Kim hadn't slept well the night before and was in no mood to chat with her fellow Fujian émigrés. In fact she couldn't recall the last time she'd had a good night's sleep. Certainly not since arriving in the colony, with its honking trishaws and motorcars, its denizens who screeched—never just spoke in normal, conversational tones—in that cacophony of a dialect.

The Fujian Association Center was crowded, with six games going at once. Bee Kim had arrived a few minutes late and been shunted to the leftover table with Mrs. Lao, a widow who was plump, guileless, and wholly uninteresting, Mr. Ng, a pensive man who only spoke when absolutely necessary, and, worst of all, Madame Tay, an unapologetic gossip who had apparently been a well-known socialite in her hometown.

At the last second, Bee Kim changed her mind and flicked her bamboo tile in the center of the table. Two tables away, Mr. Tan raised his arms in the air and yelled, "Mah jong," and his opponents let out disappointed hoots.

Madame Tay waggled her skinny, penciled-on eyebrows and cleared her throat. "Surely you've heard the news by now," she said. It was her typical opening.

"What news?" asked Mrs. Lao, who always took the bait. Back home, the widow would never have been a part of Madame Tay's clique. Here in the colony, however, in the grand tradition of exiles putting aside differences and banding together against a common enemy—in this case, the snobby Hongkies—the women had become fast friends.

"Pung," Mr. Ng said softly, reaching for Mrs. Lao's discarded tile.

Bee Kim continued to study her hand. She didn't feel like indulging Madame Tay.

Undeterred, Madame Tay turned to Mrs. Lao. "Oh, you haven't heard? About the execution on Drum Wave Islet?"

Bee Kim slowly raised her eyes. Beside her, Mr. Ng shuffled the tiles on his rack again and again.

"Oh dear," said Mrs. Lao. "There've been such a rash of them. The communists are really showing their true colors now."

"Where did you hear that?" asked Bee Kim.

"From my son's school friend's wife," Madame Tay replied. "She's from Drum Wave Islet, or maybe her mother's family is. I don't remember which."

"Who?" asked Bee Kim.

"I can't recall the wife's maiden name—"

"No," Bee Kim interrupted. "Who was executed?"

"Oh, I see," said Madame Tay, clearly pleased to have her attention. "A famous doctor and his wife."

Mrs. Lao said, "What a waste. What a sad, sad waste."

Madame Tay placed her fingers on Bee Kim's forearm in a gesture of concern.

"Hopefully they weren't people you knew?"

Bee Kim withdrew her arm. "There's more than one doctor on Drum Wave Islet."

"Certainly, but this one was supposedly quite well known. Quite high up, too. And his wife was an accomplished pianist."

Bee Kim's throat tightened. Chin Kong's last words to her daughter-in-law reverberated in her head: *We only ask that you remember us later, when you're in a position to help us.*

Mrs. Lao nodded knowingly. "I really don't understand how all these intelligent, educated people could have stayed behind."

"Not everyone had a choice," Bee Kim snapped.

Mrs. Lao's plain, square face took on a wounded expression. She looked down at her tiles.

Mr. Ng discarded his wind tile, and Madame Tay's gnarled hand, the only part of her that wasn't immaculately preserved, pounced like an iguana's tongue. "Fishing."

The remainder of the game passed in a blur. Bee Kim mechanically chose a tile, discarded another. She didn't understand how this could have happened to Chin Kong and Rose—unless they'd been caught trying to flee. But why would someone as powerful and connected as the doctor attempt something so risky? Bee Kim remembered a long-ago article in the *People's Daily*, which reported that the head doctor at a top Beijing hospital had been banished to a labor camp for twenty years for misdiagnosing Madame Mao. She could only guess at the kind of pressure Chin Kong faced.

Mr. Ng nudged Bee Kim's elbow. "Your turn."

She tossed a tile in the center pile.

Again Madame Tay pounced and sang, "Mah jong!"

Bee Kim pushed back her chair and waved for her maid, who was sitting with the other servants in a circle on the floor in the back corner of the hall.

"Where are you going?" said Mrs. Lao. "Stay for one more round."

"Yes, stay," Madame Tay said, while Mr. Ng shrugged indifferently.

Bee Kim insisted she must be off, took her maid's arm, and prepared to go out in the rain.

All the way home, she debated what to tell Seok Koon. There was no way of knowing the accuracy of Madame Tay's news, and, even if an execution had taken place, who could say for sure that Chin Kong and Rose had been the victims? The islet had several doctors, several pianists, too. Bee Kim thought of all the young women in Seok Koon's graduating class. A few of them could have married doctors, and that was just one class!

There was one line of questioning Bee Kim refused to pursue: what Chin Kong's and Rose's deaths might mean for her granddaughter. Thank heavens Seok Koon and Zhai had another rescue plan in the works, one that Seok Koon insisted was practically risk-free.

Back in the flat, Bee Kim settled into her chair with her needlepoint to await her daughter-in-law's arrival. She would break the news as gently as possible. "This is just a rumor," she'd say. "The woman who told me is an incurable gossip."

The front door opened. Bee Kim heard Seok Koon drop her pocketbook on the table in the entryway, even though she'd repeatedly warned her daughter-in-law that until they were sure the servants could be trusted, she shouldn't be so cavalier.

Bee Kim sewed the last stitches of a pale-pink lotus flower, put down her needlepoint canvas, and waited. But Seok Koon rushed past the sitting room without stopping.

"Daughter-in-Law," she called.

Seok Koon backtracked and entered, a dazed expression on her face. "I didn't expect you to be home already." Her hair was windswept, her skirt, wrinkled and streaked with mud.

"What happened to you?"

Seok Koon's mouth dropped open but no sound emerged. She covered her face with her hands and said in a muffled voice. "I'm sorry, I have a splitting headache. I really must lie down." She turned to leave.

"Wait," said Bee Kim.

Her daughter-in-law obeyed.

But how could she reveal the news now? "The girl," she said. "Everything is in place? When will we hear about her permit? When will she arrive?"

Flatly Seok Koon said, "Nothing is in place. Absolutely nothing."

Bee Kim sat up. Never before had she seen her so defeated. "What does that mean? What more must we do?"

Seok Koon shook off her stupor. Her shoulders rose to her earlobes. Her hands formed fists. "I don't know, I don't know."

"What are you saying, Daughter-in-Law?"

Seok Koon stepped into the room. She towered over Bee Kim. "That we never should have left her. That we may never get her back."

She fled down the hallway, and Bee Kim let her go. She sat with her hands in her lap, weathering the terrible pounding in her chest. What would her own mother have said? That you couldn't expect a sugarcane stalk to be sweet on both ends, that you had to sacrifice one thing to get another. But the pounding failed to cease. If only she had someone else to talk to. If only she could call Hua. All of Hua's grandchildren lived abroad, so she'd doted on Ah Liam and especially San San. Once, when Bee Kim complained about the girl's stubbornness, Hua had burst out laughing and said, "She takes after you! Someday she'll grow into a stern but loving grandma to grandchildren of her own." Bee Kim tried to picture her gangly, tomboyish granddaughter as a young lady. How much had she grown in the past month? Who would tell Mui Ah to have the seamstress come by to make her new clothes? Who would buy her new shoes? Who would sit by her bedside, telling her stories until she fell asleep? She clasped her hands over her chest and wondered if she was suffering a heart attack. When the pain finally eased, she took up her needlepoint canvas and began where she'd left off.

A fat orange carp was taking shape beside the lotus flower when her grandson trooped in from school.

"Grandson, come greet your grandma," Bee Kim called. She wanted to tell him everything—the alleged execution, the dangers San San now faced. Once and for all, he would see what his beloved Party was capable of. But just in time she stopped herself. Her grandson was still a boy, and she could not burden him so.

Ah Liam appeared in the doorway. "Mahjong got done early?"

How smart he looked in his gray tie and matching trousers, his broadening shoulders straining ever so slightly against the shirt seams. Her own mother would have reminded her not to neglect the people standing right beside her for the ones she had lost. She gestured at the settee across from her. Her grandson hesitated, a list of excuses plainly running through his head, and then put down his satchel and joined her.

"How was your mathematics test?" she asked.

"I got a ninety-seven."

"Smart boy," she said.

"Is my ma home?" he asked.

Bee Kim said meaningfully, "She's resting."

Ah Liam interlaced his fingers and cracked his knuckles, a nasty habit he'd recently picked up.

"Tell me more about this new school of yours," said Bee Kim.

"What do you want to know?"

Bee Kim sighed. Her grandchildren had once told her everything, seated around the dining room table, enjoying French pastries for tea. She saw a very young San San kneeling on her chair to reach the pastry box at the center of the table. The girl pushed a strawberry tart into her small mouth, as though afraid someone would take it away from her, and the red jelly stained her lips and cheeks like clown paint.

She batted away the image and said, "Tell me about your friends, your teachers."

"I mostly hang out with older kids," Ah Liam said. "The ones in my class are so immature."

This made her smile. "Do you miss the sweets we used to buy on the islet? I'm sure there's a decent French bakery around here."

The boy scratched his ear. "I always have a snack at school."

"Never mind, then. It was just an idea."

He leaned forward like he was about to make an excuse to leave, but then said, "Remember the summer program I was telling you about? To study English?"

"Have you decided to join?" Zhai was right; school was good for the boy.

Ah Liam said he had and that he needed to pay the fees at the first session the following afternoon. He tilted his head in the direction of Seok Koon's bedroom. "I would ask my ma, but I don't want to disturb her."

"Yes, don't disturb her," Bee Kim said. "You know how she is when those headaches strike." She reached in her pocket and withdrew the fat wad of bills her daughter-in-law had given her for her daily expenses. She counted out the bills—the program was costly—and handed them to her grandson.

He ducked his head and shyly mumbled something in English.

"What did you say?" she asked.

Ah Liam switched back to Chinese. "I said, 'I'm very grateful for your help.'" He picked up his satchel and flashed an impish grin.

He was so much happier now. Bee Kim wished there were an activity her daughter-in-law could throw herself into, something other than her work to rescue San San. Perhaps Seok Koon would consider it callous to suggest such a thing, but Bee Kim knew better. Why did they think she filled her hours with mahjong? Certainly not for the company of the other émigrés. She, too, had days when she missed her granddaughter so much, all she could do was lie in bed with her eyes squeezed shut, fervently praying that when she opened them she'd be back in the villa, a thin wall away from San San. Unlike the rest of them, however,

Bee Kim lived in the real world, where things didn't come true simply because you wished them to.

Unbidden, her sister's small face at age six rose in her mind. Full cheeks, flat nose, crooked smile. San San really did take after Bee Lian. Bee Kim felt her eyes mist over, and she forced down the memory before the tears formed. Reaching for her cane, she stood and went to the kitchen to check on dinner preparations.

22

A flash of blue caught San San's attention. Tangled in a bush was the dusty tarp she'd hidden beneath just three weeks earlier in that handcart, her heart battering her chest as she held on to Auntie Rose. How trusting and naïve she'd been, brimming with such foolish certainty that everything would go according to plan.

A rustling in the waist-high grasses drew her gaze over her shoulder for the umpteenth time since she'd fled the postmaster's lawn; she was sure the servants had somehow tracked her all the way to this deserted cliff on the islet's far edge. But when she lowered her eyes, she found the noise had been caused by a harmless reed snake, which, though by no means reassuring, was a more welcome sight than that of Cook's heavy, panting form. She jumped out of the snake's path and made for the edge of the cliff, searching the waters below for the rickety boat the students had lashed to a boulder.

All that remained was a single oar, half buried in the sand, and what use was an oar with no boat?

Across the narrow channel the Xiamen harbor beckoned, close enough to watch the tiny people working aboard a pair of graceful junks. Down below, the thin strip of beach was littered with rotting driftwood and fronds shaken loose from a row of coconut trees, none of which could be used to construct some kind of raft.

A burst of wind carried a familiar tune, sung in a high reedy voice, across the water to San San. "Waves are crashing, they scare me not. Set my course straight, I row ahead."

Out of the corner of her eye she spied a wiry figure in a wide-brimmed straw hat dragging a boat ashore. When the figure removed his hat and mopped his brow with the edge of his shirt, she recognized the fisherman she and her brother had befriended the summer before, the one who'd taught them to harvest oysters. It amused her that he'd been singing a children's song. She recalled his kind eyes that seemed to seal themselves shut when he threw back his head and laughed. But she dared not call out. Instead, she crouched behind a bush and watched him take his meager catch from the boat. He swiftly gutted and cleaned each fish and plopped it in a bucket of water. When he was done, he set the bucket beneath a coconut tree and lay down beside it. He covered his face with his hat, shifted this way and that, and went still. In the shallow waves his boat stood, ready to be nudged back to sea.

San San scrambled down the steep rock face, clinging to the wild grasses for balance, careful not to make a sound. Near the base of the hill, a rock beneath her foot gave way, and she fell, scraping her elbow and knee. But she did not cry out, and the fisherman continued to doze.

San San was close enough to touch the boat's stern when she remembered something her mother had told her: some of the islet's fishermen, she'd said, were too poor to own houses and slept in their boats at night. By stealing this boat, she would not only take his livelihood but also his home. She gazed back at the sleeping man, and thought of waking him and asking his permission. He was so friendly, so cheerful. Perhaps he would even offer to row her across. But what if he said no, as—now that she considered it—he surely would? What if he recognized her and turned her in, denounced her along with the entire town?

She rolled up her pant legs, pushed the boat into the water with little difficulty, and jumped in. Then she plunged the oars into the sea and rowed with all her might. To her amazement, the clear silky water that she so often glided through was a thick, unforgiving sludge. These oars, so long, so unwieldy, battled her every stroke. Within minutes her shoulders and arms and back burned. She'd traveled only a few dozen meters when the longing to raise the oars into the boat and rest awhile colonized every inch of space in her mind.

A voice screamed, "Hey! Come back here, you bastard, you son of a dog!"

The fisherman sprinted across the sand, his face a red knot of fury. San San put her head down and dragged the oars through the sludge, over and over, as fast as she could. Blisters formed where her fingers met her palms. She feared her arms would soon give way. Over her shoulder she saw the fisherman splash into the water and continue his chase.

Her throat was so parched she had to beat back the desire to pour a handful of ocean in her mouth. When the fire in her arms grew too excruciating to bear, she turned back to look once again, letting the oars drift in the water. What a stupid plan this was. If the fisherman didn't catch her, someone else would—either here in the channel, or later in the city. She should give up now. Let the fisherman turn her in, collect his reward. If someone had to profit from her capture, at least it was him.

She was ready to turn the boat around when Auntie Rose's face filled her mind, the lifeless eyes, the brilliant red slash against her bleached skin, the dark cave of her mouth when she dropped her jaw and wailed. Adrenaline shot through San San's limbs. Her blistered palms tightened around the oars and she pushed onward to Xiamen.

Not far from shore, the fisherman's head bobbed in the ocean. He continued to spew curses and obscenities, but he appeared to have stopped chasing her. Maybe he didn't swim well enough; maybe she was moving faster than she'd thought. She told herself to row just three more strokes, and then another three, and then another. Finally she raised the oars and caught her breath, dipping her battered hands in the bath-warm water. A sumptuously cool breeze drifted over her. The current picked up, bearing her stolen boat toward the harbor. When she regained her strength, she kept rowing.

How much time passed, she could not say. Ten minutes? Thirty? An hour? Her muscles quavered as she fought through the last few desperate strokes before leaping into the thigh-high water and dragging the boat onto the rocky sand. If not for the fishermen peering at her askance, she would have collapsed right on the shore beside her boat.

The squat, concrete open-air harbor was steps away, so close the intoxicating waft from the food vendors swelled the hollow in her stomach. She adjusted the portfolio of letters tucked in the waistband of her pants and entered the main hall, treading lightly so her soaked shoes wouldn't squeak against the floor, careful to avoid the path of a pair of patrolling policemen. Her nose led her to plump, white *moa ji* made from sweet glutinous rice flour and coated with ground peanuts, to dough sticks emitting a joyous, sizzling percussion in their bath of golden oil. Every once in a while, a well-dressed cadre would approach a vendor, jiggling coins in his palm. She watched a lanky woman with small round spectacles shove a red bean pancake in her mouth with an envy that bordered on hatred. When the woman took a swig of tea and then abandoned her tin cup on the ground, San San pounced on it and gulped down the bitter dregs.

Above the chattering passersby and the grunting laborers and the crash of machinery rose the rich, sinuous sounds of an erhu. A few notes in, the music took the shape of "The Crescent Moon Rises," a simple, well-known folk tune San San had mastered on the piano years ago. A small audience had gathered at the opposite end of the hall. Slipping between people to get to the front, San San saw a thin boy, no taller than Ah Liam, clad in ragged clothing. The boy had a large, round head with ears that jutted out from beneath his floppy hair like the handles of a jug. As he weaved his bow between the twin strings of his slender instrument, his large head bobbed in time. San San thought he played quite well, but it was when the boy opened his mouth and sang that she grasped the extent of his talent. The boy's unchanged voice was high and pure, yet tinged with shadow, like the first evening chill at the end of a sweltering late-summer day. A few food vendors abandoned their stands to join the audience, and though she considered seizing the opportunity to steal a morsel of food, the music held her in place.

The boy sang three more folk songs, one after another without pause, finishing with the crowd-pleasing *"Mo Li Hua."* Then he bowed theatrically to the warm applause. A vendor offered him a packet of rice, another, a small fish. The boy gathered up his spoils in a cloth bundle, strapped the erhu to his back, and strolled out of the hall, whistling a jaunty tune. San San envied his carefree attitude, his skill and charm, his soon-to-be-full stomach. She wondered if he played here every day and how much food he collected and why he didn't have to go to school. When he turned down the footpath lining the water, she followed.

The boy squatted beneath a shady tree, pulled a pair of wooden chopsticks from his shirt pocket, and proceeded to cram the fish into his cheeks, pausing only to spit out a few delicate bones. When he'd devoured precisely half the fish, he carefully wrapped up the remains and moved on to the rice.

San San approached with caution. "Don't you have school today?"

The boy nearly dropped his packet of rice. "You scared me to death."

"Sorry."

He raised the packet to his chin and swept more rice into his mouth in quick fluid strokes. With his mouth full he said, "It's summer."

San San had missed so much school, she'd forgotten. "Right," she said quickly. "I don't have school either." She knelt on the grass beside him.

He sized her up. "What do you want?"

She wagged her head vaguely. She just wanted to chat.

"Hungry?"

Eyeing the leftover fish, she admitted she was. But the boy dug in his pocket and held out a handful of crab apples, which she accepted all the same. The tartness of the fruits drenched her mouth with saliva. "Thank you," she mumbled as she chewed.

"More?" the boy asked, holding out another handful.

She nodded and pushed the marble-sized globes into her mouth.

He must have noticed her continuing to eye the fish because he said, "I have to bring this back to my ma."

"Oh," said San San.

"She's very sick," he said matter-of-factly. "She has a mass in her lung, and there is no cure."

It was San San's turn to reveal something. "Tuberculosis killed my family. I'm an orphan." How easily the lies came to her.

The boy set down the rice packet. "Then where do you live?"

San San hesitated. The boy didn't seem like someone who'd report her to the Housing Registration Board. "I don't really have a home."

The boy seemed to mull this over.

She quickly changed the subject. "You sing very well. Who taught you? Your ma?"

The boy nodded. "She and I used to do duets. She plays the accordion, but now she's too sick to leave the house."

San San saw an opening. "Do you need a partner?"

The boy frowned. "You play the accordion?"

"I play the piano. I'm very good. I could easily pick up the accordion." She'd once seen an accordionist perform with a military theater troupe and had noticed how a single button on the instrument produced a whole chord. The accordion seemed like a simplified piano. She hoped she wasn't overestimating her abilities.

"And can you sing?"

San San swallowed the last of the crab apples and launched into the first song that popped into her head: "The Favors of the Communist Party Are Too Many to Be Told." Compared to the boy's, her voice was nothing special, but it was loud and clear and right on pitch.

The boy closed his eyes and listened intently. When San San moved on to the chorus, he held up his hand. "Okay, okay, that's enough."

He didn't elaborate, and she asked timidly, "What did you think?"

He mulled it over. "Not too bad. Can you sing harmony?"

She'd never really tried before. "Of course. Sing anything and I'll show you."

He grinned. "I'll teach you the harmonies. You don't have to make them up yourself."

"Oh," she said. "That's much easier."

"I'll take you home to try out my ma's accordion."

She couldn't believe her luck. Once she got to his house, perhaps she could ask to stay there—just for a short while. "I swear I won't disappoint you," she said, and then added shyly, "Gor." Elder brother.

He held out the remaining rice, which she accepted at once.

"After we take out my ma's share, we'll split all food forty-sixty because I'm bigger than you. Deal?"

She was too busy eating to negotiate. "Deal."

He retied his cloth bundle. "Get up, then. We have work to do."

That evening, after San San had watched Gor perform to similar acclaim at the train station and in Commercial Square, he led her down narrow, winding streets, past crumbling tenements that would have long ago collapsed had they not been packed so tightly together.

Gor stopped in front of a dilapidated, soot-colored building and said, "We're here."

San San followed him up a dark, dank staircase that reeked of urine. She covered her nose with her sleeve, lowering it only to ask, "Are you on the top floor?"

"Kind of."

She almost added that her old home was also on the top floor, but stopped herself in time.

On the fifth-floor landing, instead of turning down the gloomy hallway to one of the apartments, Gor pushed open a door that revealed an even narrower flight of stairs.

"Where are we going?" San San asked.

"Almost there."

At the head of the stairs, Gor opened yet another door. San San stepped onto the rooftop, at the very center of which was a tent, fashioned from a length of dirty tarp. It seemed too small to house even a single person.

"Ma, I'm back," Gor called, as San San would have done upon entering her flat.

She stared at the back of Gor's head. In the twilight, she could have mistaken him for Ah Liam.

"Ma?" Gor repeated.

A strained, hoarse voice emerged from the tent. "Son, you're home. Have you eaten?"

"Wait here," Gor said. He lifted one edge of the tarp and crawled inside. "Ma, I brought a friend. She's an orphan."

"Oh?"

"She has nowhere to live. Can she stay here?"

And to think San San didn't even have to broach the question herself. She waited for a response, but all she heard was a string of violent phlegm-soaked coughs. Gor left the tent, uncovered a pail of water in the corner, and dipped a cup inside. San San hung back by the doorway

184

as if to give them privacy, but when he returned to the tent, she moved closer to eavesdrop.

"How can she stay?" his mother asked. "If someone reports us to the Housing Registration Board, just imagine the trouble we'll be in."

"Her whole family died of tuberculosis."

"It's out of the question, Son."

San San backed away. She should have expected this. She wondered if there were any chance her stolen boat remained on the beach, and how many nights she could spend in it without inviting suspicion.

"She sings pretty well and plays the piano," Gor said. "I'll teach her the accordion. You know it's pointless for me to go out on my own."

San San didn't understand what he meant. Gor played just fine on his own. Better than fine. His pleas were met with silence. More coughing commenced.

"Drink a little water," said Gor.

After the coughing faded, his mother said, "I suppose she can stay the night, if you promise to be extremely careful."

San San rose up on her toes and raised her arms in triumph.

"I will," said Gor. "You'll feel so much better once I can purchase your tea."

"Extremely careful."

"Ma," he said. "I swear I will."

San San gazed out at the tent homes that had sprouted from the surrounding rooftops. Judging from the garments hanging on the laundry line, the neighboring rooftop housed many more people than this one.

"Your friend plays the piano? She must come from a rich family."

San San pulled the hem of her sleeve over her father's watch.

"They're dead," said Gor.

"That's very unfortunate."

"I almost forgot, I brought you fish," Gor said, but his mother replied that she had no appetite and insisted he eat it.

Finally Gor came out of the tent and brought San San a straw mat and a thin blanket.

"You can sleep here tonight," he said.

She thanked him solemnly, masking the joy that fluttered wildly within her. A soft breeze kicked up, ruffling her hair. "It's pleasant up here," she said.

"I prefer it to where we lived before. It was too cramped," said Gor. "We're supposed to be relocated, but the authorities have been saying that for years, and nothing's happened yet."

A soft moan rose from the tent.

San San spoke quietly. "Your ma needs a doctor."

"It's too late. There's nothing they can do."

San San wished Dr. Lee were here to help the sick woman. He would surely be able to cure her. He was so intelligent, so calm. Her head thronged with the crazed insults of a crowd possessed—insults aimed not at Dr. Lee and Auntie Rose, but at her, Ong San San, the girl who'd caused the execution of the last of her loved ones left on the islet. Tears gushed in her eyes.

Gor placed a hand on her shoulder. "My ma's been sick a long time. Don't cry, Sio Beh."

Hearing him refer to her as "little sister" made San San tear up more. All day long she'd lied glibly and without hesitation about her family. Only now did she see the truth behind those lies. In the past days, she'd hidden from the police, escaped the servants, made it across the channel—all by herself because she'd had to; she had no one else.

She tried to smile at Gor through her tears.

"On clear nights like this, I sleep out in the open," he said. He retrieved his own bedding, which he set next to the tent. "So I can hear if she needs anything."

San San arranged her bedding on the other end of the rooftop. When Gor turned away, she removed her leather portfolio from her waistband and slid it beneath the straw mat. She wasn't sleepy at all, but she lay down anyway. Resting her hands on her thighs, she moved her fingers as if across a keyboard, as if she were playing one of her Bach Inventions. She was the best student of the best piano teacher on Drum Wave Islet; surely she'd be able to pick up the accordion.

She tapped her fingers with more vigor, and her ears filled with the corresponding notes. She heard the tick-tick-tick of Auntie Rose's metronome, smelled her sweet sandalwood scent, felt her strong compact hands beating time on her shoulder. San San played through Prelude and Fugue in C Minor over and over, until this image of Auntie Rose supplanted the others lurking in the shadows, and then she drifted off to sleep.

23

Ah Zhai pushed open the door, his nostrils twitching in anticipation of the cooking smells emanating from the ancient upholstery of this shabby Happy Valley hotel he'd called home for the past three days. Another offer on the townhouse had fallen through. Now, no matter how he insisted he could not sink another penny into the place, his realtor was pressuring him to make what he called "simple updates" to raise the house's appeal to potential buyers. "Take another five percent off," Ah Zhai told the sputtering, incredulous man. "Whatever it takes to sell it."

He nodded at the dour receptionist and climbed the spiral staircase to the second floor. He inserted the heavy brass key into the lock and nudged the door open with his toe. The spartan room was just as he'd left it, with its peeling paint and lumpy single bed and narrow shower stall that could only be entered sideways. The rank, fungal odor and the clatter of the ceiling fan he barely noticed anymore.

Without bothering to remove his shoes, Ah Zhai fell back onto the scratchy bedspread and stretched out his limbs like a starfish. He felt his blood surge in all directions to the very tips of his fingers and toes. He shut his eyes and hoped against all odds that sleep would free him, however fleetingly, from his troubles. Within the darkness, however, his mind whirred, spurring on his heartbeat.

A tentative knock on the door startled him. He sat up. No one knew he was here, not even his secretary. And that lazy receptionist should have called to make sure he was receiving guests.

Another, more insistent knock.

"Coming." He peered through the peephole at the blurred form of his wife and backed away in horror. He couldn't be seen here. How had she tracked him down? The only thing she wanted from him was what he didn't have. His first instinct was to escape through a window. It was a blessing in disguise that the hotel had withheld a room on a higher floor.

"Zhai?" Seok Koon called softly.

He would say he'd been in the neighborhood for a business meeting, that he'd taken ill—food poisoning, probably—and had decided to take a room for a few hours until he felt well enough to go home. He cracked open the door.

Her hands cupped opposite elbows as though she were holding something in. "I'm sorry to bother you. Please may I come in?" Her eyes widened as she gazed into the miserable room.

"I had a meeting," he began.

"Let's talk inside," she said.

"I'll have the money very soon."

She pushed past him, looked around for somewhere to sit, and perched on the edge of the bed. "Won't you sit down?"

"I'll stand."

She clutched her pocketbook in her lap with both hands. Her face bore a brave smile. "I have good news. Someone has offered to lend us the money."

"I told you I'll have it soon." He turned away, determined to deny everything. When had she learned of his bankruptcy? For how long had she let him spout those sorry excuses while she sat back and listened and secretly thought him a fool?

Seok Koon spoke slowly as though addressing a young child. "It's a friend of yours named Francis Low. And it's just a loan. You'll pay back every penny the instant they release San San."

More questions flooded his brain. How was his wife in touch with that arrogant, balding, bug-eyed man to whom Lulu had once been promised? The last time Ah Zhai had shown up at Cynthia's, the housekeeper had told him Lulu had moved out. He assumed she was simply trying to make him leave, but now he knew where his mistress had gone, even if he had no idea how she'd come to befriend Seok Koon.

"I don't need a loan. You shouldn't have asked him, and you shouldn't have come here."

His wife's fingertips grazed his shoulder blade. "Zhai, we all need help from time to time."

A white-hot spark within him burst into flames. He spun around with his arm outstretched. The back of his hand struck his wife's jaw with an earsplitting *CRACK*. Seok Koon fell against the bed, cupping her face. She didn't cry out.

He shook out his sore hand. His next words were a plea. "I told you not to meddle in my affairs." He was glad she would not look at him, for how did he appear to her? An insecure, good-for-nothing, ridiculous joke. He was half the man Francis Low was, for at least Francis Low had maintained his father's fortune; Francis Low would never have lost his child. Ah Zhai couldn't blame Lulu for making her choice any more than he could blame Seok Koon for despising him.

There was nothing he could say in his own defense, so he said, "Tell no one about this place."

She lowered her hand to reveal the shadow that had spread across her cheek and nodded without meeting his eyes.

He wanted to ask if Lulu had been the one who'd offered the money, if she'd spoken his name, if she'd clasped her white hands around her neck as she always did when discomfited.

He said, "Leave now."

Seok Koon stood and smoothed her dress and whipped out the door without a word.

Ah Zhai picked up the telephone and dialed reception, ready to spew the entirety of his wrath onto an easy target.

24

Day after day Gor and San San rehearsed the program for their debut performance. They began with "The Crescent Moon Rises," followed by "Mo Li Hua," and, to finish, San San would perform a solo rendition of "The Young Shepherdess." With a little help from Gor's mother, she'd quickly picked up the accordion, but even so, she wasn't thrilled about having to play and sing by herself.

"Why can't you do it?" she asked Gor.

He rolled his eyes. "I already told you, silly, it has to be sung by a girl."

"Why can't we play it as a duet?"

"It sounds better with just accordion."

"What if I make a mistake?"

"Stop worrying like a eunuch," he said. "Everyone will love you."

From inside the tent came Auntie's strained voice. "He's right, you know. You have talent."

San San blushed. After the first night, Gor had said she could stay until the end of the week. She prepared to go back to the harbor to devise a new plan, but Gor didn't point out when her time was up, and she didn't remind him. She concocted elaborate stories to explain this penniless family's generosity. Perhaps Auntie had always longed for another child, a sibling for Gor, but had been too ill to get pregnant;

perhaps, fearing she didn't have long to live, Auntie wanted a companion for her son. San San imagined that as Auntie's health deteriorated, Gor had grown disillusioned with his schoolmates' trivial preoccupations. Perhaps he'd been waiting for a friend like her, someone who truly understood what it meant to lose a loved one. She wondered where Gor's father was, but of course she didn't ask, even as she longed to share that she, too, had never really known her father.

Once, she awoke in the middle of the night, coated in sweat, unable to shake the image of Pa, moaning in pain and calling her name. Trapped in the hazy purgatory between sleep and alertness, San San raged at her mother for poisoning even her slumber with those lies.

When she and Gor weren't rehearsing, San San worked to be as unobtrusive as possible. No matter how hungry she was, she ate sparingly and never accepted more. She learned to cook and clean and wash the laundry, so that Gor could devote more time to alleviating Auntie's pain with hot compresses and massage techniques he'd learned from a sidewalk doctor.

In a matter of days, the ship with the green flag would arrive to bear San San to Hong Kong. Sometimes the yearning for that moment to arrive struck her so deeply she feared she would collapse; other times the view off the rooftop of the sun setting on the city filled her to the brim. She envisioned staying behind, becoming a part of this family; she would forget she'd ever been an Ong.

Finally, one morning, after San San had played through "The Young Shepherdess" three times from start to finish, and Auntie had found the strength to peek out of her tent and offer some pointers—"Slow down when you sing that phrase," "Draw out the pause for another beat"— Gor declared them ready.

They strapped their instruments to their backs and descended into the foul-smelling stairwell. At the entrance to the tenement, two old women sat on the front steps with their feet in the street.

The pair ignored Gor's polite greeting and peered at San San. "To what family do you belong?"

Gor and San San had anticipated this scenario, and he replied smoothly, "She's the fourth daughter of the Tan family. She lives in that building over there." He pointed vaguely down the street.

One of the women nodded. "Ah, yes, the Tans. You take after your mother, little girl."

Gor and San San hurried down the street, holding in their laughter until they were out of hearing range.

They reached Commercial Square at the busiest time of the day, when queues of shoppers clutching ration tickets snaked through the marketplace and out of stores. But the shelves in the pair of general stores that sold shoes and clothing were almost completely bare. Instead of meat, the market vendors peddled inferior short-grain rice that had been mixed with millet for bulk, and those oversized vegetables that Cook had complained about, so tough and fibrous that no amount of boiling could prevent them from catching in your throat.

San San followed Gor to the center of the square, and when he unstrapped his erhu, she adjusted her own bulky instrument in front of her—so the straps wouldn't cut into her shoulders—and ran her fingers over the keyboard. At first, no one paid them any mind. The queuing shoppers went on complaining about wait times and scarce inventory. But when Gor began to tune his strings, a few of the shoppers turned to face the square. The men smoking on benches beneath spindly yellow flame trees lowered their newspapers enough to reveal their eyes.

That familiar tingling sensation that always hit San San before piano recitals spread through her. It was as if someone had flicked on an extra lamp, or turned the volume knob up a notch. The world came into sharper focus. She stood a little straighter.

Gor mouthed the word, "Ready?"

"Ready," she mouthed back.

He launched into the first song, and even though by now San San had heard him sing plenty of times, she was once again stunned by his voice. Like all great performers, Gor saved his best for when it mattered, and today he'd found an added suppleness, a new grace.

She recovered in time to make her entrance. For the first few bars, she focused intently on moving her fingers to the right spots, but she soon saw that her fingers effortlessly found the buttons and keys. These folk songs were much simpler than Chopin and Bach.

The chorus came back around, and this time she sang the harmony to Gor's melody, which was even easier than playing the accordion. When she sang with Gor, his stunning voice seemed to enfold her rather unremarkable one, imbuing hers with its beauty, until both voices and both instruments merged into a pure, impenetrable wall of song.

At the conclusion of "The Crescent Moon Rises," Gor and San San moved right into "Mo Li Hua" without pause. ("Never give the audience a reason to disperse," he'd instructed the day before.) And then it was time for her solo.

Gor gave her an encouraging nod and ceded the stage. By now a sizable crowd had gathered, a few of whom continued to hold their ration tickets even though they'd abandoned their places in line.

San San took a deep breath, played the introduction to "The Young Shepherdess," and sang, "From dawn to dusk I roam these hills, my sole companions, my flock of sheep."

At first her voice emerged reedy and weak, but then she imagined Gor's voice pouring out of her, and her voice took on a richness she'd never heard before. She closed her eyes and felt the accordion bellows swell and empty beneath her arms like a pair of lungs. Her body undulated in time. ("Singing isn't like playing the piano," Gor had said. "You can't retreat into yourself. You have to smile, make eye contact, tell a story.")

Her eyes snapped open. She smiled at Gor who had blended into the front row of the crowd. Instead of smiling back, however, his eyebrows came together in the center of his forehead, just for an instant, and her confidence dimmed. She kept going, wondering what she'd done wrong. It was then that she saw Gor's fingers creep into the trouser pocket of the fat man beside him and pinch out his wallet. A split second later the wallet had vanished, leaving her to wonder if she'd imagined the whole thing.

Her voice quavered. Her fingers sounded a wrong note. This time she read alarm on Gor's face, and somehow, seeing his fears so plainly displayed calmed her down. She paused, started the phrase over, and got to the end of the song without making another mistake.

As the crowd scattered, Gor clapped her on the back. "Not bad for the first time."

She gazed at him flabbergasted. Did he expect her to play dumb? Was he daring her to confront him? At last she knew the truth: neither generosity, nor kindness, nor even pity had driven Gor and Auntie to take her in. It was purely a financial transaction. She'd been cheated, used.

Gor must have mistaken her silence for disappointment. "You're too hard on yourself. That wrong chord was no big deal."

She set off toward the marketplace, too shaken to speak.

"What's the hurry?" he asked.

She stopped dead, and he crashed into her back. "Of course my mistake was no big deal to you. You don't care about the music." She lowered her voice. "You're a thief."

Gor's face blanched. He dragged her to a quiet spot by a low stone wall. "Sio Beh, I can explain."

"I'm not your sio beh. We barely know each other."

"Fine. Let me explain."

"In a way, I'm glad you were just using me because then I don't have to feel so indebted to you. Now we're even."

She expected Gor to yell back, but all he said was, "If that's what you really think, you'd better find somewhere else to live."

"Fine," said San San. Even as she turned to go, she knew she was being foolish—foolish and hypocritical. For hadn't she lied to Gor and Auntie to convince them to take her in? At the end of the week, she would disappear without a word, never to see them again. What did she care about their secrets and schemes?

She turned back. Gor was already walking briskly in the opposite direction. She hurried after him, ready to call out, but something in his bearing—the defiant jut of his chin, the purpose in his gait—silenced her. After a few steps, she slowed, continuing to tail him.

At the main intersection, instead of veering east toward home, he veered west, and she quickened her pace. Weaving through pedestrians and bicyclists and some kids kicking a tin can back and forth in the dirt, he led her down an alley curtained off from the sky by rows of laundry draped from bamboo poles. Near the end of the alley, he slipped through a gap between two buildings and emerged onto a street so narrow, the awnings of the tenements on opposite sides nearly touched. Gor whirled around to make sure he was alone, and San San leapt inside a doorway just in time. She waited a few moments and then resumed following him. On the back side of one of the tenements was a door that appeared to lead to a ground-floor flat. He must have already gone inside. She peered through the frosted-glass shutters of the window by the door, but a faded floral sheet had been tacked up as further insurance against prying eyes. Pressing her ear to the shutters, she heard muffled voices, polite laughter. She couldn't make out what was being said. Never before had Gor mentioned any relatives or friends, but of course he and Auntie could not be all alone in this big city. After a while, she crouched down on the gravel beneath the window to wait.

A sharp crash drew her to her feet.

A voice cried, "Please have mercy."

The voice was high, tremulous; it couldn't have been Gor's. Perhaps he wasn't even inside that flat. Perhaps he'd gone into another unit altogether.

"Hold the boy before he breaks anything else," someone growled, and then San San heard the sounds of one heavy blow followed by another.

This time, Gor's cry was unmistakable. San San ran out to the street to find help, but the only person in sight was a bent old woman on bound feet, fanning herself in the doorway of her home.

"Grandma, who lives in the flat back there?"

The woman's eyes glazed over. "No idea," she muttered.

"My brother's in trouble," said San San. "I need to get help."

She backed into her flat. "I can't help you."

"Is anyone else home?" San San pleaded.

"I can't help you," she repeated and shut the door.

"Please," San San said, pounding on the door, but it remained closed—as did all the other neighboring doors. In fact, she'd never seen a street so deserted in this overcrowded city.

She ran back to the tenement, at a loss for what to do. Should she knock on the door and demand to be let in? Scream for help and hope someone would hear? She didn't have to make a decision because there, kneeling on the gravel with his head in his hands, was Gor.

She gasped. The skin around his eyes was red and swollen and quickly darkening to purple.

He stood. "Did you follow me here? Were you spying on me?"

"I wanted to say I was sorry," she said.

He took her hand and pulled her onto the street. His palm was hot and rough, and she hoped the gesture meant all was forgiven.

Back on the street, however, Gor dropped her hand and said, "This is not a place for kids."

She touched his sleeve. "Who did this to you?"

He turned away, and she reached for his arm. "Gor, tell me what happened."

He shook her off and started down the street. "Don't follow me. From now on, you and I are strangers."

She tugged on his arm with all her might, and finally he slowed. Again she asked who had beaten him.

"Someone I owe money to, all right?"

"Is that why you stole?" she asked. "Are you in trouble?"

He waved a hand at his battered face. "This may look bad, but it's nothing compared to my ma's suffering."

San San cocked her head, confused.

He looked up and down the empty street and then leaned in. "Do you know what the black market is?"

She nodded. She'd heard Grandma say that their daily teatime petits fours had been purchased "on the black market," though she'd never given the term much thought.

Gor explained that the man in the ground-floor flat sold medicinal herbs. He'd gone to buy a special powder to ease his ma's pain; this, despite the fact that he still owed him money from last time. "I was hoping, stupidly, that the herbalist would make an exception this once," he said.

San San wished she could take back her earlier accusations—and that there was something she could do to help Auntie.

Gor went on. "He warned that if I came back without the money, he'd be forced to give me two black eyes." He gestured to his face and smiled weakly. "So really, I only have myself to blame."

San San asked how much money he needed.

"What does it matter? More than I have."

She pushed back her sleeve, wrenched the bangle down from her elbow and over her hand, and held it out to Gor. He squinted at the bangle's delicate scrollwork but made no move to take it. "Sio Beh, is this real gold?"

"Yes. My grandma gave it to me before she died." She thrust the bangle into his palm, and he tried to give it back, saying, "It's too much."

She held her hands behind her. "It's yours."

"I can't accept it. It's too much."

"We're family," said San San.

A tear welled in the corner of Gor's swollen eye and trickled down his discolored cheek. He wiped it with his sleeve and winced in pain. "I can't thank you enough, Sio Beh."

"Family members don't thank each other." She felt a wild desire to blurt out her plan to board the ship with the green flag. If only Gor and Auntie could come along to Hong Kong.

He grinned through his tears, wiped his nose on the edge of his shirt, and then together they returned to the herbalist's flat.

Gor told San San to wait outside because strangers made the man jumpy.

"Be careful," she whispered.

Gor knocked on the door, which opened a crack. "The bloom is not a bloom, the mist not mist," he said—the first line of a famous Tang poem that she had learned in school.

The door opened all the way, and he went inside.

From underneath the window, San San listened for any sounds of trouble and was relieved when none came. She'd meant every word she'd said to Gor. For the next few days, at least, he was her family, and she was his.

25

After the heat and smog of city streets, the Peninsula Hotel's cool, perfumed air was a balm. It was just before three. The tearoom was packed with ladies in slim dresses and coiffed hairdos. They chattered like songbirds in high, melodious voices and clinked heavy silverware against fine porcelain. On an elevated platform in the center of the lobby, a pianist played a sentimental Gershwin tune, and Ah Zhai caught himself humming along.

A waitress with swaying hips led him to a corner table. He pulled the brim of his hat low over his eyes to avoid having to stop and make small talk, and then sat with his back to the room, even if it meant missing Lulu's entrance.

In the past seventy-two hours, his mood had ricocheted between extremes. Three nights earlier, reeling from his wife's visit and the news of what his mistress had done, Ah Zhai had parked himself at the bar of the Parisian Grill, hoping to catch Lulu's angular profile in the long mirror above the shelves of bottles, to hear her throaty laugh wafting down the hallway to the powder room. The longer he sat on that hard, unforgiving stool, the more he agonized over what to say if forced to speak to Francis Low. Only the scotch tempered his anxiety, and he downed glass after glass, until the music from the swing orchestra blurred in his ears and the dangling lights of the chandelier danced like raindrops.

He stumbled outside just in time to vomit in the gutter, much to the amusement of the idling chauffeurs.

But the following day his luck turned: an English banker expressed interest in the townhouse, and even though everyone knew the Brits to be penny-pinchers, Ah Zhai immediately asked his secretary to invite Lulu to high tea. She didn't love Francis Low, that much he knew. Now he just had to convince her that once the townhouse sold, even for an absurdly low price, and he had the money in his account, and San San was finally rescued—after all that, they could start over. He'd buy a modest but well-appointed condo in Mid-Levels. He'd start to pay off his debts. He'd finally take Old Wu's advice and downsize his factories. It would take some time to regain his former wealth—in truth, he might never get it back—but he could give Lulu his word that they would always live comfortably and he would never deceive her again. Once San San crossed the border, he would divorce Seok Koon and marry Lulu. She would have another child. They would be a real family.

He felt a pang in his chest for his two daughters: the one he'd held in his arms only a handful of times, and the one he'd never laid eyes on. He even thought fondly of his insolent son. It was too late for him to be a good father to San San and Ah Liam, but the new baby would give him a chance to try again. This time around, with Lulu by his side, he would be the kind of father who was warm and affectionate and stern only when necessary. The baby would look up to and adore him.

The efficient click-click-click of high heels against marble drew his attention. He caught a whiff of Lulu's intoxicating perfume. There she was, a vision in an emerald silk-shantung column dress with a matching pillbox hat perched atop her sculpted waves of hair. He stood, lightly touched her shoulder blades, tried not to mind the way she stiffened when he leaned in to kiss her cool, powdery cheek.

"You look marvelous, bunny," he said.

"Thank you." Her low, husky voice thrilled him. "I'm sorry I'm late. Traffic was abominable. I hope I didn't keep you waiting long?"

He looked at her in disbelief. Why was she talking to him like an acquaintance, like one of those friends she only pretended to like?

The waitress arrived to take their order.

Lulu didn't glance at the menu. "I'll have a pot of orange pekoe."

Ah Zhai had been looking forward to scones and clotted cream, but said, "Same for me."

The waitress swayed off.

He held out his cigarette case, which he'd filled with her brand. She lifted out a Pall Mall without comment, and when he leaned in with his lighter, she said, "Thank you kindly."

He was determined to make her drop the act. "Bunny, I've missed you so much. Tell me how you've been." He'd already decided he would not bring up Francis Low.

"I moved out of Cynthia's house."

His smile strained the corners of his mouth. "Indeed."

Lulu twisted the pearl cocktail ring on her finger from side to side. "I know this is awkward, Zhai."

"Awkward?" he said. "I'm so happy to see you. Don't you feel the same way?"

"I'm just going to come right out and say it. I live with Francis now."

He leaned forward, bumping his knees on the edge of the low table, and covered her hand with his. "It doesn't matter," he said. "I don't care. We've both made mistakes."

She extracted her hand. "That's not what I meant."

He had to take control of the conversation before it was too late and so he blurted, "I'll get a divorce."

She stared at him. "No."

"Yes," he said ardently.

"No."

"I've made up my mind."

"I don't want that," she said. "Don't you see? It's too late."

205

But how could that be true? She couldn't have moved in with Francis more than a week ago. "We'll start over," he said. "I'll never lie to you again."

"I can't unknow what I know." She violently stubbed out her cigarette.

He didn't want her to elaborate, so he said, "I love you. Come home."

She raised her napkin to the corners of her eyes. "Stop, please."

If only he could take her in his arms and kiss away her tears. Why had he waited so long to act? He should have fought harder to see her at Cynthia's. He should have slept on the floor by her hospital bed until she was well enough to come home. "I need you, Lulu."

Their eyes locked, and for a moment, he thought he'd made himself heard.

She opened her pocketbook and retrieved an envelope, which she slid across the table.

"What's this?" In all their years together, Lulu had never once written him the kind of florid, sentimental letter he'd written her. She'd left him little notes and reminders, of course, but never anything more.

"For you and your family," she said.

Pressure mounted in Ah Zhai's ears.

"From Francis and me."

The din in the tearoom became a buzz of white noise. He pushed the envelope away like it was tainted. "No. Never. No."

"Zhai, it's just a loan."

"I said no."

Their tea arrived. He watched the waitress set down the teapots and sugar bowl and milk pitcher, and arrange the strainers over the cups, and finally, finally pour out their tea, and all the while he resisted the urge to send the whole elaborate setting crashing onto the floor.

As soon as the waitress retreated, Ah Zhai said, "I don't need his money. An English banker wants the house."

"Oh," Lulu said. "I'm glad to hear it. When will you sign?"

"Everything was dealt with yesterday." He knew that she knew it was a lie.

"These things take such a long time to go through." She touched the envelope. "Take this for now."

The back of his neck blazed. "Tell him I don't need his money."

"It's not for you, it's for your little girl."

Everything about Lulu, from her weak-tea eyes to her soft, pliable mouth to her white hands encircling the base of her throat exuded pity. He knew then that any remaining traces of affection she'd felt toward him he'd successfully obliterated with his failure to rescue San San. Perhaps Lulu had never truly loved him, not the way he loved her. Perhaps, over the years, her feelings had transformed from a teen-ager's girlish infatuation into a longtime companion's restrained—and resigned—affection, bypassing love altogether. He wondered if his wife's love had ever been pure, unsullied by duty and convention. Though what did it matter, now that she hated him, too.

Gently, patronizingly, Lulu said, "Once you sell the house and pay him back, the whole thing will be over. No one will ever know. I'll make sure of it."

He tried again. "I love you."

This time she simply shook her head.

He thought of his daughter in that large, rambling villa. His last trip to the islet, San San had run to him, a man she couldn't have rec-ognized, as fast as her chubby little legs would carry her, hurling her soft, tender body fearlessly, wholeheartedly into his embrace. Moments later, she would grow shy, but Ah Zhai would always remember her squawking laugh as he lifted her into the air, her unbridled delight. His San San. The only one he hadn't yet had the chance to wound and push away.

His fingers crept toward the envelope. He watched his hand as though it were something separate from him. He took the envelope with his thumb and first two fingers, weighing the full cost of tucking it into his breast pocket. One side of the scale sagged beneath his wife, mother, son, daughter, along with his father and grandfather and all the other ancestors he recognized only from their dark, dreary portraits; the other side held Lulu.

"Thank you," he managed to say.

"I couldn't stand the thought of Seok Koon losing her." Her eyes watered.

He saw no point in defending himself. At that moment Lulu might have been thinking of Marigold, but he could think only of her, his willful, impulsive beauty who'd left him once and for all.

26

Once Gor's breathing had deepened, and San San was sure he was asleep, she reached beneath her mat for her letters and loosened the grosgrain ribbon holding them together. In the darkness, she could barely make out her mother's neat hand, but that mattered little, for she knew the words by heart. She ran her fingertips over the thick, grainy paper like a blind man reading braille. Here, her mother described San San's room with its pink-curtained canopy bed, the Broadwood baby grand that would go untouched until she arrived; there Ma wrote of a man in the colony, someone she'd come to respect and trust. A few of the lines had been blacked out by censors, so San San wasn't sure if Ma was referring to her father in some oblique way, or to someone else altogether. *He is intelligent and so very kind,* Ma had written. *He will help reunite our family.*

San San carefully folded the letters along their creases and returned them to her hiding spot beneath her mat. Evidently this man her mother spoke so highly of hadn't succeeded in rescuing her. But on this warm, starless night, less than twelve hours before she was to board the ship that would take her to her family, she didn't want to think about all the ways in which they'd failed her. She rolled onto her back and spread her arms and legs, the position that best shielded her knobby bones from the concrete floor. Her tangled, sweat-matted hair caught on the straw weave, and she smoothed out the strands with her fingers. Soon, soon, she would trade in this life she was growing accustomed to for one filled with hot baths, soft mattresses, warm featherweight quilts. This time tomorrow, if she so chose, she would bury her face in the softness of her mother's abdomen, relax every muscle in her body, and let someone else bear the weight of her.

The next time her eyes darted open, the sky was fading from black to lavender. She lay very still. Soon she would rise and prepare breakfast, heating yesterday's leftover sweet potatoes on the small woodstove. After breakfast, she would leave with the basin of dirty dishes, but instead of going to the communal tap, she would lay the basin on the staircase landing for Gor to happen upon when he eventually went looking for her. By then San San would have made it to the harbor and disappeared onto her ship. Once in Hong Kong she would send money and medicine and those multicolored lozenges that had filled her mother's packages. She pictured Gor opening the box, crying out as the candies poured into his lap.

Across the rooftop, Gor stirred. San San stretched her arms overhead, yawned audibly, and pushed herself upright. As though it were any other day, she folded and put away her straw mat before she started a fire in the stove and boiled a pot of water for Auntie's tea. At first, the powdered herbs that Gor had purchased with her grandmother's bangle had seemed a miracle cure. Auntie was well enough to sit out in the sunshine, take a sponge bath. The day before, however, the powder had abruptly lost all healing powers. Auntie had stayed in her tent, refusing food and Gor's repeated offers to massage her feet.

Still, San San dutifully mixed a pinch of the powder in hot water and took the cup to Gor. He was squatting before the belly of the stove, blowing on the smoldering wood to get the fire to catch once more. The discoloration around his eyes had faded to a deep ochre, a few shades darker than his skin. "Will you take it to her?" he asked.

San San paused at the opening of the tent she'd never before entered. In fact, she typically refrained from looking inside, for Auntie's pallid, emaciated body and its stale odor frightened, even repulsed her.

"Auntie," she called softly. "Auntie, I have your tea."

Auntie responded with a moan. San San gingerly pulled back one side of the tarp. The stink of decay hit her full in the face. Auntie lay on her side, her thin limbs swathed in blankets.

Holding her breath, San San crouched at the tent's opening and offered the cup. But this morning, Auntie was too weak to sit up. San San had no choice but to crawl inside, prop up her lolling head, and hold the cup to her pale, chapped lips.

"Thank you, child," Auntie said, blinking. The whites of her eyes had yellowed like aged piano keys.

A flurry of footsteps pounded up the stairwell, and the door to the rooftop flew open. San San managed to steady her hand before she tipped the hot dregs all over Auntie's blanket.

"Housing Registration Board," a gruff voice said.

San San froze. If Auntie hadn't fingered the edge of her blanket, signaling for her to burrow beneath it, she wouldn't have known what to do.

Gor's voice shook as he spoke. "Uncles, what can I do for you?"

San San wondered how many of them there were.

"Where is your mother, boy?"

"She's in the tent. She's an invalid."

Breathing heavily, Auntie rolled onto her side, and San San nestled into the curve of her bony back. The air beneath the blanket was hot as a furnace. An angry rash spread down San San's nape and she longed to scratch it.

"We've received reports that you've been harboring an unregistered individual in your home."

"There must be some mistake. Only my ma and I live here." Gor let out a tremulous laugh. "And as you can see, there's hardly enough room for the two of us."

Once they found San San, it wouldn't take them long to discover her true identity. Perhaps whoever had reported her had offered a description, and they'd already pieced everything together.

Footsteps neared the mouth of the tent. "Comrade," the gruff voice said, "you may be ill, but we must do our job."

San San pressed her cheek to the spot below Auntie's shoulder blade. Auntie's surprisingly robust heartbeat reverberated through her entire body like a warning signal.

Auntie said hoarsely, "Of course, come in."

The officer raised the tarp, letting in a gust of air. He breathed loudly through his mouth, and San San squeezed shut her eyes like an ostrich jamming its head into the sand.

After a moment, the officer said softly, "Forgive my disturbance, comrade. I hope your health improves."

The officer rounded up his team.

Gor said, "Sorry, Uncles, for wasting your time."

"Don't give us a reason to have to come back." With that, the officer and his team trooped down the stairs.

Tension escaped from San San in a shudder. The stench and the heat and the itchiness faded away. She was snuggled against her mother in her soft, roomy bed, with her brother on the other side. Outside a cold wind blew, but Ma's warmth was more comforting than any quilt.

Auntie lowered the blanket. "Child, are you all right?"

San San opened her eyes, almost sorry to have to get up. One corner of the tarp lifted, and Gor squeezed into the tight space. Wrapping his strong, skinny arms around them both, he released a maniacal laugh. At first the strange, screechy sound disturbed San San, but when Auntie joined in, her laughter husky and clipped, San San let go. Wave after wave of laughter rolled out from deep within her abdomen, shaking her chest and shoulders.

"Who do you think reported us?" asked Gor.

The laughter drained out of San San.

"It could have been anyone in the building," said Auntie, "but I'd put my money on that busybody, Mrs. Chan."

Gor murmured in agreement, and San San tried to remember which neighbor was Mrs. Chan.

"I told you both to be careful," Auntie said. "This can't happen again."

Sunlight sliced through a gap in the tent, and San San sat up. How much time had passed? If she hurried, might she still make the boat?

"We'll be careful, we promise." Gor looked at San San. "We'll never leave the building at the same time. She'll only use the back entrance and the back stairs."

As casually as she could, San San said, "All right. And now I must wash the dishes."

"Leave it for later," said Gor.

"No. If I get there too late, I'll spend ages waiting in line." She crawled over the tangle of limbs and out of the tent. "I'll be home soon," she said cheerfully, hoping neither of them noticed the way her voice cracked.

Inside the stairwell, San San dropped the basin on the landing and flew down the steps and out the front door. She crossed the overpass leading to the harbor just as the largest ship she'd ever seen pulled out of the docks. The ship was as long as one of those brand-new dormitory buildings lying on its side. The deck of the ship was filled with uniform steel crates, stacked neatly in threes, like a child's building blocks. Surely this couldn't be her boat, for if it were, the university student with the cross pendant would have made sure to mention its size.

The ship gained speed and rotated counterclockwise, churning the ocean in its wake. There, perched on the very tip of the back deck, was a bright green flag. Her heart contracted violently, as though an invisible hand had plunged into her chest cavity, engulfed the pulsing organ, and squeezed. She squinted into the sunlight, tracking the square of fluttering fabric as it shrank and finally vanished into the distance. Calmly, rationally, like a mere observer to this tragedy, she considered falling to the ground, cursing her mother and grandmother and brother, bemoaning her poisoned fate. Instead, she dropped her head and trudged back the way she'd come.

The next time she turned to look, the flat expanse of ocean was marred only by gentle ripples flowing with the breeze. It was as if the immense ship had never come at all.

She crossed Commercial Square, where her reflection in a grimy shop window slowed her to a stop. Her greasy, overgrown bangs were pasted to her forehead. Her once smooth, round cheeks were all angles and planes. Her skin had lost its luster and was sallow, stripped bare. And yet her eyes glinted like dark, polished stones, and she sensed this starkness was her true face, excavated from beneath its old layer of flesh. She brought her nose to the glass for a closer look at this not-quite stranger, and her reflection vanished, replaced by a bored salesgirl halfheartedly shooing her away.

Outside the marketplace, she passed a sidewalk barber and doubled back. "Uncle, will you cut my hair?"

The barber tossed his cigarette butt on the ground and motioned for her to sit on his stool. "How do you want it?"

"Cut it all off," she said. "As short as you can."

"Little sister, are you sure?"

"Very sure," she said before she could change her mind.

He said, "All right, then. It's just hair, after all."

It was just hair—a clump of lifeless fibers shrouding her head, no different from a wig, which was no different from her old face that had revealed itself to be a mask.

The barber raised his rusty scissors, tugged a thick lock of her hair, and snipped.

She couldn't help it, her eyes filmed over, as though the scissor blades had pricked her flesh.

He tugged another lock and snipped again.

"Wait," she said. "I have no money." She looked around for a mirror and wondered how much he'd cut, if she could hide the short pieces beneath her longer strands.

He lowered his scissors and sighed. "Well I can't send you home looking like a lunatic, can I?"

She gazed back at him, the correct answer beyond her reach.

"Just this once, it's free."

She held very still and listened to each sharp snip that would bring her closer to her essential self.

When he was done, he held up a mirror. She ran her fingers through the short crop and broke into a grin. No longer was she the missing daughter of the Ong family but a street urchin with whatever name she chose.

At Gor's building, she entered through the back door and climbed the back stairs. On the top-floor landing, Gor sat in the darkness beside the basin of dirty dishes with his knees pulled into his chest.

"Sio Beh, what did you do to your hair?"

She sat down beside him. "I don't want to cause any more trouble for you and Auntie. This way no one will recognize me."

He rubbed his palm over her head. "You look like a boy."

She said, "That's the point."

"I wasn't sure you'd come back."

"I wasn't sure you'd want me back."

He jabbed his elbow in her side. "Where would you go? You're too small to go off on your own."

She studied Gor's earlobe, fleshy and long. The kind that was said to bring good fortune. Amid the bleakness crowding in on all sides, he was a single shining spark of luck.

"We're brothers now," she said.

"You've gotta be kidding. You still kick like a girl."

She punched his arm. "How about that? Did that feel like a girl?"

He laughed and lightly returned her punch.

Her ship wouldn't return to the harbor for another fortnight, an eternity as far as she was concerned. Anything could happen in that time. Gor could get caught stealing. Auntie could get weaker, maybe even succumb to her illness. Despite her best efforts, she could be discovered and sent back to the islet, unless she found another way to get to Hong Kong.

She stood and lifted the basin of dishes.

"I'll come with you," said Gor.

She shook her head. "You stay and take care of Auntie."

Right now, what she wanted more than anything was for her life with this, her temporary family, to go back to normal. Besides, there was no point in both of them waiting in line.

27

B ee Kim set down her needlepoint canvas and reached for the ringing phone. "Yes?"

"Good afternoon. This is Mr. Ong's secretary. May I speak to
Mrs. Ong?"

Bee Kim knew the girl meant Seok Koon, but she feigned dimness.
"This is Mrs. Ong."

The girl hesitated and then evidently decided against challenging
her. "Mr. Ong said to inform you that the money is in his account."

Bee Kim hurriedly thanked her and slammed down the phone.
"Daughter-in-Law," she called. "He took the loan. Zhai took the loan.
San San will be fine."

Seok Koon ran in the room. "What? Impossible! Who told you?"

Again they counted the days that had passed. Seok Koon's letter
detailing the need for San San to collect her inheritance in person would
have reached the villa about a week ago, which meant that a response
from Cook—hopefully reporting that the girl had received her permit
and was leaving on the next train—could arrive any day now.

Seok Koon clasped Bee Kim's shoulders, her eyes shining. "She
won't have packed more than a small bag, so we must have some new
clothes made."

Bee Kim pressed her daughter-in-law's hands. "Better to wait until she arrives. The girl grows like a weed."

Ah Liam poked his head into the sitting room and asked, "What's going on?"

Bee Kim and Seok Koon announced that the plan was finally in place. They took turns drawing the boy near, smoothing his hair, tripping over words as they raced to finish each other's sentences and take control of the story.

"For all we know," Bee Kim said, "San San could be on her way here as we speak."

Her grandson looked slightly dazed. In a measured tone he said, "That's wonderful news."

Bee Kim's giddiness faded. She exchanged a look with her daughter-in-law. The boy was right; it was too early to celebrate. They mustn't let themselves get carried away.

"Now there's nothing more to do than wait," said Seok Koon.

Bee Kim hobbled to her chair and motioned for Ah Liam to sit down, but he declined, explaining he had to get back to his homework. His summer school teachers were relentless. Zhai was right: Hong Kong schools were much more demanding than those on the islet.

"He's a good boy," Bee Kim said.

"They're both good," said Seok Koon.

One day and then another passed with no response from Cook and San San. Seok Koon worried that her letter had been destroyed by the censors, or had somehow gone missing before it had even reached the islet. Bee Kim learned to calm her down by repeating in a soothing tone that the response would probably come the following day. She'd swiftly change the subject to San San's arrival. How would the girl react to their new flat? What was the first thing she'd want to eat? What would they take her to see? The view from The Peak? The beach? The zoo, which was said to be world class? The two of them could while away hours in the sitting room, speculating, planning. In contrast, Ah Liam rarely asked for news of San San. He spent more and more time in his room, and once, when Bee Kim went to see if he wanted a snack, she found his door locked—by accident, he claimed.

But there was no time to worry about him, for the following afternoon, a letter arrived. Bee Kim watched her daughter-in-law draw the letter opener across the top of the envelope with such haste, she pricked her finger and drew blood. She offered her handkerchief, but Seok Koon waved it away. She pulled out the letter, marring the onionskin-thin sheet with crimson dots.

"What does it say?" Bee Kim asked.

Seok Koon's eyes raced across the sheet of paper. She let out a shrill cry and hurled it onto the Persian rug.

Bee Kim's knees cracked as she bent to retrieve it. She sped through the lines and then returned to the beginning, a tiny part of her believing that she could somehow will the characters to rearrange themselves into saying something new. But there was the same appalling message from Cook, doubtless written with the aid of a professional letter writer: *It is with a heavy heart that I inform you that San San disappeared from her bedroom on the night of June 14th. Rest assured the police department of Drum Wave Islet is working tirelessly on the case.*

Bee Kim shook her head until her vision blurred. She closed her eyes and prepared to read the letter again. This time the message would be different.

"Ma." Seok Koon forced open her hand and took back the letter before helping her to her chair. "Cook is spouting lies. I knew we were wrong to trust him."

Bee Kim gazed into her daughter-in-law's glinting eyes, trying to decipher if she truly believed what she'd said.

"Look here," Seok Koon went on. "The letter says San San disappeared weeks ago, which can't be true. How could she have gone missing without anyone else noticing? Rose would have told me at once."

Bee Kim's head reeled.

"What, Ma? What is it?"

She didn't answer. Maybe she'd been wrong to hide the news of the execution. Maybe, if she'd told Seok Koon, she would have written to neighbors and friends to make sure others were watching out for the girl besides those wretched servants.

Seok Koon knelt before her and seized her hands. "Do you know anything about this? What have you heard?"

Somehow Bee Kim broke free of her grasp. If she'd doubted her daughter-in-law could have handled the news back then, this was an even worse time.

"Answer me, Ma."

Her daughter-in-law's voice sliced through her. What choice did she have? "I fear your friend is dead."

Seok Koon fell back on her seat, her face a white mask. "Where did you hear such a thing?"

"They executed her and Chin Kong for attempting to flee."

"That's impossible," Seok Koon said. "Who would concoct such vile gossip?"

"I'm sorry, Daughter-in-Law. I'm so sorry." Bee Kim stared at the Persian rug until the red-and-navy pattern blurred into a dark mass.

"No," said Seok Koon. "I won't believe any of these lies."

Bee Kim said, "I'll phone Ah Zhai."

"For what? Haven't you learned by now that he's as powerless as the rest of us? We're at the Party's mercy. If only we'd accepted that from the start."

"Fine," said Bee Kim. "Then what do you think we should do?"

"How should I know?" Seok Koon roared back. "Haven't I proven, once and for all, that I know absolutely nothing? That I'm not fit to be a mother?"

Bee Kim didn't refute her. She pounded her forehead with the heel of her palm to dislodge the images taking root—gruesome images, multiplying exponentially, of her granddaughter's painfully thin body floating in the channel, or stashed behind a shrub, or hastily buried in the earth for any wild beast to happen upon and tear to shreds.

28

"See you downstairs," Gor said, strapping his erhu to his back. San San clipped the last of the wet laundry to the line. Ever since the visit from the Housing Registration Board, she and Gor had stopped rehearsing on the rooftop. They avoided being seen together in and around the tenement, and she came and went using only the dilapidated back stairs. She didn't know if their precautions satisfied Auntie, who had grown too weak to speak up.

"Goodbye, Ma," Gor called. He paused, hoping for an answer, and when none came, he hung his head.

Over the past week, Auntie's health had deteriorated precipitously. She hadn't kept down food in days. Her breathing was ragged and labored. Her hands and feet were ice cold. Gor never discussed his mother's condition except to say, "When we have enough money, we'll go back to the herbalist to buy the most potent thing he has." By now San San doubted the herbalist's expertise, but she kept that to herself. Every so often she forced Gor to take a break, and she took over massaging Auntie's extremities. Sometimes, she simply sat with her in the tent, holding her hand.

Gor disappeared into the stairwell. San San took up her accordion and went over to the tent. "Auntie?" she whispered. She peeked inside.

Auntie's ashen face and slack jaw made her pulse jump beneath her skin, but then Auntie let out a buzzing snore.

"Goodbye, Auntie." San San opened the door to the stairwell and listened to make sure no one was there before descending one flight and running through the corridor to the back stairs. She met Gor at the end of the lane, and together they set off.

It was an ordinary summer morning, and yet pedestrians packed the streets. As she and Gor neared Commercial Square, a wall of people standing shoulder to shoulder blocked their path.

"What's going on?" Gor asked a petite, almost child-sized woman standing on a bench.

"Parade," she said.

Above the chattering rose clashing cymbals, blaring horns. San San was too short to see over the other spectators, but Gor reported that three men wearing tall conical caps and paper robes were being led down the street by their leash-bound hands.

San San asked who they were and what crimes they'd committed, and Gor stashed their instruments beneath the bench and hoisted San San onto his shoulders so she could see for herself. From the characters scrawled in black ink across the men's paper robes, she gleaned that they were doctors at the city hospital who'd committed counterrevolutionary acts. The doctors' colleagues and staff filed behind them, shouting insults and sounding their instruments. The elderly doctor at the very front was clearly the guiltiest of them all, for his cap was a full head taller than the others. The nurse leading him down the road treated him with particular contempt, jerking his leash to make him bow low before the crowd.

Right in front of San San and Gor, the nurse yanked the leash so suddenly that the doctor tripped on his own feet and sprawled onto the ground. The spectators clapped and jeered. Gor's shoulders shook with laughter, and San San lost her balance. She would have crashed upon the pavement like the poor doctor if Gor hadn't managed to catch her.

He asked if she was all right, but she couldn't speak. The cackles and the taunts and those earsplitting horns wormed their way through her ears, deep into her skull, until the unbearable cacophony seemed to be emanating from inside of her.

"Sio Beh, what's come over you?"

She swallowed hard, sure she was going to be sick, and then she was elbowing her way through the spectators, fleeing the parade.

"Where are you going? Sio Beh, stop!"

"Resolutely purge all counterrevolutionaries!" the doctors and nurses chanted. "Lenience to the enemy is cruelty to the people!"

Somehow San San found herself inches away from the marchers. A pair of nurses held a banner that read: "Nurses of Drum Wave Islet Stand in Solidarity with People's Hospital of Xiamen." One of the nurses was young and pretty with dimples in her cheeks. San San regarded her for several moments before placing her: the head nurse at the maternity clinic across the courtyard from her home.

When the tail end of the parade had trooped past, the crowd scattered, but San San followed the Drum Wave Islet nurses. They gathered beneath a banyan tree, and one of them passed out hard-boiled eggs, while another poured tea from a large thermos.

Instead of collecting her meal with the others, the pretty head nurse edged to one side. With her colleagues distracted, she turned and walked quickly away.

San San trailed her into People's Park. She had so many questions for her, if only she could reveal her identity. Were the police still looking for her, or had they given up? Did the nurse ever talk to Cook and Mui Ah? Had anyone notified her ma of her disappearance? Did her ma's letters still arrive every other day?

At the center of the park was a pond covered with water lilies. A man sat on a stone bench facing the pond. The nurse stealthily approached the bench and clapped her hands over the man's eyes. He leapt to his feet with a roar of delight. He was tall and clean-cut with black-rimmed spectacles. The nurse and her friend grinned and squeezed each other's hands. Together they sat down on the bench, and the nurse laid her head on his shoulder, just for an instant, before looking around to make sure no one had seen. She didn't notice San San, pretending to admire the lush pink blooms of an azalea bush.

San San touched her boy-short hair. She inspected her calloused palms and dirt-caked fingernails, the torn seams of her tattered pajamas. Even if she were foolish enough to go up to the nurse and reveal her own name, the nurse would never believe she was the girl from Diamond Villa. She belonged to the slums now—like Gor, and like Auntie, wasting away in her rooftop tent. If the nurse could examine Auntie, would she be able to help her? Would she know doctors who could? In fact, this companion of hers looked rather doctorly.

Someone tapped San San's shoulder, and she whirled around.

"There you are," said Gor. He had his erhu on his back and her accordion strapped to his chest. "How did you end up all the way over here?"

San San said, "Sorry, I couldn't stand the racket."

He peered into her face. "You were acting so strange. I'm just glad I found you."

"I feel better," she said. "Why don't we play here?"

Gor sized up their potential audience and agreed. They positioned themselves by the foot of the bridge spanning the pond and started in on "The Crescent Moon Rises."

A pair of elderly gentlemen smoking pipes stopped before them. One of them nodded approvingly when she and Gor perfectly struck the high notes.

Next they launched into "Purple Bamboo Melody." San San played the introduction on her accordion and Gor sang the opening line. It was then that the nurse and her companion wandered over, just as she'd wished.

San San's vague hopes for Auntie sharpened into a scheme. She lost track of her left hand and sounded a wrong note, drawing a look from

Gor. She refocused on the music. Gor drew his bow across the strings in short, quick strokes, injecting an extra dose of playfulness into the song's coda. Holding the final note, he muttered that they'd play "The Young Shepherdess" next, San San's solo.

She knew what she had to do. Gor lowered his instrument and joined the audience, and San San played her first line. When her vocal entrance neared, she filled her lungs, opened her mouth, released every muscle in her body, and fell to the ground. Her shoulder landed first, sending a bullet of pain straight through her center. Her accordion followed, the keys smashing into a deafening dissonant chord. With her eyes closed, she felt Gor's rough palms on her shoulders, heard his voice, high and frantic, urging her to get up. She was sorry that the only way she could think of to help Auntie involved putting him through this.

"Stop shaking her," a commanding voice said. "Stand back, all of you. Give her air."

When the crowd kept closing in, shouting advice, the same voice said, "Let me through, I'm a nurse."

The nurse knelt over San San. She pressed her ear to her chest and felt her pulse. She held an index finger under her nose and gauged the strength of her breathing.

"Is my little sister going to be all right?" Gor asked. The quaver in his voice was unmistakable, which only made San San more determined to see her plan through.

"She's breathing fine," the nurse said.

San San fluttered her eyelashes and asked weakly, "What happened?"

"You fainted," said the nurse. "It could be dehydration, or low blood sugar, or maybe anemia."

The crowd thinned, disappointed, perhaps, by the anticlimactic outcome.

San San opened her eyes fully. The nurse was leaning in so close, she spied a smudge of pink lipstick on her front tooth. Beside the nurse was Gor, his face pale and streaked with tears. Meanwhile, the few

remaining onlookers offered their own medical theories. She'd probably drunk bad water, or consumed too many warming foods in this
hot weather.

"Do you think you can stand?" asked the nurse.

San San said, "I think so." She didn't want to appear too ill, for fear
of being deposited at the hospital.

The nurse gripped San San's left arm and told Gor to take her right
one, badly bruised from the fall. San San winced convincingly as they
lifted her to her feet.

Gor told the nurse he could get San San home; they only lived a
few blocks away.

Upon hearing this, San San listed to one side, saying, "I feel a little
dizzy."

Immediately the nurse offered to walk them home. Before they
set off, the nurse sent her companion to the pharmacy at the People's
Hospital to obtain a few nourishing herbs.

Together the three of them climbed the tenement's back stairs,
which were so narrow the nurse had to let go of San San's arm and walk
behind them.

"I feel much better," San San said when they reached the rooftop.

Auntie's hacking cough greeted them.

"Who's that?" asked the nurse.

"That's my ma," said Gor. "She's not well."

"What's the matter with her?"

"A mass in her lung."

"Son?" Auntie wheezed. "Home so early?"

The nurse listened intently to the proceeding string of coughs and
said, "Would you mind if I took a look?"

Gor went to inform Auntie she had a visitor, and San San hid
her glee. "They say there's no cure," she said, hoping the nurse would
contradict her.

"That may well be true, but we can try to make her more comfortable."

San San remembered that she, too, was supposed to be sick. She limped over to her straw mat, unfurled it, and lay down.

Midway through the nurse's examination, her companion arrived with a package from the pharmacy. The nurse told Gor to boil water for San San's medicine, and he went to light the stove.

Curled up on her mat, San San heard the nurse say to Auntie, "You're so fortunate to have such good children to take care of each other—and you."

Auntie's pain must have clouded her thoughts, for she replied, "The girl's not mine. She's an orphan. Her family died of tuberculosis."

San San sat up.

"An orphan, you say?" said the nurse.

Should she cry out, kick over the water pail, anything to interrupt this dangerous conversation? But maybe she was overreacting. The nurse may very well have assumed that Auntie had cleared everything with the Housing Registration Board.

The nurse said, "That's good of you to take her in."

Now San San was glad she hadn't interrupted; she waited for Auntie's response.

"I did it for my boy. He'd be all alone otherwise."

Gor approached with a steaming cup. The strain must have shown on San San's face because he crouched beside her and said, "The nurse said you have nothing to worry about. You'll be well in no time."

San San took a small sip of the bitter brew.

Upon concluding Auntie's examination, the nurse crawled out of the tent and came over to them. San San's hand trembled, shaking the cup and scalding her tongue.

"I know it tastes bad," said the nurse, "but it will make you strong."

San San took another sip, keeping her face lowered over the cup.

"Good girl," the nurse said. She handed Gor a piece of paper. "Get this filled at the hospital pharmacy. The pills should make your ma feel better."

Gor took the paper with both hands and bowed deeply. "I can't tell you how grateful we are."

"Yes, thank you," said San San. She decided she ought to be too weak to stand.

"It was nothing," said the nurse. Her gaze seemed to linger on San San, and she ducked her head and scratched the nape of her neck.

As the nurse and her companion walked out the door, the nurse said, "The little girl reminds me of someone I knew on the islet."

San San's eyes cut to Gor to see if he'd heard, but he was crawling into the tent to talk to Auntie.

"Oh?" said her companion. "How odd."

The nurse said, "The little girl I knew lived in the mansion across from the clinic. She wouldn't survive in a place like this for more than a minute."

San San downed the rest of her tea in a single gulp. The intense bitterness coated her tongue and throat and made her gag, but at least nothing came back up.

29

I n the taxi, Seok Koon's fury grew. She'd been a fool to believe she could outsmart the Party. What distinguished her from all the other mothers who'd lost children to war, disease, poverty? What made her think she deserved more?

Again came Father Leung's voice, as though he were murmuring right in her ear. *"Promise me you'll pray. Promise me you won't try to face this on your own."*

"I did everything you said," Seok Koon told the priest.

"Hah?" the driver called back.

She ignored him and went on with her conversation. "I came to church every Sunday. I prayed morning and night."

"Madame, you talking to me?"

In her ear Father Leung whispered, *"He is our refuge and our strength, an ever-present help in trouble."*

But none of that had been true. What kind of God let a little girl be taken from her family? What kind of God let good, kind people be executed before a crazed mob?

"Madame?" said the driver. "Madame, we're here."

Seok Koon paid for the ride. She charged through the double doors of the cathedral, vacant on this weekday afternoon aside from Father Leung and the organist, who were chatting in the choir loft.

"Madame Ong," the priest called down. "Is there news?"

She tucked her wayward strands of hair behind her ears. Her voice faltered. "In a sense."

"I'll be right down."

He and the organist descended from the choir loft. Once the organist had left, Father Leung came up the aisle, saying, "Tell me what's going on."

All of her rage and confusion and desperation coalesced upon this kind, compassionate man. She flew at him and beat her fists on his chest. "Liar," she screamed. The word echoed through the soaring nave. "You told me to pray. You told me to have faith. You told me God would not mete out more hardship than I could handle."

The priest shielded himself with his hands. "Please calm down."

An ache spread down her arms. Her fists continued to strike his chest.

"Madame Ong, please, we can't talk like this."

"Liar. You lied, and I believed you."

The priest caught her wrists and gently lowered them. "Tell me what happened."

Seok Koon unclenched her fists. "San San's gone missing."

"Oh no." The priest lowered his head and turned away.

"Look at me," she said sharply. "No one else can help me. Look at me."

He turned back slowly. "It's not I who can help you, it's God. Surrender your grief to the one who 'heals the brokenhearted and binds up their wounds.'"

"What is that supposed to do?" she heard herself snarl. "My daughter's missing. Tell me something that will actually make a difference."

"You're hurting, I know, but we can't make demands on Him. That's not how it works."

Seok Koon stepped back, incredulous. "Then why am I here? Why are any of us here?"

"Your pain is intolerable. You feel entirely alone. But trust that whenever you're ready to turn to Him, He'll be waiting for you."

She stuffed her fingers in her ears. "Stop, please, stop, I shouldn't have come." She stepped around him and made for the door, but he caught her by the elbow.

"No, you were right to have come."

His touch made her shiver, and the instant he let go, she missed the weight of his hand. When was the last time her husband had been driven by an emotion other than rage to touch her? Her fingers stroked her cheek and jaw, still tender when she pressed down, the last places her husband had touched.

And yet Zhai had swallowed his pride and accepted the loan, shocking them all. The day they'd received the good news, Seok Koon had decided that if bearing the full brunt of her husband's wrath were the price of her daughter's rescue, she would gladly pay it many times over. Indeed, she and Zhai had both held up their sides of the bargain. But what good had it done? Her daughter was gone, and she had no way of finding her.

She fell onto a hard wooden pew and gazed up at the rudimentary figures depicted in stained glass.

"Shall we pray?" the priest asked.

She'd forgotten he was there. "Leave me alone," she said. "Please."

He complied.

Her eyes shifted to the crucifix atop the altar: two lengths of bronze, nailed together, painted gold. She couldn't pray. She couldn't even cry for her daughter, for Rose. Her head was a hollow cave, her body, a cracked and brittle shell.

30

The tablets were small and white and utterly ordinary looking. Within hours of swallowing one, however, Auntie's moaning ceased. Her ragged breaths grew smooth and steady. The following day, after what she said was the first full night of sleep she'd had in as long as she could remember, Auntie was able to sit up and swallow a morsel or two of sweet potato. By the end of the week, she'd vanquished her near-constant cough and emerged from her tent to soak in the sunshine.

Given these miraculous developments, San San shouldn't have been surprised to awaken one morning to find a tall figure, ghostly in the early-morning light, standing before the stove. She'd never seen Auntie upright before and was stunned by the sheer length of her body, the ethereal quality of her bony limbs without their protective swathe of blankets.

Gor looked on with pride and delight. When he noticed San San, his grin split his face in half. "You're up. Come eat."

He insisted that San San and Auntie sit on a pair of overturned buckets, while he squatted beside them. The addition of a few bits of salted cabbage made the watery gruel taste delicious.

"I'd forgotten what hunger feels like," Auntie said. Despite her frailness, her complexion was bright.

"It's all thanks to Sio Beh," said Gor, and San San demurely lowered her gaze. "If she hadn't fainted, the nurse would never have come up here in the first place."

They sat together, talking and laughing, and when San San placed the dirty bowls in the basin, Auntie said, "Leave those. You children have done so much for me. Go out and play."

Auntie's fingertips brushed San San's cropped hair, making her scalp tingle. San San's heart fought to break free of her rib cage. Someday in the future, after she'd solidified her place in this household, she would finally confess how she'd lured the nurse to the rooftop to examine Auntie. Gor and Auntie would admire her craftiness; they'd marvel at her convincing acting. *"She hit the ground so hard,"* Gor would tell Auntie, *"Her shoulder was bruised for days!"* Their lives would be humble but filled with joy.

Only five days remained until the ship with the green flag returned, but such fantasies filled San San's head. Once she made it to Hong Kong, she'd find a way to rescue Gor and Auntie. Perhaps they could board that same ship a fortnight later and come live with her family— didn't Ma owe her that much?

"Go on," Auntie urged. "Go play."

San San recalled a poster she and Gor had seen a few days earlier, advertising a military theater troupe's performance of "The White-Haired Girl," an opera based on the story recounted in one of her brother's comic books. Now she suggested they go to the square to catch the performance, and Gor agreed.

They descended separate stairways and met up down the lane. The morning was crisp and cool. San San's belly was full and her footsteps felt light and effortless. Her mother and her grandmother and her real brother were far, far away.

She and Gor arrived as the opera was beginning. The quick, quivering notes of the violins in the small orchestra circled up by the stage set an ominous tone. A stooped old man, clad in rags, was helped onstage

236

by his beautiful daughter. The pair prostrated themselves before a wealthy landlord and begged him to forgive their debts, but the ruthless man showed no mercy. He yanked the beautiful girl from her father's arms and made her his property.

San San watched in rapt silence as the girl bade her father a final farewell. And when the old man, driven insane by grief, hanged himself, she wiped her eyes on her sleeve.

Not long after her abduction, the beautiful girl became pregnant. Instead of marrying her, the cruel landlord sold her to a brothel. Her first night there, however, she managed to flee with her baby and return to her village, only to discover it occupied by the Japanese. To escape further brutality, the beautiful girl and her baby hid in a cave. Two years passed, and the girl's black, waist-length mane turned a pure, snowy white.

Finally, just as the girl had resigned herself to living out her days alone with her child in the cave, the communists arrived to liberate the village. The ruthless landlord stood trial, and the gathered peasants shouted the verdict: death penalty!

San San and Gor cheered madly and hugged each other.

"What a show," Gor said. "I wanted to jump onstage and strangle that landlord."

But San San was fixated on the father who couldn't go on living without his beloved child. She wondered how it felt to be truly indispensable, the way Ah Liam was to Grandma and Ma, the way Gor was to Auntie. Being indispensable meant being treasured above all else. It meant never having to prove your worth. San San would never be indispensable to her real family, or to Auntie, but she wondered if perhaps she was growing indispensable to Gor. He didn't stay mad at her when she played wrong notes. He'd shed actual tears when she'd pretended to faint.

"What are you thinking about?" he asked, looking askance at her.

"Nothing," she said.

They ran home to tell Auntie about the opera, and to see if she felt up to attending that evening's repeat performance.

When they arrived at their building, Gor entered through the front while San San went around the back. She tugged and tugged at the door, but it would not budge. It hadn't rained in days, so the wood couldn't have swelled into the ground. She wondered if someone had locked the door, though she'd never encountered another person on those back stairs.

She had no choice but to use the front entrance, where she immediately encountered nosy Mrs. Chan of the first floor. San San took the stairs two at a time, ignoring the woman who shouted, "You, boy, I've seen you here before. Who are you visiting? Where did you come from?" Luckily, Mrs. Chan's bad limp kept her anchored to the bottom step.

Up on the rooftop, the concrete floor had been swept and mopped. Blankets and bedding sagged on the laundry line; the straw mats had been draped over the railing to air.

"Auntie, did you do all this?" she called out.

She heard Auntie and Gor murmuring inside the tent, and then Auntie said, "Give us a moment, San San."

She gazed around the spotless space in wonder. Auntie's recovery had truly been a miracle. And then it hit her: Auntie never used San San's given name. To them, she'd always been "Sio Beh."

Her eyes flitted from her straw mat folded over the railing to the spot on the floor where it usually lay. She ran to the mat and patted down every inch of it, verifying what she'd already known to be true: her mother's letters were gone.

Her mouth and throat went dry. Her body grew cold but sweat sprouted beneath her arms. Aimlessly, helplessly, she spun around, wishing someone would tell her what to do.

Auntie came out first, and then Gor took his place behind her. From his hand dangled the pink grosgrain ribbon that had bound her letters.

"San San," Auntie said.

At the sound of her name, her knees buckled, and she fell onto an overturned bucket. Had they already sent someone to notify the authorities? Were the police on their way?

"Do you have any idea of the danger you've put us in?"

San San studied the hairline crack that snaked across the floor. All this time, she'd been so focused on her own survival that she hadn't truly considered the risks she'd forced onto Gor and Auntie.

"Have you ever thought of anyone besides yourself?"

She looked up, stricken. The answer, she feared, was no.

Auntie went on. "We let you stay because we believed you were an orphan. You told us you had nowhere else to go. Don't you know what they'll do to us for harboring a fugitive?"

San San drank in each and every one of Auntie's words and held them deep within her. She understood that she had no right to respond.

Auntie raised her face to the sky. "The daughter of counterrevolutionary capitalists. We could be executed. My son could be executed. Did that ever occur to you?"

She shook her head no because it was the truth. Could she really cause another execution? How did she end up destroying every soul who tried to help her? What deadly venom ran through her veins? What toxic blackness?

Finally Gor spoke. "What do we do now, Ma?" His eyes were soft and sad.

San San knew then that they hadn't contacted the authorities. The realization almost disappointed her, for a part of her yearned to be punished, imprisoned on the islet, forced to write enough self-criticisms to fill a wall of encyclopedias. A part of her would have gladly given up all hope of reuniting with her family if it meant that she and Gor and Auntie were even. If it meant they would forgive her.

Auntie took a step forward with her arms akimbo, forming a human barrier between San San and Gor, and between San San and this rooftop she'd thought of as home.

There was only one thing San San had to offer: to spare them any further anguish.

She rose from the bucket and went to gather her belongings. But aside from the watch on her wrist and those letters, which she never wanted to see again, nothing in this place belonged to her.

She walked slowly to the door, training her eyes straight ahead, knowing that if she so much as glanced at Gor, she would start to cry.

Her hand touched the doorknob.

"Sio Beh."

She couldn't help it; she turned. Gor's cheeks were flushed, his eyes wide with alarm.

Auntie said quietly, "Let her go," and he scrunched his face and looked away.

Alone in the darkened stairwell, San San couldn't hold back. Tears flooded her eyes, stealing her sight. With her hand on the wall, she felt her way down the steps, both fearing and hoping she'd trip and tumble to the ground, for then she could curse and wail and otherwise bemoan her miserable state, and no one in the world would fault her for it.

31

Dear Mrs. Ong,

You may not remember my name, but I am the head nurse at the clinic across from Diamond Villa. I am writing to express my condolences over the disappearance of your daughter. I am not yet a mother myself and thus can only imagine the grief you must be experiencing. Rest assured that our fine comrades in the Drum Wave Islet police department are working tirelessly to find her. I have utmost faith that they will bring her safely home.

In the meantime, I wanted to share an interesting encounter I had in Xiamen yesterday. I was taking a stroll in People's Park when I heard the most enchanting music performed by two young buskers. The boy played the erhu and the girl, the accordion. Both had lovely singing voices. The girl not only looked to be your daughter's age, but also very much resembled her in appearance. (Though, of course, she could not have been her.) In the middle of the performance, the girl fainted from dehydration, or, perhaps, low blood sugar (none of which are serious conditions). After tending to the girl, I escorted the children back to their home. Their household is poor but full of love. The girl appeared happy and content.

I recount all this as a way of saying that wherever your daughter is, I am certain that one of the many kindhearted souls in our glorious nation has taken her in and will care for her until she can be returned home.

I hope your husband's health has improved, and I eagerly await you and your family's return to the Fatherland.

Your fellow comrade,

Nurse Ho

The nurse, a mere acquaintance, hadn't made the long list of neighbors and friends Seok Koon had written to in an attempt to scrounge up news of San San. Seok Koon was well aware of the great risk the nurse had shouldered by entrusting this letter to a friend to carry across the border. From there, the letter had found its way to the Fujian Association and into the hands of one of Bee Kim's mahjong friends, a Mr. Ng, who had personally delivered it to the flat.

For all this, Seok Koon should have been grateful. Grateful that this woman she barely knew had gone to such lengths to give her this message. Grateful her daughter was alive.

And yet, her mind swirled with numbers and calculations, what-ifs and why-nots. How likely was it that the nurse had come across San San and not some look-alike child? Was it better to know one's daughter was alive but forever remote than to know nothing at all? Could she cleave her family in two to go in search of her daughter? Were they even a family without her? Seok Koon could tell herself that eventually she and San San would make it back to Hong Kong. But how long would that take? Months, maybe years? Her son would be a man when she next saw him; he would have learned to view her with his father's disdain. Maybe that was a fair price to pay to have both children by her side, but she also risked ending up with nothing, with no one. To whom would she go to with her complaints then? From whom would she demand compensation?

She tore the letter in half and then in half again. Methodically she shredded the paper into smaller and smaller pieces, until each was no larger than her thumbnail, until she was certain no one could put the letter back together again. She could not face another unsolvable equation, another impossible quandary.

32

Days San San spent roaming the harbor, pouncing on food scraps that the vendors didn't bother to sweep up, careful never to stay in one spot long enough to attract the attention of the patrolling police. Nights she sneaked back to the tenement and slept at the foot of the back stairs, secretly hoping Gor would come looking for her.

But the only person who came for her was Mrs. Chan, who poked her awake one morning with the handle of a broom. When San San sprang up, Mrs. Chan grabbed her arm. "You might be able to fool the Housing Registration Board, but you can't fool me."

Before San San could process what she was about to do, she reared back her free hand, gathered her strength, and slapped the woman across the face. Mrs. Chan howled and let go. As San San sprinted away, she didn't dwell on the brutality of her actions, or on the peculiar rubbery density of the woman's flesh.

Outside, thick clouds padded the sky. The air was pregnant with moisture. She'd taken no more than a few steps when fat raindrops beat the crown of her head like marbles. She covered her head with her hands—which slowed her down considerably—until its futility became clear. She dropped her hands and kept running, and the unrelenting raindrops stung her eyes and drenched her hair and clothes.

In the harbor, she huddled in a corner of the main hall, trying to wring out her blouse and pant legs. A policeman materialized before her, swinging his baton. His mouth twisted in contempt. "Beat it. You can't be here."

She hurried back into the rain, guessing that an important official was due to arrive at the harbor. Why else was the waiting area so orderly, the floors so clean and free of perfectly edible food scraps?

Plodding past a row of sampans, she wished for a fisherman to peek out his window and invite her in for a little while, maybe offer her a small bite to eat. But all the shutters were sealed against the downpour, which served her right, given how she'd stolen a boat from one of their own. She stuffed her hands into her pockets and walked on.

Across the wide avenue from the harbor, she settled on the doorstep of an abandoned shophouse. The instant she relaxed, she was engulfed by a profound ache stemming from the pit of her stomach. She fell onto her side, clutching her belly, wondering if this were how it felt to die. Moments passed before she concluded she wasn't dying: the ache was deep, merciless hunger.

Gazing out at the soggy, windblown city, she drew her knees into her torso, as if she could somehow trick her body into thinking she'd filled the gaping hole. When the ache persisted, she stepped out from under the shophouse eaves, lifted her face to the sky, and gulped down the murky-tasting rain, mouthful after mouthful, until the skin of her belly stretched taut. Then she settled back on the steps to wait. All she did these days was wait.

The whine of sirens filled the air. A long black car, flanked on all sides by a quartet of motorcycles, sped down the avenue toward her. The important official had arrived.

At the traffic light, the motorcade stopped, giving San San a clear view of the portly, well-groomed man in the car's back seat. No doubt he was being whisked away to a fancy banquet. She couldn't stop herself from imagining the exquisite dishes awaiting him: crispy roast duck, and tender garlic-scented greens, and endless bowls of fluffy white rice.

The official gazed blankly out his window. He didn't seem to see her. But then he leaned away and said something to an aide and pointed right at San San. She thought to shrink back, duck her head, make herself invisible. Instead she stared back at him.

A long-ago memory returned to her: the time she demanded to quit the piano like her brother, kicking over a vase of pussy willow branches and facing her mother without fear. It was then that Ma told her she was too ugly to find a husband. She'd burst into tears, not because she longed to be more beautiful, but because she hadn't thought her appearance mattered to her mother.

The traffic light turned green. The motorcade drove on. The important official had no reason to devote any more attention to a ragged child who bore little resemblance to a missing girl on a forgotten poster on a tiny islet's marketplace wall.

Eventually, the rain slowed and trickled to a stop. San San went back to the harbor. In the short space of time since the official's arrival, the main hall had returned to its normal state of disarray. Already the floors were littered with paper and cigarette butts, and smeared with spittle and phlegm. The food vendors once again hawked their wares, filling the air with the heavenly scent of grease, but she couldn't find any good scraps. Instead she swooned over the fried dough sticks, with their glistening golden-brown crusts. She inhaled deeply and felt the void in her belly expand.

"Shoo," the vendor said. "Paying customers only."

San San slunk off to her corner. She didn't have the heart to retort that as far as she knew, smells were always free.

Just then, the strains of an erhu drifted over from the opposite end of the hall. A voice both achingly familiar and strangely new sang, "Half a moon climbs in the sky."

How had Gor's voice changed so dramatically in the few days they'd been apart? His was no longer the hauntingly clear soprano of a boy, but the rich, faintly husky falsetto of a man. And like a fruit just past its peak, it was a voice that was almost unbearably sweet.

When Gor neared the end of the first verse, San San's hands tensed involuntarily, preparing for her entrance. She moved her fingers across an imaginary accordion, and to her great surprise, the corresponding notes filled her ears. She craned to see across the hall, and there, standing beside Gor, with San San's accordion strapped to her torso, was Auntie.

The accordion bellows swelled and emptied between Auntie's thin arms in a sensuous, supple dance. Mother and son turned to each other as their voices merged in harmony: "My sweetheart, please make haste, open the window and pluck a rose and gently throw it down."

San San saw then that she'd been nothing more than a temporary, second-rate substitute, and a deluded one at that. This family was a single, complete whole. There had never been any space for her.

She walked out of the main hall and kept going until the music no longer reached her ears, coming to rest by a garbage heap not far from the public latrines. The fetid odor attacked her nostrils and knocked her off balance. Even the policemen would have to agree that her presence here disturbed no one.

At sunset, a trio of fierce, feral-looking kids tramped toward the garbage heap. The oldest, a boy, appeared to be about San San's age, the youngest maybe only three or four. At first San San guessed they'd spied her from a distance and wanted to talk to her. But then she watched in horror as they ventured right into the putrid pile and picked through the trash for anything remotely edible.

Even though the smell no longer bothered her, San San's stomach spasmed. She turned away, determined to hang on for one more day, to choose starvation over eating garbage.

"There's nothing good left," the oldest one said. "Someone must have gotten here before us." He stared at San San, and she backed away, not from fear, but from shock that he viewed her as one of them.

She ended up on the strip of pebbly sand by the water, pacing back and forth, afraid that if she sat down to rest, she would fall asleep and get herself arrested. She paced for what seemed like hours, until her ankles had swollen to twice their size and her feet were scarred with blisters. By now her hunger was so intense, it seemed to emanate not from her gut but from deeper inside, from the very marrow of her bones. She had to make it stop. Her chin fell against her chest. She walked as though aimless, unable to acknowledge where she was headed.

As she rounded the latrines, she saw the same kids camped out by the garbage pile. They'd built a small fire and were kicking a piece of trash back and forth in its glow. She edged timidly toward them.

The boy squared his shoulders and placed his hands on his hips. "You again."

San San stood as tall as she could. "I'm just taking a walk. The last time I checked, you didn't own this path."

The two younger ones joined their brother. The boy sneered, "Walk where you like. Just stay away from our garbage."

San San gazed longingly at the reeking heap, the contours of which were just visible in the dim firelight. Her eyes registered a flicker of motion at the top of the heap before her brain comprehended that what stood before her was a writhing pile of rats.

The scream coursed up molten and lethal within her. She turned and fled, too revolted to respond to the wild, spiteful laughter that chased her.

33

Of all the comic books still standing on the bookshelf in Ah Liam's old room in the villa, the one he longed to flip through right now was *The Boy Who Defeated an Army*. The book told the story of a boy his age who, with the aid of an improvised flotation device—fashioned by knotting off and blowing into his uniform trousers—managed to swim out undetected to an enemy ship and set it on fire.

He stared at the rain drumming the windowpane, regretting all the times he'd scolded his sister for stealing the book and creasing its pages. Was it only a couple of months ago that she'd knocked on his door in the middle of the night because she'd had a bad dream? Instead of letting her climb in bed, he'd kicked his bedspread to the floor and made her lie there. Ma insisted San San would be found. But while she and Grandma shouted into the telephone and spat veiled accusations at each other, only he was taking real action.

For the past weeks, he and his friends had plotted their return to the mainland. They met at Li An's house to study and discuss pamphlets containing the Chairman's latest speeches and essays, which Ah Tek procured from an underground communist at Hong Kong University. They returned to their homes to steal small, barely noticeable sums of money from family members to put toward their train fares. When the money accumulated too slowly, Fatty took a job at a bookstore in Sheung Wan and pledged his entire salary to the cause. Ah Liam tricked his grandmother into handing over a large sum of cash for summer school fees. Li An pawned a ruby ring that her parents had given her on her fifteenth birthday. And finally, they'd reached their goal.

The clock on the nightstand read a quarter past five. By the time the typhoon hit—that afternoon, according to the evening news—Ah Liam would be back on the mainland to join the revolution. Once he received his dormitory and school assignments, he would get permission to go back to the islet and find out what happened to his sister. Surely the neighbors and the servants would have useful information that the grown-ups couldn't get from this far away.

He pulled on his raincoat and rubber boots and shouldered his school satchel. Then he reread the note he'd written minutes earlier and left it tented on his pillow.

In the dark hallway Ah Liam paused in front of his grandmother's room. Pressing his ear to the door, he thought he discerned her low, rumbling snore—from this distance, as soothing as a kitten's purr. Although he'd tried his best to explain his actions in his note, he knew that nothing he wrote would make her accept that his lies and betrayals were neither about nor against her. For this, he was truly sorry. If only she could see what he saw: that the revolution was so much larger than him and her and the rest of the family.

He hurried out the front door. The elevator chimed as it released him into the lobby, startling the night guard who'd been dozing with his chin in his hand.

The guard rubbed his eyes. "Where are you off to so early this morning?" He plopped his cap on his head.

"Football practice," Ah Liam answered without slowing.

Before the guard could point out that no one in his right mind would hold practice in this weather, Ah Liam slipped out the door. The narrow twisting street was empty. The only noise came from the rain beating upon the hood of his coat. He walked briskly, stepping over puddles. Thunder crackled overhead, and he cringed and then felt ashamed. The boy who defeated an army would never display such cowardice.

Even the downtown district was eerily quiet. The buses and street-cars lurching down the boulevard were hollow boxes of glass and steel. The hawkers that typically blocked off whole sections of the sidewalk to sell pig's blood congee must have decided to sleep in. The few remaining ramshackle tents built from aluminum sheeting and burlap sacks looked in danger of being blown away any second now.

As Ah Liam waited to cross the street, he watched a bony woman lift a tarp off four ragged children, sleeping head to toe right on the ground. The children scowled and covered their faces and blinked up at the rain in confusion. Here, right before him, was living proof of the evils of capitalism. Look at how the rich—his family included—cosseted themselves behind high gates and in tall towers, while the poor suffered mere steps away. He longed to take those children by the hand and drag them to the station. "Paradise is just across the border," he'd say. "The Party will see to all your needs, and you'll grow tall and strong."

In contrast to the rest of the city, the train station was in a state of chaos, as though the denizens of Hong Kong had all spontaneously descended upon this single spot. Travelers lugging heavy suitcases hurried as best they could from one end of the hall to the other and pleaded with ticket agents to get them on the early train and lamented to each other that they simply had to make it out before everything shut down. Laborers with muscled forearms passed heavy crates down an endless human chain, seemingly oblivious to the rain streaming down their faces. Uniformed porters pushing dollies piled high with luggage tried to cut paths through the hordes. A clump of construction workers crouched by a tea stall, sipping from steaming tin cups and smoking cigarettes and peering up at the sky. Ah Liam reveled in the activity. He wanted no part of his parents' pristine, secluded life. Soon he would join the pulsing throng of workers, sweating and grunting and panting as one. Soon he would be useful.

He weaved through the masses until he reached the newsstand at the end of the platform, their designated meeting point. Li An and Ah Tek were already there, clutching thick folded blankets to their chests. Ah Liam's exuberance gave way to alarm. Somehow he'd forgotten his bedding, the one thing all overseas students had been instructed to bring. He wondered if there was time to take a trishaw back to the flat, and how he'd avoid the servants who were no doubt awake. He would have sought his friends' advice, but Ah Tek's wild gesticulations and Li An's plaintive expression made him slow. What could they possibly be arguing about right now? Even through his fog of worry, Ah Liam appreciated Li An's simple navy-blue tunic and trousers, visible beneath her open raincoat. What would have looked dowdy on anyone else, on her appeared effortless, elegant. He could already see her photograph in the *People's Daily* above the caption: "Model Overseas Student Returns to the Fatherland." Perhaps the four of them would be photographed together.

"There you are, Ah Liam!" Ah Tek shouted. "He came. He's here. He came."

Whom those reassurances were meant for, Ah Liam didn't know.

"Thank goodness," Li An said, waving him over.

Ah Liam glanced down at his watch. He was only a few minutes late. "Fatty isn't even here yet."

Ah Tek scowled.

Li An shot Ah Tek a look and said, "Well, Ah Liam, it's just going to be us three."

"What do you mean?" Ah Liam asked.

Ah Tek spat on the ground. "She means Fatty's a coward. A no-good chickenshit."

Li An folded her blanket in half again and shoved it under her arm. "Look, Fatty pulled out and I don't blame him," she said. "Not everyone is cut out for this. 'A revolution isn't a dinner party,' right?"

Ah Liam couldn't still the tremor in his voice. "When did he change his mind?"

"It doesn't matter when," said Li An.

"Last night," said Ah Tek.

She glared at Ah Tek. "What matters is that the three of us are ready and committed."

"Right," Ah Liam said, but inside him something threatened to explode. Had his mother found his note? Had she and Grandma called Pa? Maybe even the police? Were they rushing to the station to keep him from boarding the train? He wondered if the police had the power to halt all outbound trains.

Li An balanced her blanket atop the suitcase on the ground beside her and placed both hands on Ah Liam's shoulders. Her index fingers grazed his neck, and all he could think of was the weight of her palms, the coolness of her skin.

"I'm glad you came instead of Fatty," she said.

A train barreled down the tracks, whistle blaring.

"Come on," said Ah Tek. "That's ours."

Ah Liam followed his friends into the swarm, but his eyes defied his brain, scanning the terminal for Ma's pale frantic face beneath the nest of hair she wouldn't have had time to comb. He heard Li An ask if they thought a Party representative would meet them at the Guangdong station, but he didn't catch Ah Tek's response.

A group of students also clutching blankets squeezed in front of Ah Liam. They were followed closely by a Western couple clad in shabby, ill-fitting shirts and trousers. Li An called for Ah Liam to keep up.

"I'm trying," he yelled back.

A woman with a sleeping baby strapped to her chest bumped his shoulder, while a young man supporting an old man with a cane closed in on him from the other side. Ah Liam dropped back and let them pass.

The train came to a halt, and everyone surged to the doors. He had no choice but to surrender to the throng. He lost sight of the back of Li An's head. The sharp point of an elbow jabbed his ribs; the toe of a shoe grazed his heel. As he boarded the train, he tripped on the rain-slicked steps and fell against a man who cursed and told him to watch where he was going. Instead of moving into the belly of the train, Ah Liam paused on the top step and flattened himself against the thin metal banister.

"What the hell," someone said, pushing past him.

"Stop blocking the goddamned door," said another.

Ah Liam squeezed his way down to the lowest step. He tightened his grip on the banister and craned around the outside of the train. Squinting through the rain, he was pretty sure he spotted Li An's shiny cap of hair in the nearest window. "Li An," he screamed. "I forgot my bedding, Li An!" It was the only thing he could think to say.

"Crazy kid," a woman said, swiping his side with a large, soaking-wet shoulder bag.

His friend didn't respond.

"Li An!"

The train whistled, signaling its imminent departure.

"Goodbye! Good luck!" cried the people who remained on the platform.

Ah Liam pulled himself back inside the train, planting his feet as firmly as he could on the slippery bottom step.

The train gained speed. The people on the platform waved harder. Even the ones with tears in their eyes looked strangely happy and carefree. Once the train left the station, they would hurry home, change into clean, dry clothes, fill their stomachs with hot tea and steamed buns.

"Don't forget to write, Little Treasure!" called a woman, her jaw stretched wide to display gold molars.

The train continued to accelerate. Beyond the platform, travelers bustled around the waiting hall. Ah Liam picked out a disheveled figure running through the main entrance, her mouth a cavernous hole beneath an unruly nest of hair. His heart leapt. He closed his eyes, let go of the banister, and jumped.

His feet slammed the concrete and his right ankle twisted, sending him tumbling onto his side. Screams filled his ears. A crowd formed around him.

"Are you all right?"

"Are you insane?"

"What kind of stunt was that?"

Steeling himself against the pain, Ah Liam rose and pushed through the crowd, ignoring their questions and insults. Twice he limped up and down the full length of the waiting hall, but his mother was nowhere to be found. Perhaps he'd conjured her up in his head; perhaps he'd seen a ghost.

34

The sky was still dark when San San, bleary eyed and fatigued to the point of delirium, climbed the overpass to track the arriving ships. The last time her boat hadn't left the harbor until late morning, but she could not risk missing it again.

At first she could barely discern where the sky ended and the ocean began. As the morning wore on, however, she studied every vessel that approached, from humble, stripped-down fishing boats to oversized cargo ships that looked like towers tipped over on their sides. None of them flew a green flag.

By the time the sun shone directly above her, and her shadow was a squat shape encircling her feet, she began to wonder if she had the wrong date, or if the university student with the cross pendant had mixed up the boat's schedule, or if the boat had changed its route. It dawned on her that there were an infinite number of reasons why her boat might never come. Still, she remained glued to the blazing concrete.

On a patch of yellow grass below the overpass, boys kicked a football, a circle of seated women mended garments. After hours beneath the beating sun, San San's thirst was a roaring, implacable beast, and yet she dared not abandon her post. Uniformed workers leaving factories and job sites streamed past. A cool breeze kicked up, providing a trifling measure of relief. She waited and waited until it was too dark for her to decipher the colors of the flags on the last few straggling boats. Only then did she finally turn and head in the direction of the garbage heap. With any luck, the feral kids had moved on.

Shuffling down the unlit path toward the latrines, she tripped on a rock and narrowly missed landing in a stinking, swampy pool. Mud splattered her face. Her stubbed toe screamed in pain. She spun around, looking for someone or something to blame. But here in the darkness there was only her. Even those kids by the garbage heap had each other. Even the white-haired girl had her baby. Even the little match girl had her matches.

The low moan of a ship's horn lulled San San deeper into her misery. How very tired she was. Why not give up, collapse right here, let the mud ooze through her pores, let the earth bear the weight of her. The horn blasted three more times, in quick succession. She turned toward its call. And then she scrambled back to the harbor, moving as quickly as her swollen legs and wounded feet would carry her.

She arrived just in time to watch her ship—massive as a citadel, flying a green flag—plow past the harbor without slowing. All the same she ran after it. It wasn't too late for her to take a running leap, dive like a dolphin into the ocean, and swim for her life.

At the edge of the dock she stopped dead. Two dockworkers peered at her.

"That ship," she said. "The one with the green flag. Why didn't it stop?"

The dockworkers traded looks. "Must be a change of route."

"How can that be? Why would it pass through here then?"

One of the men shrugged and said, "Save that question for the big boss," and the other chortled. "Now, shoo. We have work to do."

A second cargo ship, smaller than the one that had left her behind, but still sizable, approached the dock. She walked off, dragging the worn rubber soles of her canvas shoes against the ground. She would walk all the way back to the islet, if only it were possible. All the way back and straight to the police. And if they sent her to a labor camp, at least she would no longer be alone. At least she could finally stop hiding. She wondered if they'd let her see Cook and Mui Ah one last time, because weren't they the closest thing to family she had left?

An image surfaced in her mind: she was lying face down in bed, her mother seated beside her, swearing they'd be separated for just a few days. The memory knocked the wind out of her. She sank to the ground behind a wall of empty crates that stank of fish.

Even back then, San San had sensed her mother was lying, trying to appear more certain than she was. Why had she let her family leave? Why hadn't she at least put up a fight?

And then the answer came to her. Nothing she could say would have changed Ma's mind. Ma had abandoned her because she loved Ah Liam more. That was the simple truth. San San had always known her worth in comparison to her brother's, as surely as she knew her own name. But somehow, amid the turmoil of the past weeks, she'd lost sight of this immutable fact; somehow, because of all she'd suffered through, all she'd seen, she'd convinced herself that she deserved more.

Truly, it was time to go home.

Beyond the wall of crates, a dozen crewmen streamed onto the deck of the cargo ship. They directed the dockworkers to roll barrel after barrel into large nets hooked up to complex pulley systems. With their drab work clothes and identical buzz cuts, they formed an army of clones.

A pair of crewmen passed right in front of San San's hiding spot, hauling a dolly stacked high with burlap sacks. The arms of the man at the head of the dolly were covered with beautiful pictures that had somehow been inked into his skin. Here was a long, sinuous dragon unleashing tongues of fire from its mouth, there, a beautiful maiden whose legs had been replaced by the lower half of an emerald-scaled fish. The man shouted something in Cantonese and gestured for his partner to pick up the pace. San San's eyes fell on the picture inked on the underside of his forearm: a slender, half-naked foreigner impaled upon a cross. It was nearly identical to the pendant that had dangled beneath the university student's shirt.

She told herself to cut it out. She'd made up her mind, once and for all, to return to the islet. And yet she couldn't snuff out the flicker of optimism within her. This time would be different; this time she knew where she stood. The laws that governed her world were absolute: she would always be second place. Her family owed her nothing, and would give her nothing more. And if she chose to flout those laws, as she would in attempting the journey once again, she understood that she could fail. When that happened, if it happened, the authorities would deposit her on the islet to face the consequences—the same position she'd be in if she gave herself up today.

Now, if only she knew where this Hong Kong ship was going next.

For several hours, the men worked to unload barrels and replace them with new ones. They hauled wooden boxes and metal drums back and forth, yelling to each other in Cantonese, which she had trouble deciphering. Every once in a while, the inked man led the others through rousing tunes about sun and sea, paying no deference to the late hour. She wondered if she should try to board the ship even without knowing its destination. But wouldn't it be worse to end up in some other port city like Quanzhou or Guangzhou? And how would she sneak aboard with so many people around?

When the sun peeked over the lip of the horizon, the crewmen stopped to take a tea break. They were joined by a group of boys, clearly affiliated with the ship, some of whom were only a few years older than San San. The boys squatted on the ground and smoked—even the very youngest one—just steps away from her hiding place.

She channeled all her energy toward trying to understand the peculiar, lilting syllables that poured from their mouths. She picked out words like "kitchen" and "wash" and "dishes." The boys seemed to be arguing about which of them was the most efficient dishwasher, and she concluded that they ran the kitchen aboard the ship. Teacher Lu had told her that outside the mainland, children were often enslaved and forced to labor as adults, so she wasn't entirely surprised.

The oldest boy appeared to be the head cook. He hacked up a wad of phlegm and spat it at the feet of the boy they called Turtle, who jumped back and hollered, "Watch it, bastard!"

She almost cracked a smile. Their easy, good-natured mocking reminded her of her brother and his football teammates. How many times had she trailed shyly behind them after school, wishing to be in on their jokes, to be teased and to tease back? A ship like this one would have a plethora of suitable hiding spots, and wouldn't it eventually make it back to Hong Kong, no matter the stops along the way?

Like the crewmen, the boys wore old, plain clothing that was quite dirty, not all that different from her own. She swiped a palm over her short prickly hair and shook out her limbs, like a runner preparing to race. When the group, responding to some invisible signal, got to their feet, San San slipped out from her hiding spot and merged with them, careful to linger behind the boys while still remaining in touching distance. She mimicked their long, buoyant strides, their jauntily swinging arms.

The crewmen chattered and told jokes. Already it seemed as if her comprehension had improved, although maybe it was because the men spoke and gestured so expressively. They trooped up the gangplank, their heavy boots drumming rhythmically upon the metal ramp.

"Don't let Ah Ling hear about it," one said.

"Cheh!" the other replied, a universal expression of scorn.

"You're a real scoundrel," said someone else.

"Cheh!"

San San mouthed the word, longing to feel it explode on her tongue. She noticed too late that the boys had split off and were heading below deck. She hurried after them. The boys went down a flight of stairs and through a corridor. She followed, treading as lightly as possible. The youngest boy was recounting a complicated riddle about two elephants in a circus, and the bigger boys interrupted periodically to poke fun at him.

On the shore, workers in a nearby dormitory were being called to their morning exercises. Loudspeakers blared "Hymn to Chairman Mao" on a continuous loop:

Oh! Most honorable Chairman Mao, may you live long!

You liberate all with your brilliance. People now are happy, full of blessings!

All people look to you as a kind protecting mother!

May you live in the world forever and point us down the peaceful road!

San San had never paid attention to the song's lyrics, but now, after all that incomprehensible babble, each word seemed to call out to her. This wasn't the time to let herself get distracted. What she needed was a supply closet of some sort, a room the crewmen would visit sparingly. She passed a door and tried the doorknob but it wouldn't budge. She passed a second door, and this time the doorknob turned. Grasping the doorknob with both hands, she pulled with all her body weight, and the door opened, groaning against the floor.

She jumped back, but the boys were already coming for her.

"Hey you," the head cook shouted.

Her first instinct was to run, but it was clear they would catch her almost immediately.

"Who are you, boy? How did you get down here?"

"Please let me come with you," she said in Mandarin, hoping they'd understand. Her high, trembling voice horrified her; she lowered it at once. "My pa is dying in Hong Kong. The rest of my family is already there."

"What's he saying?" the head cook asked.

Thankfully, the boy called Turtle spoke Mandarin. But after he translated, the head cook only smirked, as if to say, *"How is this my problem?"*

"Just give me a place to hide," San San said. "I swear I won't cause any trouble."

The youngest boy said, "No way, no way. If anyone finds out we'll all be in deep shit."

Turtle said, "Can't we maybe hide him in the kitchen?"

Footsteps sounded on the deck above, and the head cook said, "We can't discuss this out here." He headed down the corridor.

The other boys followed, and San San did, too. She had to somehow convince them to help her, or to at least not rat her out.

Inside the kitchen, the youngest boy said, "It's too dangerous. They'll definitely fire us. My ma will kill me if I lose another job."

Turtle said quietly, "His pa is dying. What would you do if it were your pa?"

"Stop talking all of you. I need to think," said the head cook.

A voice spoke in accented Mandarin on the floor above. "After I show you the cabins for the crew, I'll take you downstairs to see the kitchen and mess hall."

"All right, comrade," another voice replied.

The boys' eyes bulged. "Shit. Inspection."

The youngest boy grabbed San San by her shirt collar. "Get out of here. It's too dangerous," he said, just as Turtle contradicted him. "Hide him in the storage room. Why would they look there?"

The head cook's eyes passed from one boy to the other. San San had to tip the balance in her favor, and she had to do it now. She pulled back her sleeve and fought to unbuckle her watch.

The youngest boy shoved her. "Scram. Go."

She thrust the watch at the head cook. "Take this. It's from abroad and worth a lot."

The head cook snatched the watch from her hand. Why hadn't she thought to clean it? He spat on the strap and rubbed off the dirt and crowed, "What a girly color."

Tears filled her eyes—it was the last thing her father had given her—but she managed to blink them back. She was a boy now, and one thing she knew for certain was that boys didn't cry. She changed tactics. "If you don't help me, I'll tell them you let me on board, and then"—she pointed at the youngest boy—"he's right, you'll all get sacked."

Turtle quickly translated. Footsteps pounded down the corridor toward the kitchen, closer and closer. The youngest boy began to cry. Again Turtle urged them to stick San San in the storage room. But the head cook continued to hold up the watch, gazing at it like a sacred talisman that would somehow tell him what to do.

35

B ee Kim awoke to rain splattering across the windowpane. These modern flats were so flimsy, outside noises passed right through them like water through a sieve. A crack in the drapes told her it was still dark, and she shut her eyes, determined to fall back asleep.

Down on the street, a vendor hollered for the neighborhood housewives to bring him their broken ceramics. "Don't throw away money. I can make your old ones as good as new."

At this hour? In this weather? Wasn't a typhoon supposed to strike? With a sigh she pushed herself upright and eased her legs off the bed.

In the hallway, she paused with an ear to her grandson's door. Her hearing may have worsened, but she swore she could hear Ah Liam's long steady breaths—the pure, deep slumber of a child who'd never suffered and who'd always been loved. What a sweet, handsome little boy he'd been, adored by everyone he encountered. What a thoughtful, intelligent young man he was growing into. *This*, Bee Kim thought. *As long as I have this.*

She quietly pushed open the door, and her grandson's empty bed was so confounding, it took her a moment to notice the sheet of paper on the pillow. She lunged for the note.

My family,

I have gone to rebuild the Fatherland. Our country needs its young people, and it is my privilege and my duty to join the most important revolution of our time.

Please don't worry about me. I'm not alone. My friends and comrades are with me, and the Party will see to all our needs.

I'm sorry I didn't say goodbye. I hope someday you will come to believe in the revolution and will understand why I had to deceive you. Know that everything I've done stems from love for my country, and that I'm sorry for any pain I've caused. As soon as I'm settled, I will look for San San. You'll hear from me then.

Your loving son and grandson,
Ah Liam

"Daughter-in-Law," Bee Kim cried. "Come here! Now!"

Seok Koon appeared, holding her dressing gown closed with one hand. "What is it, Ma? Are you hurt?" She looked around. "Where's Ah Liam?"

The servants scurried down the hallway, repeating variations of the same questions.

Bee Kim thrust the note at Seok Koon.

She read it and crushed it to her chest. "I must go to the train station." She turned to the maid. "Go flag a taxi. Hurry!" She ran to her room and emerged with her pocketbook dangling from one wrist. She belted her dressing gown and shuffled to the front door in her bedroom slippers.

With the aid of her cane, Bee Kim followed. "I'll come, too."

"No," Seok Koon said sharply.

Never had she spoken to Bee Kim in that tone of voice.

"You stay. I can't waste any more time." She was already out the door.

Bee Kim said, "Let me help."

Seok Koon whirled around and jabbed a finger in her face. "You've done enough damage to this family. I won't lose my son, too."

Bee Kim staggered back against the wall. The door slammed. So this was what her daughter-in-law truly thought of her, after all the kindness she'd shown her through the years. After all they'd weathered together.

The cook, who'd taken in the whole scene, said, "Madame, please sit down. I'll bring you a pot of tea."

Bee Kim brushed away the woman's hand and closed her eyes. How could Ah Liam have planned this whole thing behind their backs? Where did he get the money to pay for his ticket? Nausea rippled through her. She clutched her stomach. No, she refused to believe it. It couldn't be true. He couldn't have looked her in the face and lied.

"Madame, is something wrong?"

Her insides roiled. Her cheeks and forehead blazed.

"You don't look well. Do you need medicine?"

"I'm all right." She mopped the perspiration from her hairline.

"Are you sure? Shall I call the doctor just in case?"

"No."

"Shall I call Master?"

Somehow it hadn't occurred to Bee Kim to telephone Ah Zhai. And then she wondered what he could possibly do. He couldn't stop the trains. He couldn't cross the border to bring back his son. He couldn't even take care of his own family. Why was he living in that cheap hotel? Why wasn't he here where he belonged?

"Sure, call him. Tell him everything." She hobbled down the hallway. "I don't want to be disturbed. Not until they find the boy."

36

Seok Koon's waterlogged bedroom slippers were a pair of iron shackles. She kicked them off and ran into the station. She had never seen it so crowded. It was as though the entire city had spontaneously descended upon this spot. She scanned the departures board and pushed her way to the platform for the train to Guangzhou, but the only person there was a janitor, sloshing dirty water across the floor with a mop, who told her the train had long gone. The janitor's eyes lingered quizzically on her, and she folded her arms across her chest. Barefoot, in her dressing gown, she must have looked like she'd escaped a mental institution.

Back in the main hall, a bored-looking policeman stood in a corner, surveying the crowd and smoking. Instinctively she hurried toward him, and then stopped short. What did she expect him to do? Cross the border and drag back her son?

Most of the travelers, she noted, seemed to be moving in one direction toward some common goal. She traced their paths as they joined the serpentine queue before the single ticket window with its light on. Beyond the glass, a bare fluorescent bulb hung above the weary attendant's bald pate, and she stared at the glowing halo as though it were a distant guiding star. She joined the back of the line. She would get on the next train. She would follow her son back to the mainland, and together they would go to Xiamen to find San San.

She planted herself behind a young couple with a wailing newborn. The wife bounced the baby in her arms and made hushing noises, but the cries persisted.

"I can't take it anymore," the husband said. "Go over there where I can't hear her."

Seok Koon gave the woman a sympathetic smile. She craned to see if the line had moved, but the same red-faced man was shouting at the attendant and slamming his ticket against the window.

She felt sorry for the poor attendant, and for the young mother, and even for the grouchy father and the red-faced man at the head of the line. She felt sorry for the frantic people dashing past and for the desolate few who'd given up and now sat huddled together on the dirty floor. Compassion flowed out of her, pure and strong, abundant enough to span the entire station. In her mind, she'd already crossed the border and found her children. "It'll just be the three of us now," she'd say, smothering them with kisses. Her flimsy bathrobe no longer embarrassed her. She was glad she'd brought nothing with her. She wanted no reminders of her previous life. She and her son and her daughter would start anew. It had been a long time since she'd taught piano, but a diploma was a diploma, and she was sure she could find students. A sob crept up her throat as she thought of dear Rose.

"Next," the attendant called.

Seok Koon gathered herself, stepped up to the window and asked for a ticket on the next train out.

"You're better off leaving tomorrow, or even the day after."

"No," she said. "I'll stand the whole way if I have to."

"There's one seat left, but the rain's getting worse. This train has almost no chance of running."

"I'll take it," she said, thrusting all her money through the hole in the glass.

The attendant shrugged and slid over the ticket.

For the first time in a long, long while, Seok Koon felt her whole body exhale.

Several hours remained before the train would arrive. She searched for a place to sit, but tired bodies filled every inch of the long wooden benches. She wandered toward the back wall, and an elderly woman invited her to share the suitcase she was using as a seat. Given Seok Koon's bizarre and disheveled appearance, she was shocked the woman had offered.

"Thank you," she said. Her aching feet were black and filthy, and she tucked them beneath her. "My shoes got completely soaked. I kicked them off so I could run faster."

"You were trying to make the early train?" The woman took out an orange and began to peel it.

"Yes," said Seok Koon. The fresh scent sparked her hunger, but when the woman offered her a segment, she politely declined.

The woman chewed and nodded at Seok Koon's pocketbook. "You travel light."

"It's a long story," she said, and then added, "Everything I need is on the other side."

The woman finished the orange and wiped her fingers on her handkerchief and asked Seok Koon to watch her things while she went to the lavatory. Seok Koon leaned back against the wall and felt her eyelids grow heavy. How long it had been since she'd slept a full night. She reached in the pocket of her dressing gown and fingered the edge of her ticket. The instant she and her son reached the islet, she'd go to Nurse Ho and ask to be taken to the little girl in the city. What had the nurse said? That the girl sang well and could play the accordion. Of course she was San San. How could Seok Koon have ever questioned it? The whole plan was laughably simple. She couldn't believe her luck.

The suitcase's owner returned from the lavatory and reported that the wind had picked up even more. "What will you do if the trains stop running?"

"We'll get out before then," said Seok Koon.

The woman waggled her head to show she wasn't so sure, and Seok Koon grew indignant. "The typhoon's coming from the south, and we're going north. These bureaucrats are being skittish because they don't want to be held responsible if something goes wrong."

Again the woman waggled her head. "It all depends when the storm hits."

Seok Koon was sick and tired of preparing for the worst. She had to get away from this woman and her pessimism. She stood and stretched her legs and tried to think of a polite way to make her escape. She rolled her head in a circle to loosen her neck, and out of the corner of her eye, she spotted a boy fighting through the crowd.

"Ma!" That single high, sweet syllable pierced her heart.

She pushed her way to meet him. "Son!"

Ah Liam threw his whole body against her, and she buried her nose in his hair, breathing in the stale odor of sweat as though it were the sweetest perfume.

"Ma, I'm sorry."

"It's all right, Son. It's all right."

"How did you know I was still here?"

"I didn't," she said, taking his face in both hands, pressing her forehead to his. "But I hoped. I just kept hoping."

Someone bumped into Ah Liam, making him gasp, and Seok Koon took his arm and pulled him outside.

"Where are your shoes?"

"Don't worry about that," she said.

The wide multilane thoroughfare was strewn with tree branches and metal garbage cans and the odd umbrella carcass. Wind whipped Seok Koon's hair about her face. Even beneath the awning, rain pelted their backs. But at least they were alone.

She said, "Don't ever do that again. Promise me."

Ah Liam pulled away and began to cry. "I'm a coward."

She wrapped her arms around him and said fiercely, "You're not a coward. Whoever told you to go back to the mainland filled your head with lies."

The boy was sobbing so hard, he could barely get out the words. "It's my fault San San's missing."

She tightened her arms around his shaking body and whispered things to calm him down.

He gulped at the air. "I'm the one who reported Grandma and got the whole family in trouble. I thought I was a revolutionary, but I'm just a selfish, worthless coward."

"You're a child," she said. "This is my fault. I'm the one who left San San behind."

In a small voice he said, "What if they never find her?"

Something broke open inside Seok Koon. She turned her son to face her. "You cannot run away ever again, do you hear me?"

He drew back, perhaps surprised by her vehemence, and she shook him again. "Do you hear me?"

"Yes."

"Swear it."

"I swear, Ma, I'll never run away again."

She released her son. "I'm the one who left her, and now I must live with it. That's all we can do—live with our mistakes."

He laid a hand on her back and awkwardly patted her, and she saw the uncertainty on his face. His questions were hers: What if a mistake was too grave to live with? What if the guilt wormed its way deep into the flesh and grew more and more potent, devouring tissue and fat and skin, until one day, you looked down, and your whole self had been ravaged and nothing remained?

She drew her son near and pressed her lips to his damp forehead. "Let's go before this typhoon arrives."

Arm in arm they walked into the storm. Seok Koon's hand slid into her pocket and found that her ticket had soaked through. She wadded up the limp, soggy slip, dropped it on the ground, and kept going.

37

And now, here Seok Koon was, sitting at the dining table, pre-tending to read the paper. Today is Sunday, she told herself. I am enjoying an ordinary morning with my family. This is my family. This is ordinary.

Sunlight spilled through the window, but she didn't get up to draw the curtain. The pristine, porcelain-blue sky held no remnants of yester-day's storm. From behind her paper shield she watched her son spoon congee into his mouth and chew and stare into the distance. Was he thinking of the friends who'd gone off without him? He would make new friends; of that, she had no doubt. He would join the football team and learn to speak English and excel at school. Was he thinking of his sister? If so, there was nothing she could offer him, except to say, "This is our family now."

Her husband turned a page of the business section and coughed lightly. She didn't understand how he could sit there so calmly, read-ing and absorbing the latest stock numbers. Last night he'd moved his things into the guest room, and for that, she was grateful. He'd hovered in the background with a mildly shell-shocked expression on his face as she'd tended to her son and fed him double-boiled beef broth. Seok Koon saw how superfluous her husband felt, and his vulnerability gave her strength. As a peace offering, she'd stayed home from church this morning. In fact she knew she'd never go back there again.

Her mother-in-law was still asleep. She hadn't left her bed since Seok Koon had returned with Ah Liam. And when she and Zhai had gone to Bee Kim's room to tell her the good news, she'd merely said, "Make sure he never does that again. Now leave me alone." Her forehead felt hot, but she wouldn't let the doctor examine her, insisting she felt fine. "Old, tired, but fine."

Seok Koon folded her newspaper and announced, "I shall go to the market. We'll have a nice family meal tonight."

Her son grunted noncommittally. Her husband turned a page and said, "All right."

She washed and dressed and left the flat. She was wading through sludge, or maybe swimming through air. Her brain was swollen taut like a glossy balloon. But she would buy the freshest fish, the plumpest chicken, the glossiest vegetables, something special for dessert.

Passing through the lobby, she noted that the guard had left his desk. This wasn't the first time he'd gone missing at random hours of the day. She'd have to remember to ask Zhai to have a chat with the manager.

A cry pulled her gaze beyond the glass doors of the building. She stopped with a hand on the door handle, stunned by the commotion outside. There the guard stood, swinging his nightstick in a circle above his head. His menace was aimed at a vagrant, quite young—just a boy, really. The boy tried to run, but after a few steps, his legs buckled, throwing him upon the sidewalk. The guard struck the boy again and again. Seok Koon clutched her skull, unable to bear his wounded-animal cries. She pushed open the door and rushed in the opposite direction. She would hail a taxi at the end of the road.

"Ma!"

The word daggered her between the shoulder blades.

"Ma, it's me."

The guard continued his assault. Blindly Seok Koon charged at him, a part of her marveling at the ease with which she dragged him off her daughter. But could this really be San San? Oh, she was so brittle and so frail and what had happened to her hair?

"You moron," Seok Koon screamed at the perplexed guard because she didn't know whom else to blame. "You prick, you son of a whore"—insults she'd never said out loud.

She fell to the ground and cradled her daughter, afraid to jostle her precious delicate bones. "San San, is it really you? How did you get here, my treasure? Where did you come from?"

"Ma," her daughter said, closing her eyes.

Seok Koon touched her handkerchief to her girl's bleeding palms, her scraped elbows and knees. Her lips moved continuously, murmuring soothing phrases of comfort and love, even as a single thought colonized her mind: her daughter deserved better—a mother who could have rescued her, a mother who knew every last inch of her face.

38

She let them fuss over her. She let them speak to her in voices filled with warmth and concern. She let them wash her and bandage her and feed her and stroke her hair and face and arms. She let them carry her to a roomy bed beneath a pale-pink canopy, let them tuck her in a soft, light quilt. Sometime soon, maybe tomorrow or the day after, she would tell them about the boys she'd bribed to hide her in their kitchen aboard a cargo ship, about the typhoon that had forced them to dock in Shantou, about a kind boy called Turtle who'd ferried her by trishaw to this flat at 72 Fontana Road. It exhausted her to think of recounting all the details, and all the questions they would have—and this was before she'd even mentioned the boy with the magical voice, the rooftop tent, the denunciation session that haunted her dreams, the truck stuffed with tea pallets that had set in motion the whole chain of events. So, it would have to wait until tomorrow, if not the day after. Her eyelids closed. She was engulfed in a thick, almost solid blackness. Her slumber was deep and unrelenting.

In the morning, when her mother opened the door, the first thing San San asked was, "Can I see Grandma now?" She didn't understand why she'd had to wait this long.

Ma shook her head. "She's still asleep. I told you she's under the weather."

She kicked off the covers. "I won't disturb her. I just want to see her."

"Have breakfast first. The cook made century egg congee."

Her stomach rumbled, but she said, "No, now." Somehow she knew she wouldn't have to plead or whine or raise her voice.

She followed her mother to Grandma's room.

Her mother knocked softly. "Ma, are you up?" She gently pushed open the door.

The curtains were tightly drawn, and the room was dark, as though the sun had somehow overlooked this tiny corner of this strange city, crammed with so many tall buildings you couldn't see the sky. Her grandmother blinked open her eyes and struggled to sit up, and San San ran to her. "Grandma."

"Bee Lian," her grandmother croaked. "Little Sister is it really you? Who did this to your hair? Why did they say you died?"

San San backed away in alarm. What was wrong with her grandmother's voice? Who was Bee Lian?

Her mother swiftly intervened. "Ma, she's not your sister. She's San San. Your granddaughter."

Her grandmother waved her mother off and kept talking. "I'm so sorry, Little Sister, I didn't know the dog would attack. It was so thirsty, I just wanted to give it some water." Grandma took San San's arm. Her hand was cold, and San San tried to warm it in both of hers.

"Bee Lian died a long time ago," her mother said.

But Grandma didn't appear to have heard her. "I shouldn't have left you with that dog. It was bigger than you! I should have known better. I'm the older sister."

San San squeezed her hand and said, "Grandma, it's me."

Ma smiled reassuringly at San San. "Grandma's confused. A high fever can do that."

Her grandmother scowled. "You think I wouldn't recognize my own sister? The one I love so much?" She turned to San San. "Oh, the blood that poured from your face. So much blood for such a small girl."

San San sucked in a breath.

"All right, Ma, that's enough," her mother said.

Her grandmother tightened her grip around San San's hand. "Please, Little Sister, can you forgive me?"

The air in the room seemed to thin. Her grandmother's form grew hazy before her. She felt herself list forward, and she clung to the edge of the headboard with her free hand to steady herself.

"Grandma needs to rest," said Ma.

Tears shone in her grandmother's eyes. "Can you?"

San San loosened her grandmother's fingers, placed her hand atop of her stomach and stroked the knotted blue-green veins. Grandma lay back, and San San edged toward the door.

Her mother said, "I'll have the maid bring a cold compress, and if the fever doesn't break soon, we'll call the doctor."

"No doctor," said her grandmother.

San San let her mother steer her into the hallway. When the door had shut behind them she whispered, "She's dying."

Her mother crouched down so they were eye to eye. "Nonsense, it's just a fever, that's all."

But San San knew that wasn't all. She'd held Grandma's icy hand and seen her waxen complexion and heard her ragged breaths. She chewed on her bottom lip and said nothing. She knew her mother knew that she didn't believe her.

Ma said, "Sometimes, a person can suffer so much stress that it's hard for her to recover fully. Sometimes her body can't take anymore."

San San blurted, "I gave my friend my bangle so he could buy his mother's medicine."

At first Ma said nothing, and then she urged, "Go on."

She tried again. "A barber cut my hair for free."

"Yes," Ma said, cupping San San's face in her palms.

She slipped out of her grasp. "I bribed some sailors with my watch."

"Yes, go on."

But her mother's gaze was so probing, so invasive, that San San couldn't go on. She shrank back until her shoulder blades hit the wall, her throat throbbing with all the things she had no words for, all the things she couldn't speak aloud.

Ma enveloped her with startling ferocity, smothering her face. San San tried to push her off, she didn't think she could breathe.

"All that matters is that you're here now," Ma said. "We'll never let you suffer again."

Each stroke and kiss sent a bolt of pain through San San's center, but she was powerless to stop her. Arms pinned to her sides, she couldn't even stuff her fingers in her ears to block out those inane phrases her mother spoke over and over, as though afraid of what the silence would bring.

ACKNOWLEDGMENTS

Thank you to my family, Michelle Brower, Carmen Johnson, Al Woodworth, Scott Calamar, Little A, Kim Liao, Beth Nguyen, Vanessa Hua, Reese Kwon, Aimee Phan, Claire Vaye Watkins, Pamela Painter, Paul Douglass, Nick Taylor, the Steinbeck Fellows Program, and Hedgebrook. To Matt Salesses, for his wisdom. To Eunice Chen, for sharing her reminiscences. And to Jon Ma, for telling me an unforgettable story many years ago.

So many books helped me complete this novel, especially *Escape from Red China*, by Robert Loh and Humphrey Evans, *Discover Gulangyu* by William Brown, *The Private Life of Chairman Mao* by Dr. Li Zhisui, *The Secret Piano* by Zhu Xiao-Mei, *The Bitter Sea* by Charles N. Li, *The Tragedy of Liberation* by Frank Dikötter, and, last but not least, *The Amazing Adventures of Kavalier & Clay* by Michael Chabon, which, in its author's note, contains a line that became my guiding star, pulling me through those times when doubt and insecurity threatened to derail my work. In writing his novel, Chabon states, "I have tried to respect history and geography wherever doing so served my purposes as a novelist, but wherever it did not I have, cheerfully or with regret, ignored them." I wholeheartedly concur.

ABOUT THE AUTHOR

Photo © 2017 Sarah Deragon

Kirstin Chen is the author of the novel *Soy Sauce for Beginners*. Born and raised in Singapore, she currently lives in San Francisco.